CRIME MIGHT PAY

Robert Archibald

Cactus Mystery Press
an imprint of Blue Fortune Enterprises LLC

CRIME MIGHT PAY

For information contact :
Blue Fortune Enterprises, LLC
Cactus Mystery Press
P.O. Box 554
Yorktown, VA 23690
http://blue-fortune.com

Book and Cover design by Gretchen Bedell, Odd Moxie

ISBN: 978-1-948979-59-7
First Edition: March 2021

DEDICATION

I would like to dedicate this book to my siblings. They put up with a great deal from their brother.
David Archibald
Richard Archibald
Beth Lewis

Fiction by Robert Archibald:
Roundabout Revenge
Guilty Until Proven Innocent

Reviews for Roundabout Revenge
Fascinating plot, thoughtfully developed. Looking forward to what story
twists his next book will bring.
Fred Cason, Amazon review

I loved Roundabout Revenge. Author Robert Archibald is a retired
college professor whose writing demonstrates that he is a scholar not
only in his professional field of study, but also in his observations on
society. In this engrossing novel, he sheds light on why law and justice
are sometimes at odds with each other. There also are wonderful
discussions among the characters about sports, diversity in schools and
society, and about how conservatives and liberals have come to hold their
beliefs. I look forward to the sequel.
CW Stacks, Amazon review

Reviews for Guilty Until Proven Innocent
Another Archibald masterpiece... This quality page-turner encompasses
a number of adventures that sometimes end not as anticipated. The
expected becomes the unexpected...
If you enjoyed "Revenge," you'll enjoy this too. If you missed "Revenge"
pick it up with the knowledge that you'll have two enjoyable books to
occupy your time.
Wilford Kale, Virginia Gazette review

ACKNOWLEDGEMENTS

Crime Might Pay is a work of fiction. Any resemblance between the characters of this book and anyone I have known or met is a complete coincidence.

This book benefited from the efforts of several individuals who read and commented on drafts. I would like to especially thank my friend Kirk Lovenbury who has carefully read all my fiction. Also, I would like to apologize for misspelling his last name in previous acknowledgements. Members of two writer's groups have provided useful comments: Sharon Dillon, Tim Holland, Elizabeth Lee, Barbara McLennan, Caterina Novelliere, Christian Pascale, Dave Pistorese, Patti Procopi, Peter Stipe, and Susan Williamson. None of these people deserve blame for any remaining errors or awkward phrases.

I would like to especially thank Narielle Living for a superb edit.

Finally, everything I do benefits for the help of my wife, Nancy.

CHAPTER ONE

AT HER SMALL women's shoe store in Pittsburgh, Sybil Watson congratulated herself on unloading the outrageous spike heels on the woman who'd just left. The shoes were among the most expensive Sybil carried. The woman had even worn them out of the store. Just as Sybil turned to go to the back room to get something to replace the spike heels in the window display, she heard a scream from outside. Sybil rushed to the front door and saw the woman who'd just left sprawled on the sidewalk. Sybil hurried outside to see what had happened.

The woman looked up at Sybil. "I tripped on a crack in the sidewalk and hurt my ankle. It's bad!"

"Can you stand up?"

"Why?"

"Look, if we can get you standing up, you should be able to hop into a chair. We can't leave you where you are. Wait a second. I'll get a chair for you to sit on." Sybil turned and hurried inside.

Within seconds, Sybil returned with a chair and went to assist the woman. "Don't put any weight on the foot you hurt," she instructed. "I'll do the lifting. When we get you up part way, just push up with your good leg."

When the woman was settled on the seat, they both heaved a sigh of relief.

Sybil had already sized up the woman while selling the shoes. She appeared to be a fading beauty in her fifties hanging on as best she could. Her obviously dyed raven hair was nicely styled. Her legs suggested a considerable amount of time in some gym. She wore too much makeup and perfume for Sybil's taste, and her now-rumpled dress didn't look appropriate for her age—too short and cut too deep in front. Then again, the shoes Sybil had just sold her weren't appropriate for her age either.

When Sybil saw the woman had regained her composure, she asked, "Do you want me to check out your ankle?"

"I guess so. It's hurt real bad."

Sybil knelt down. She had to agree with the woman. It looked bad. Her ankle had already started to swell. It might be a sprain or maybe even a break. Sybil decided not to touch anything. She got up, retrieved the woman's purse and the shoe box with the shoes the woman wore into the store.

"You need an ambulance. I'll get some ice. The only thing we can do is put ice on it until they come."

"Please," the woman pleaded. "You can't leave me out here in the heat. If you support me for balance, I can hop into your store where there's air conditioning."

"Okay, sure. Just put your arm around my shoulder."

The woman winced with every hop, and Sybil saw tears in her eyes. *The injury must be very painful*, she thought.

When the woman settled in a chair inside the store, Sybil retrieved the chair from outside, along with the woman's purse and the shoe box. Back in the store, she said, "You need to call an ambulance. You have a cell phone, don't you?"

The woman nodded.

"I'll get some ice."

Returning with ice, Sybil could tell the woman hadn't done anything. Maybe she's in shock. Sybil slipped the shoe off the injured foot before she put on the ice, which she'd wrapped in a towel. Then she said, "I can call the ambulance if you want, or do you want to call someone else? You might be able to get into a car. Still an ambulance would be better. Your ankle needs to be supported somehow."

The woman didn't respond.

Sybil didn't have any idea what to do, so she backed off. Maybe the woman just needed time to compose herself. After a couple of minutes, the woman extracted a tissue from her purse and dabbed her eyes. Then she retrieved a small mirror and checked her makeup. She didn't look happy with what she saw.

After a few minutes another customer entered the store, so Sybil went to help. The second customer tried on several pairs of shoes but in the end didn't find anything. Leaving shoe boxes scattered by the bench, Sybil went to the woman who'd hurt her ankle.

As she approached, she asked, "Is the ice helping?"

Pausing, the woman didn't answer. She simply said, "It still hurts real bad."

She didn't sound strong to Sybil. "Why don't I call an ambulance for you? You need a doctor to look at your ankle. The medics can stabilize it for the ride. Is that okay?"

"Sure, I guess," she responded. The woman's voice sounded weak.

The ambulance arrived ten minutes later. Sybil was on the phone when it arrived, so she didn't have a good look at the action. As the medics were loading the woman on the stretcher, Sybil saw they'd stabilized the injured ankle. Just as they were leaving, Sybil rushed up and handed one of the medics the new shoes she taken off the woman, the purse, and the shoebox with the old shoes.

That evening at home, Sybil told her husband, Dave, all about the excitement. "I hope the woman's going to be okay," he responded. "Frankly, those spike heels are a hazard. I can't figure how women stand up in them. It serves her right for buying them."

"Oh Dave, your age is showing. You're being a middle-aged fuddy duddy."

"Watch your mouth, woman. You're fifty-five just like me."

Sybil continued with a smile. "High heels are perfectly safe if you know how to walk on them. The bigger problem is what they do to your feet if you wear them too often. This woman, Cynthia Calcott, I looked at her name on the credit card receipt, is younger than us, and she's the kind whose been wearing high heels for most of her life. Her old shoes were pretty high, too."

"She fell on the sidewalk, right, not in the store?"

"Yes. In fact, that made it worse. There was nothing out there to break her fall. I'm afraid she'll find she has some bruises as well as a bad ankle. I did the right thing to get her the ice."

"You're going to call Beth tonight. She'd be the one who knows if icing the ankle was the right thing. I'm just happy the fall didn't happen in the store. We might be liable for the accident if it happened there."

"There's no problem. And yes, I'm already planning on calling Beth. It's good to have a nurse in the family."

CHAPTER TWO

ON FRIDAY NIGHT three weeks later, Beth Watson and Ralph Williams walked to dinner at Phil Philemon's house. Ralph had known Phil since his undergraduate days at Lackey College. Phil had helped him with an independent study critical for his on-time graduation, and Phil had always been a faithful customer at his computer store. Ralph had sold a couple of computers to Phil's wife, Mary Jane, too. Tragically, she'd died in a traffic accident a couple of years earlier. *Wow, a lot has happened since Mary Jane's death*, Ralph thought.

Beth had her own thoughts during the walk. She'd become friends with Phil and Sherry Ahearn when the four of them had been involved in a plot to get justice for women who were being sexually harassed. At first, Beth had been intimidated by Sherry. She was so gorgeous, with long hair, strong cheekbones, clear skin, dimples, and a flawless figure. Phil, on the other hand, looked more-or-less like an ordinary guy. He was taller than Sherry and thin, and he'd started turning gray-haired and balding. She wondered whether he'd be totally bald before he turned completely gray. Beth understood Phil and Sherry were close to the same age, somewhere in their upper fifties. Nevertheless, Phil looked much older.

Unfortunately, the project to help victims of sexual harassment ended.

An FBI agent got wind of what they were doing, and she forced them to stop. Their activities didn't involve breaking any federal laws. Still, they were guilty of violating many state and local laws, mostly breaking and entering. While the FBI agent had been willing to look the other way, she told them she'd report them if she ever found they'd started their activities again.

With Sherry moving in with Phil, meals at the Philemon house were something to look forward to. After the four of them settled in the living room with wine, cheese, and crackers, Beth started the conversation by informing everyone her parents recently learned they were being sued.

"What happened?" Phil asked. "Did one of your father's car repairs go bad?"

"No," Beth answered. "A woman who bought a pair shoes at my mother's store fell on the sidewalk outside the store and broke her ankle. She's claiming the shoes were defective, and she fell inside the store. The lawsuit is for a million dollars—medical bills and pain and suffering."

"That sounds terrible," Sherry said, leaning over to spread some cheese on a cracker. "I hope your mom has liability insurance."

"She does, but it's not very good. There is a high deductible, and it only covers losses of up to half a million. If they lose the suit, it'll wipe out almost all their savings. My parents are really worried."

Phil interrupted. "The woman fell on the sidewalk outside the store. In the suit, she claims she fell inside the store. It sounds like she's lying."

"Yes. My mom's sure the woman is lying through her teeth. The lady fell outside the store, and the shoes weren't defective. My mom's very careful. She always inspects a shoe before a customer tries it on. Her store's one of those old-fashioned ones where individual service is part of the deal. She, or one of her employees, helps people try on the shoes. She doesn't just hand out shoe boxes."

"So, the lawsuit doesn't have any merit," Sherry concluded.

"Yes, and my mom's really disgusted. When she heard the woman screaming, my mom ran out to help her. She even helped the woman get to a chair inside the store and put ice on her ankle. My mom called the ambulance. Mom felt she'd gone out of her way to help the woman. The lawsuit came as a big surprise to her."

"Were there any witnesses?" Phil leaned back and sipped his wine.

"No. I asked the same question. The street was empty when the woman fell, and only one customer came into the store during the whole episode. That customer didn't buy anything, so there's no way to identify her. And even if mom knew who she was, it wouldn't help. The customer came in after my mom got the injured woman back in the store."

"I've been wondering about this since you told me about it earlier," Ralph commented, as he rose and started pacing. "It might not be so easy to prove the lawsuit's bogus. It's going to come down to one person's word against another's. The lady says she fell in the store and claimed the shoe had a defect. Your mom says the lady fell on the sidewalk, and there were no problems with the shoe. They'll agree on one thing—the ambulance picked up the woman in the store. How come she was in the store if she fell on the sidewalk? A lawyer would hammer at that."

"And," Phil said. "If these people are lying about what happened, they could easily have doctored the shoe to make it look defective. I bet they're the ones who have the shoe."

"I guess they do," Beth replied. "You guys are making me nervous. Do you really think there's a possibility my parents will lose?"

"I'm afraid so," Sherry offered. "Look, they're dealing with unscrupulous people. The woman is willing to lie. I don't see how anyone can prove she isn't. Like Ralph said, it's going to come down to two conflicting accounts. I hope your parents have a good lawyer."

"Their insurance company has a lawyer," Beth said. "My parents are relying on him to handle things."

"It might pay for them to get their own lawyer," Phil conjectured. "You say their insurance coverage won't cover the whole amount if they lose, right?"

"Yes."

Phil repeated, "They should get a lawyer."

Beth looked at the other two, and they nodded in agreement.

When they moved to the dining room for dinner, the conversation turned to Sherry's finances. Several months ago, the farmhouse Sherry lived in with her mother had burned down as the result of arson. While Sherry and her mother had managed to escape the fire, the house had been a total loss. Since she didn't have a house to return to, Sherry's mother decided to move into a continuing care retirement community close to her son, Trick, in South Carolina, and the family decided to sell the farmland.

After they started eating, Ralph asked, "So, what's the latest on the sale of the Ahearn land, Sherry?"

"There's big news," Sherry replied. "Phil has been marvelous. The offers we were getting were from oil companies, the ones doing fracking. We started to wonder how much they'd make if they found oil on our property."

"I suspect they'll find plenty," Ralph interrupted. "Several nearby farmers have sold out, and I hear the wells on those properties are productive. The Spiveys and the Nelsons have taken the loot and moved to Florida. Their farms are close to yours, aren't they?"

"Yes, they are. So, like I just said, Phil helped a great deal. He pointed out the local paper lists all property sales. He went to the archives and pulled up all land sales in the last two years. Then he narrowed the list down to those involving oil companies. This way we went into negotiations with a good idea of how much these guys were willing to pay."

"There were big payments in some cases," Phil added. "Based on this evidence, we suspected the averages we calculated underestimated the most the oil companies would be willing to pay. I bet a lot of those farmers didn't bargain very hard."

Sherry continued. "First, we learned the companies gave us low-ball first offers. We turned them all down. Two days ago, we sort of held an auction.

Three oil companies participated. It started when one of them came back with a more reasonable offer. I did it on the phone with Phil's coaching. When we had the higher offer, I called one of the other companies and told them. They bid higher. Then I called the third company, and they came up with an even higher offer. I don't remember how many phone calls were involved. Finally, two of the companies dropped out. While the companies clearly didn't like being squeezed, I really enjoyed it."

Sherry got up at that point and cleared the dinner plates. When she came back with dessert, strawberry short cake, Beth asked. "So, it's finished, the land sale I mean?"

"Not quite," Sherry answered. "We have to sign the papers. It's scheduled for this coming Tuesday. It's hard to believe everything worked out for us. I mean, none of us has ever had any money to speak of. Some years my parents made money farming, and other years they lost money. Librarians and county police chiefs don't make big money either. Now we'll have ten million to split up."

"Wow," Ralph and Beth gasped, almost in unison.

"Yeah, Sherry's money makes the windfall I had from the life insurance seem like nothing," Phil said. "While taxes will take a big chunk, there'll be plenty left over."

"I remember your worries about being able to pay for the retirement place your mother's in," Beth added. "I guess that'll be a piece of cake now."

"It'll be no problem. It took my mom a little while to understand just how much money we were going to receive. I told her to consider seriously what she'd do with her money. She'll have a lot left over after she pays the retirement community monthly fee. She's always wanted to give more to charities. She'll be able to now."

"We've advised her to be wary of talking about her newfound wealth," Phil said. "If she tells everybody, there's no telling how many people will try to get a piece of it."

Beth had a sour look on her face. "Your mother's problems aren't anything like my mother's. Being sued is really different than wondering what to do with millions of dollars."

"Oh, I'm so sorry, Beth," Sherry said. "I guess it's really insensitive for me to be talking about our good fortune given what your parents are facing."

"No, I'm happy for you. I'm just saying it's really different."

When they got home from Phil and Sherry's, Ralph knew Beth was close to tears. He took her in his arms and asked, "Do you want to talk about it?"

Beth sniffled. "It's the lawsuit business. You guys think I should call my parents and advise them to get a lawyer. You're right, but still it's hard. I mean, they're my parents, and they don't have all that much money. Lawyers can be expensive."

"It's hard, but you should do it."

Breaking out of Ralph's embrace, Beth continued. "I should be going to them for advice. It seems all wrong. This is the first time I'm the one giving advice. It feels weird, and the more you three talked about it, the worse I felt for my parents."

Ralph came to Beth and put his arms around her again. "I'm so sorry, honey. It's upsetting. The whole thing is. What kind of person must this woman be? She's willing to lie."

"I guess lots of people might be willing to lie if they thought they'd be able to get a million dollars. It's just incredibly bad luck she had to trip outside my mom's store. I'm not sure how my folks will handle it if they lose the lawsuit. I'm scared for them."

"It's too late to call tonight. Call them tomorrow. Ask if there's any way we can help. For now, try not to dwell on it. There's a lot we don't know yet. It won't do any good to worry."

Back at Phil and Sherry's, the couple had finished cleaning up and loading the dishwasher. After he checked to be sure the doors were locked, Phil joined Sherry in the bedroom. "So, have you thought about what you want to do with all your money? I used to wonder what I'd do with a big windfall. I can't remember coming to any conclusions—just daydreaming."

"I've had those same daydreams. Now it's real."

"So, have any ideas?"

"I've got some thoughts. I don't want to share them just yet. It's all so new. I don't really have a firm idea about what I want to do. I'm reluctant to change a lot. I'm in such a good place now. And you're a big part of it."

Sherry finished her little speech by shedding her dress and going to Phil. After a big kiss, she said, "When I've come to some conclusions, you'll be the first person I'll tell."

CHAPTER THREE

SYBIL AND DAVE were stunned as they walked out of the courthouse. They'd lost the case. Lost it big time. The judge awarded Cynthia Calcott one million and fifty thousand dollars. Sybil and Dave's lawyer, Thornton Reed, who trailed them out of the courthouse, also seemed to be having a difficult time believing the result. He caught up with the Watsons. "Listen, this is awful. I don't know about you, but I need a drink. Let's go to Sam's place across the street."

Sybil saw Beth and Ralph approaching. Still reeling from the events in the courtroom, she marveled at the changes in her daughter. Beth had lost a ton of weight, and she'd recently had her hair styled. Sybil figured it had to be the influence of either her boyfriend, Ralph, or the upcoming wedding. Whatever, it worked. The two young people joined the group. After hugging Beth, Sybil did the introductions. "Thornton, this is my daughter, Beth, and her boyfriend Ralph Williams."

Beth interrupted. "Fiancé not boyfriend."

"Excuse me. Anyway, Beth and Ralph, this is our lawyer Thornton Reed."

As the three of them shook hands, Sybil continued. "He's suggested going to that bar."

"Sounds good," Beth said, looking across the street.

As they walked toward the bar, Thornton saw a resemblance between Mrs. Watson and her daughter. Sybil Watson hadn't done as good a job of fighting a tendency to gain weight as her daughter. And her daughter was a couple of inches taller, which helped. Still, their dark coloring and basic facial features were similar. The boyfriend came from different stock. He had fair hair and looked a bit short, maybe five eight, not much taller than his girlfriend.

After they were seated, Ralph spoke up. "Thornton, isn't it a bit weird for the judge to award more than the plaintiff asked for?"

The bar maid interrupted them, and they settled on a pitcher of beer.

After she scurried off to fill their order, Thornton spoke up. "To answer your question, Ralph—it's Ralph, isn't it?"

"Yes."

"Anyway, it's very unusual for a judge to award more than the original amount in the suit."

"Didn't the whole proceeding seem really odd?" Beth asked. "The judge took the Calcott's side the entire time. He let them place the shoe in evidence even though you argued, I thought convincingly, it shouldn't have been. The shoe had been in the possession of the Calcott's the whole time. Also, he seemed to be blaming my mom for selling Mrs. Calcott a shoe with a spike heel. Hell, Mrs. Calcott is old enough to choose her own shoes. The entire proceedings appeared tilted toward them. Is there any way to appeal based on the notion the judge is biased?"

Thornton responded. "No, the only basis for appeal would be the judge's ruling about the admissibility of the shoe. Frankly, I wouldn't advise an appeal. Even a successful appeal comes with no guarantees. The result would be another trial. There's no way to be sure how a second trial would turn out. Cases like this with conflicting witnesses are difficult."

"It still looks to me like the judge was biased. He made a completely bogus justification for increasing the award," Ralph argued.

"I agree," Thornton responded. "And it might be possible to appeal on that basis. Listen, the expenses involved with an appeal might well be more than you'd gain in a reduced judgement. And, if the appeal is unsuccessful, all the fees would be money down the drain."

"You're arguing yourself out of a job, aren't you?" Dave asked.

"Yes, I guess I am. Still, it's the best advice. I don't want to take people's money based on false hopes."

The beer arrived. Dave poured for everyone.

After taking a sip, Sybil spoke up. "It's best to forget about the trial and not dream about any appeals. Right now, we need to figure out how to cobble together the money we need. Our insurance company is on the hook for almost half of the judgement, and we've got a little savings."

"You're right, honey. There's no way around it," Dave said. "It looks like my recent brilliant financial move doesn't look so brilliant."

"What do you mean, Dave?" Ralph asked.

"When we sold our house and downsized, I had a big capital gain. I decided not to put it all in the new house. I figured the new mortgage payments would be easy and putting the money from the old house in the stock market seemed like a good idea. Now it looks like a bone-headed move."

"Why?" Ralph asked.

"I'm sorry to say, Dave's right," Thornton answered. "The Calcott's lawyers can't come after the equity in the house, however they can come after more liquid assets."

"Look, Mom and Dad," Beth said. "I'm aware you have some savings set aside for my wedding. I don't need it. Ralph and I can take care of the expense. And I have some savings, I'd be willing to loan at no interest."

"That's sweet, Honey, and I guess we'll have to take you up on the wedding," Sybil said with a wan smile on her face. "Your dad and I wanted to throw you a big bash. I guess that's not possible now."

"It's okay, Mrs. Watson," jumped in Ralph. "Beth and I can handle it. Don't worry. I wasn't too keen on the big bash idea anyway."

The little gathering settled into an uncomfortable silence as they focused on their beer. Finally, they said their goodbyes and left.

Beth started the conversation on the drive to their apartment in Lackey. "I feel so awful for my parents. The whole thing turned out as bad as possible."

Ralph said, "I can't get over the feeling the judge was biased against your folks from the get-go. I mean, he seemed bound and determined to rule against them at every turn."

"I agree. Didn't it seem strange how confident the Calcotts looked during the entire proceedings? They acted like they knew they were going to win even before the trial started. I guess it was odd a week ago when they didn't take the settlement the insurance guy offered. According to my parents, they were cocky then, too."

"I didn't want to say anything in front of your folks, but I think they rigged the trial. The Calcotts paid off the judge."

"Ralph, you're being a little extreme. You have no way of knowing about any payoffs. Still, if you're right, a lot of things fall into place. The judge always ruled for the Calcotts. The Calcotts weren't nervous at all, and the judgement turned out to be for more than they asked. It all fits if they bought and paid for the trial."

"Yes, and it really makes me mad. Did you notice the car the Calcotts were driving? I did. It's a Mercedes S class. Those cars cost a mint. The Calcotts are rich already. They didn't need the judgement, let alone the extra the judge added on. I bet the extra is the judge's commission."

"You're getting a little crazy."

"Maybe I am. Still, the whole thing stinks. It's put your folks in a terrible bind."

After a several mile pause, Ralph broke the silence. "You know the old saying: crime doesn't pay. It's sure wrong in this case. Mrs. Calcott perjured herself plain and simple. That's a crime, and it's paying off for the Calcotts."

"You're right. Crime sure paid off this time," Beth said.

The rest of the way home they drove in silence.

CHAPTER FOUR

THE NEXT DAY when Phil arrived at the computer store, Ralph was in the back room, busy with a repair.

Ralph poked his head out. "Good, I thought it might be you. Can you come back here? There's something I want to talk over with you." Phil worked part time at Ralph's store. He'd quit his job as a history professor at Lackey College after he received a large payment from a life insurance policy on his wife.

"Sure. What's up?" Phil asked.

With Phil settled in the spare chair, Ralph started. "Did you hear what happened to Beth's parents? They lost. Beth and I went to the courthouse yesterday. It turned out to be a travesty. A totally biased judge found in favor of the other people, the Calcotts. I told Beth last night on our ride home it seemed like the judge had taken a bribe from them."

"So, Beth's folks have to come up with a million dollars."

"No. Actually the judgement turned out to be a million and fifty thousand dollars. The judge added the fifty thousand himself. The Watson's only have to pay a little over half of it. Their liability insurance covered the first five hundred thousand."

"Can they handle a loss that big?"

"It's going to be tough on them. The judgement will wipe out most of their savings. Recently they moved into a smaller house. They got a good price on the old house, and they didn't put a large down payment on the new one. They put the extra money from the old house into the stock market. Now it looks like they're going to lose all that money. Beth and I told them we'd pay for our wedding. We can take care of it."

Phil jumped in. "Sherry and I would like to help with the wedding. We've been meaning to tell you we'd host the rehearsal dinner."

"That's nice, thanks. I guess you're both rich now. It's not why I wanted you back here. I strongly suspect the Calcotts paid off the judge, and I want to see if I can prove it. I'm going to get out the surveillance equipment we used before and maybe some new stuff. I can't get over the feeling there was something fishy about the whole trial."

Phil looked at him skeptically. "Wait a minute, Ralph. Sherry made a firm promise to the FBI lady. We're finished. Melissa, that's her name, did us a favor looking the other way about the breaking and entering. She said she knew we hadn't broken any federal laws, nothing in the FBI's jurisdiction. Still, she's supposed to tell other jurisdictions about any law breaking she observes."

"Only you and Sherry," Ralph replied with a smile.

"I guess so. Yeah, you're right. We didn't tell her anything about you two. Sherry and I were the ones who promised Melissa. I guess you're off the hook. What do you plan to do?"

"Actually, I planned on asking you to help with the internet investigation. We need to find the homes and offices of Quinn Calcott, the husband of the woman who fell, and Thaddeus Moss, the judge. You are really good at scouring the internet to find things."

"Sure, I'd be happy to help, and maybe I'll enlist Sherry. She's finished with the land deal, so she's sort of at loose ends. She's planning to go to part time at the library, and I'm sure she'd be willing to help. There's only so much you can do on the internet. You're going to have to do scouting missions to Pittsburgh."

"Yeah. Would it be possible for you to come on some of those trips? It wouldn't be breaking any promises you had with the FBI lady. And I don't want to tell Beth about this for a while."

"I can come on some scouting missions with you. No problem. I'm not sure why you want to keep this from Beth."

The bell rang, alerting them that a customer had come into the store. Phil went out to take care of it.

That evening Sherry and Phil talked over what Ralph had asked and agreed they would have no problem helping. Phil gave Sherry her choice, and she chose Thaddeus Moss, the judge. That left Phil with Quinn Calcott.

After an hour on their computers, they gathered to compare notes. "You go first," Phil said.

"Okay. I learned quite a bit about Thad, that's what his friends call him. Thad is fifty-six years old, and he became a judge six years ago, so he has four years before he faces an up or down vote to retain his seat on the bench. Before running for judge, he had a partnership in a small law firm. He comes from some small town in eastern Pennsylvania. He went to Pitt undergrad and then Duquesne Law School. Two years ago, he moved into a new home in Squirrel Hill North. It's quite a place. The real estate listing is still up. I don't understand why they don't take them down after the house sells. Anyway, it's huge, just a little more than four thousand square feet, on a big lot with old trees. Also, he owns a vacation cabin in the mountains in northern Arizona. It's near a town called Show Low."

"How does he afford it?" Phil asked. "I don't know about cabins in Arizona, but the house in Pittsburgh must cost a bundle."

"It surprised me too. I looked up what judges make, and as far as I can tell, Thad must make about a hundred and seventy thousand. That's a nice salary."

"Yeah," Phil interrupted. "I'm surprised he can afford a house like the one you described."

"What about private law practice before he became a judge? Maybe he made a lot there."

"What else did you learn?" Phil asked. "I'm going to get a drink, do you want something?"

"Yes, a glass of water would be nice."

"Coming up. Go ahead, I can still hear you."

"He's divorced," Sherry continued. "It happened five years ago, before he moved into the giant house. There were two kids from the marriage. One, the boy, Christopher, is grown and out on his own. I did a little searching, and he's an airline pilot for a charter outfit in Pittsburgh. The other, a girl, Linda, is in college. It appears she stays with the mother."

"Does the ex-wife work?" Phil asked, handing her the glass.

"Not that I can tell, at least not now. It looks like she sold real estate for a while. There's no evidence she has any job now."

"I wonder where he got the money for the big house," Phil mused. "He's probably paying alimony. I bet his wife's still living in the house they lived in together. That means it wasn't possible for him to use the equity on that house for a down payment on the new house. While it's not proof by any means, it looks to me like the judge has some outside income."

"Unless he made a great deal of money while he worked at the law firm," Sherry repeated. "Or he might have come from family money."

"I guess that's possible."

"Yes, particularly the big money in a law firm. Sometimes lawyers share big awards in tort cases. I'll investigate that possibility later. I haven't had time yet. On the other hand, there might be something funny going on. So, what did you learn about our Mr. Calcott?"

"Quinn Calcott owns a string of jewelry stores in the Pittsburgh area,

Diamond Times."

"Oh, I've bought some stuff in one of those stores," Sherry interrupted as she got up to stretch.

"Anyway, he and Cynthia live in a big house in the Point Breeze neighborhood. Point Breeze is adjacent to Squirrel Hill where Judge Moss lives. It doesn't look like they have any kids. The jewelry stores are quite successful. His house is impressive, too. I couldn't find any real estate listing. It looks very nice on Google street views. The Calcotts have lived in their house for several years. Quinn has an office in one of the jewelry stores. His business address is different from his home address. It might even be the original store. It's right downtown. Anyway, that's all I learned."

"I suspect it will be enough to help Ralph," Sherry concluded. "You guys are going to go to Pittsburgh and scout out these locations?"

"Yes, that's the idea."

"We made promises to Melissa, so you can't do any breaking and entering."

"I talked to Ralph, and he understands. If there's any breaking and entering, he's on his own. The only weird thing is his not wanting to tell Beth. I don't quite understand."

"Yeah, Beth will have to be told if this gets beyond just a scouting expedition."

CHAPTER FIVE

PHIL AND RALPH left for Pittsburgh two days later. Ralph had the surveillance cameras and phone intercept gizmo he'd used before, and, as he explained to Phil during the drive, he had a microphone capable of picking up sound through walls.

"So, if this thing is positioned correctly, it can record sounds from inside a house?" Phil asked.

"Yes, but it doesn't have a great range. The people have to be in the room next to it, and if the walls are too thick, the sound might not carry. While I'm not counting on it, it just might work."

"There are problems. You're required to put the microphone on the actual building, right? It's different from the cameras and the phone intercept. They can be mounted outside the houses on trees or fences or something. I guess it's not breaking and entering, but it's not as simple as the other devices."

"This is just exploratory," Ralph commented. "I don't have enough to go on to risk actual breaking and entering. And if sticking the microphones on the house is chancy, I'll back off. Right now, I've just got a hunch. I don't want to do anything risky unless I have evidence, not just a hunch."

Phil and Ralph decided to make their first stop in the Squirrel Hill neighborhood where Judge Thaddeus Moss lived. As they approached the city, Phil asked, "Isn't Squirrel Hill close to Carnegie Mellon? I've been to some seminars there. The neighborhood is nearby."

"I'm not sure it's all that close to Carnegie Mellon," Ralph replied. "The school is farther toward the center of the city. I've got Judge Moss's address on the GPS. I'm sure it'll get us there."

Ralph's phone guided them to the Moss house. Though they'd both seen pictures of the house, it still impressed them—huge and on a large, heavily wooded lot.

"At least it's not made out of brick or stone," Phil commented. "That should give your listening device a better chance."

"Yeah, you're right. I bet we won't be that lucky with the Calcotts. Their house is brick. Anyway, we'd better not hang around here too long. My car doesn't fit this neighborhood. Let's park on one of the streets where there are stores. We can make it to the house on foot. I just hope there aren't very many people at home this time of day."

They found a parking spot about four blocks from Moss's house. After walking by the house to check for any activity, Ralph went to work. He had no trouble planting a camera on a tree in front of Moss's across-the-street neighbor's house. It would give a good view of Moss's front yard. Next Phil kept watch while Ralph climbed the fence surrounding Moss's yard. Just when Phil started to get nervous, Ralph reappeared at the top of the fence and jumped down with a smile on his face.

As they walked away, Ralph reported, "Piece of cake. I put up a camera focused on the back patio, and the phone intercept device went on a nearby tree. Those big trees are right near his house."

Phil interrupted. "What about the new microphone? Did you have the guts to stick it on the house?"

"Yeah, I did. We had a look at the floor plan. I got the microphone on the room I suspect is the judge's office. At least, it's not a bedroom."

"I remember. You and Sherry thought it had to be an office because it had such a small closet."

"All we can do is hope with the microphone. Based on our experience, the cameras and the phone intercept should provide a lot of information. If the microphone works, it'll be a bonus."

Being cautious, Phil and Ralph didn't retrace their steps, so it took them quite a while to get back to their car. When they got there, Ralph entered the next address in his phone. "My phone says it's only an eight-minute drive from here to the Calcott's house."

"Yeah," Phil responded. "I knew the neighborhoods were close."

They took a quick drive by the Calcott's big brick house, slowing slightly when they were across from the house. "Should we try to find another parking place?" Phil asked.

"No, I'm going to park in the next block, and we'll trade places. You can drive back toward the house and drop me off. I'll plant the equipment, and you can come pick me up after five minutes. I'm not going to even try to plant a microphone here."

After they swapped seats, Phil did a u-turn and dropped Ralph off. Then he drove around for five minutes before heading back toward the Calcott house. When Phil approached the house, an elderly gentleman was walking a dog along the sidewalk where he'd planned to pick up Ralph. He figured Ralph must be hiding somewhere, so he just kept driving. Three minutes later he came back, waving at the dog-walker who'd made it a block past the Calcott's by this time. At the pickup spot, Ralph stood waiting for him and jumped in.

"I had to hide from that guy walking his dog," Ralph said.

"That's what I figured. Did everything go well?"

"Yeah, like the other place, these big trees made it easy, particularly since I didn't actually have to go up to the house.

"Now it's diamond time," Phil said with a smile.

"Very funny," Ralph replied. "We have to head downtown. I'm putting the address in now."

It took thirty-five minutes to get to the area close to the Diamond Times store. After searching for a parking place, they finally parked in a garage three blocks from the store. Phil put on his black hair and mustache disguise in the car before leaving the garage. They'd decided he would go into the store while Ralph checked out the back of the store from the alley.

When they met in the car fifteen minutes later, Ralph looked excited. "I put one of the microphones on the back of the store. Just as I entered the alley, Calcott got into his big Mercedes and drove off. Getting him located was blind luck. Since I knew where he was, I went right up and peeked in the window. It's his office for sure. I put the microphone high on the window frame. And I mounted a phone intercept device on one of the buildings across the alley. I've got his office bugged two ways."

"Good, because I completely struck out. The jewelry store is sort of small, and the merchandise is clearly well guarded. There were two people working there: a middle-aged woman and a young guy, a big, young guy. If you ask me, he looked more like a guard than a salesman. He hung back while the woman came up and asked me if I needed help."

"That's okay. We didn't expect to learn much from looking at the inside of the store."

"It's not like I learned nothing. There were two doors at the back of the store, one labeled 'office', and the other labeled 'storeroom'. I saw a safe in the storeroom."

"I only saw one window on the alley side," Ralph said. "It makes sense. You wouldn't want a window in the storeroom."

That evening Beth asked Ralph how his day went.

Ralph paused, trying to figure out just what to say. Before he opened his mouth, Beth put her hand over it. "Stop. I'm aware of what you did today."

"What?" Ralph blurted, his heart pounding.

"I ran into Sherry at the grocery store. I went there on my break to grab something for lunch. Anyway, I asked where Phil was, and she told me the two of you had gone to Pittsburgh."

Ralph looked at her, dumbfounded.

"Look Ralph, I'm peeved at you right now, not because of what you did. I'm mad because you didn't tell me. We're going to get married. We can't have secrets. Why didn't you tell me?"

After a pause, Ralph spoke up. "I guess there were two reasons. First, I didn't want to bring up my hunch that the judge had been paid off. You didn't appear to think much of the idea. And second… actually, it's the same thing. I didn't want you to tell me not to go."

"So, you went to the judge's and the Calcott's houses?"

"Yes, we did, and Calcott's office too. I planted cameras and phone intercept equipment like we did when we were trying to get evidence on the sexual harassers."

"You didn't break into the houses or the office."

"Right. We just stayed outside, and I added something new this time."

"What?"

"I got a small microphone capable of picking up conversation through walls. I placed one on the home office of the judge and the business office of Calcott. When we check them in two weeks, we'll learn quite a bit."

"Do you really think the Calcotts bribed the judge?"

"Of course, nothing is for sure, but the whole thing bothered me. I couldn't get it out of my head. I feel so sorry for your folks. You were there. Didn't it feel to you like the trial was rigged? While your folks were nervous, it didn't look like the Calcotts were sweating at all. They seemed cool as cucumbers. I'm not sure we'll find anything based on what I did today, but I had to try."

"Okay, fair enough. Next time, just tell me. We can't have secrets from each other."

"I sure will."

CHAPTER SIX

WAITING TWO WEEKS to go back to Pittsburgh irked Ralph. He knew the Watsons didn't have to make their payment until fifteen days after the trial, so any payoff from the Calcotts to Judge Moss would likely happen late in the first week or early in the second week of surveillance.

Beth's folks scratched together the required payment. They wouldn't have been able to do it without the liability insurance. Still, it hurt. They now had very little savings. Beth found it painful to see her parents struggle, and Ralph hated to have Beth so upset. Going to pick up his surveillance equipment gave him something to do.

He and Beth made the trip to Pittsburgh together this time. Picking up the equipment was always easier than setting it up. He knew where to look, because he'd taken pictures of the installed equipment with his phone. The only chancy part involved the trip up to the judge's house to retrieve the microphone near his home office. At each location, Beth dropped Ralph off and came back five minutes later to pick him up. Everything went smoothly.

After picking up Ralph as he came out of the alley behind Calcott's office, Beth heaved a big sigh. "Wow, this is the first time I've been involved like this. I mean, I've done a lot of computer work, hacking and what all.

Now I'm a field operative, if that's what you call it."

"I hadn't thought about it that way," Ralph responded as he looked at her. "I guess you've been behind the scenes in the other operations. How does it feel?"

"It's different," Beth replied. "It's not a big deal dropping you off and picking you up. Still, it feels different. I felt keyed up the entire time. I kept wondering what I'd do if you weren't there at the pickup point, or if a police car came by, or if a dog started barking when you went up to that house. I kept going over what might go wrong. It's nerve wracking."

"I guess I've gotten past that kind of nervousness. I can tell where you're coming from. I remember being awfully nervous at the beginning. I remember once when I had to deliver a pizza we'd doctored. I sweated bullets when the guy we were after wanted to start a conversation. I guess I'm getting used to it now."

"Well, it's over. In my view, now comes the fun part."

"So, you like being a voyeur. You like looking at other people's lives."

Beth laughed. "Yes, I guess I do. We get the Calcotts, don't we?"

"Yeah, I asked Phil and Sherry to look at the stuff from Moss. It didn't matter how we split things. With the equipment up for two weeks, there will be lots to look at. It's going to take quite a while to review all the information."

The next evening the foursome gathered at Beth and Ralph's to discuss what they'd found. After Beth brought them all a beer, they settled into chairs arranged around Ralph's computer in the spare room.

"The guests go first," Ralph announced.

"Okay." Sherry inserted a thumb drive into the computer and took the clicker. "First, we'll show you what we found from the cameras, then the phone intercept and the microphone."

The first picture showed the front of Judge Moss's house. "I only have four things to show you. First, Thaddeus Moss drives a new Lexus. Here it comes now. Second, he has a girlfriend. She drives the little Fiat parked in front of the house in this picture, and this is her coming out of the house one evening. Later we learned her name. It's Catherine, Catherine Forbes. Forbes is a big name in Pittsburgh. Maybe she's from the family the street and the stadium are named after. We'll get further details on her in a few minutes. Third, this is Moss's grown son, Christopher, coming up to the door. He's a pilot for a charter airline. We only saw him once in the two weeks of video. We saved our most interesting finding for last. Moss only had one other guest," Sherry said as she restarted the video.

"That's the Calcott's Mercedes!" Ralph interjected.

"Yes, you're right. That's Quinn Calcott knocking on the judge's front door. He's carrying a briefcase, which we learn more about later. He only stayed in Moss's house for eight minutes." The four of them watched Quinn come out, get into his car, and drive away.

"Does his briefcase look any lighter as he's walking out?" Ralph asked.

"Honey, you're grabbing at straws," Beth said. "Have patience. Sherry told us we'd learn more about the briefcase later."

"Yes, we'll get to that," Sherry commented. "To finish up, we didn't get anything from the camera focused on the back porch. Moss doesn't ever use the porch. Now Phil will tell you what we learned from the audio sources."

Sherry handed control of the computer to Phil. "There were lots of phone intercepts, and the microphone in Moss's office worked too. Basically, we learned the same thing from both sources. I am just using the phone intercepts here because they were a little clearer. I've eliminated a great deal of phone conversations that aren't of interest to our investigation.

"The first conversation is from a call Moss made to a lawyer, Jim Simmons. The call is short. Here goes. Moss is speaking first."

"Jim, I'm getting antsy, I haven't been contacted by Wilson. I expected him to get to me yesterday. That's what we agreed."

"I'll get right on it. It isn't like Wilson to miss a deadline."

"We agreed on fifty K, right? And you know how I need it. Tell him he'd better come through."

"He's good for it, Thad. I'll let him know how important this all is."

"You do that."

As Phil stopped the recording, Beth asked, "So what's this all about, and how'd you learn the lawyer's name?"

"We had those same questions, so we did some research," Sherry replied. "Show them the next slide, Phil."

Phil clicked to the next slide. It showed a story from the *Pittsburgh Post Gazette* about a suit brought against a construction company, Wilson Enterprises. Tenants of one of the buildings they'd built sued them because the tenants claimed it had been poorly constructed. Despite what appeared to be mountains of good evidence, the tenants lost the suit.

Phil interrupted as the others read. "Look at the end. The Wilson company's lawyer is Jim Simmons, and the judge is none other than Thaddeus Moss."

"Look at the date, Beth," Ralph said, jumping up to point at the screen. "The Wilson suit finished just two days before your parents were in Moss's court."

"And there's more to it," Sherry said. "Jim Simmons is from the same law firm as the guy, Frank Martin, who represented the Calcotts."

"So, Moss is a crook, just like I thought," Ralph exclaimed, still standing.

"It looks that way to us," Sherry concluded.

"And the Wilson business isn't the only evidence," Phil added. "Listen to this. It's a conversation between Quinn Calcott and the judge. Calcott's the caller, and he goes first."

"Would it be okay if I came by in about a half an hour, Judge Moss? We got the payment from the Watson's lawyers this afternoon, so we can finish our business. I drained the cash registers in my stores, so I've got it in the form you want."

"Sure, Quinn, I'll be home. I'm looking forward to seeing you. You know I want it crisp, nothing worn or crumpled."

"No problem."

"So the call came just before Calcott's car showed up?" Ralph asked.

"Yes," Phil answered. "And I can't figure out why Quinn Calcott would have any business with Judge Moss unless it involved a bribe. It sure sounded like a bribe—in cash. Moss wanted crisp bills. I guess they pack more easily."

"Phil's right," Sherry added. "Look, the Wilson call is maybe clearer. I mean, he mentioned an amount. Still, the thing with Calcott is pretty clear too."

"Anything else show up on the phone?" Beth asked.

"There were several calls between the Judge and his girlfriend, Catherine," Phil said. "It looks like they haven't been in the relationship for long. They've gone out fairly often in the last month or so. She's slept at his house a couple of times. Moss would like to have her move in, but she's resisting. It doesn't have much to do with our dealings with Judge Moss."

"We did find out another interesting thing about Judge Moss," Sherry added. "Tell them about it, Phil."

"Moss is planning a trip to the Cayman Islands three weeks from now. At one point, he bragged to Catherine about having a bank account there. We learned about this trip by listening to a conversation he had with a travel agent."

"Who uses a travel agent anymore?" Ralph asked. "I thought everyone made their own trip arrangements online."

"Judge Moss does. We can play it for you if you want."

"No, that's all right."

Phil handed the clicker to Ralph. "There's only one other thing. Moss called a lawyer in Grand Cayman and set up an appointment for the day after he's scheduled to arrive. He said something about setting up another LLC. Do you know that's about?"

"Nope. Here, Beth, you take this," Ralph said handing her the clicker.

"We didn't find anything useful the way you guys did. At least nothing you guys didn't find," Beth said. "We heard the same conversation between Calcott and the judge. Calcott made the call from his office. Other than that, we saw them going in and out of the house. Quinn drove the Mercedes we already knew about, and Cynthia didn't drive. She's still laid up from the injury she got outside my mother's store. She's bored silly, and she phoned a lot of friends. We heard more about the goings on of the social set in Pittsburgh than we wanted. Otherwise, we didn't learn anything. There's no reason for you to hand me this clicker, Ralph. We've got nothing worth showing anyone. While we prepared some stuff, Phil and Sherry have already shown us the good stuff. What we have wouldn't add anything useful."

After a pause, Phil spoke up. "I guess I'll state the obvious. Ralph's hunch turned out to be right. Now we're left with a problem—what to do about it."

"You're right, Phil," Ralph concluded. "While I really want to do something, at the moment I don't have any ideas."

"Let's all sleep on it," Sherry offered. "Maybe someone will come up with a good idea. We're under no time pressure. Let's let it perk for a couple days."

CHAPTER SEVEN

THE NEXT DAY, Phil found Ralph rearranging some things on the shelves in the store when he came in. Ralph turned around. "Let's go to the work room, I've got something to run by you."

"What's up?" Phil asked as he plopped into a chair.

"I have an idea for what to do with Judge Moss."

"You were fast. What is it?" Phil had a surprised look on his face.

"I want to steal his money."

"Huh?"

Ralph continued. "I stayed up half the night thinking about it. Look, Moss is getting his bribes in cash. That's clear from the phone intercepts. And I figure he's taking the cash to the Cayman Islands. You can't make large cash deposits in a bank here without arousing suspicion."

Phil interrupted. "You're right. Banks have to notify the government if anyone makes a cash deposit over ten thousand dollars."

"Yeah, I looked it up. And if someone makes two cash deposits in a year totaling more than ten thousand dollars, they trigger the same report, even if the deposits are in different banks."

"So, Moss is never going to get people to write him a check for bribes like the fifty thousand dollars mentioned in the call with Wilson's lawyer.

It would leave an audit trail. He has to get his bribes in cash. Then he's got a problem. He can't just deposit the cash in the bank. It would leave another audit trail."

"You got it. We can be pretty sure Moss takes the cash to a Cayman Islands. I don't think they have limits on cash deposits. Taking that much cash out of the country is probably illegal. Nevertheless, I bet he can get away with it. He can figure a way of getting the money back into his US account at some later date."

"No doubt he can," Phil said. "Still, I don't understand where you're headed."

Ralph got up and started pacing. "If I'm right, he carries a briefcase, or maybe a suitcase, full of cash to the Cayman Islands. We should figure out how to steal the briefcase. The fact that he's carrying it to the Caymans makes him vulnerable. And the great thing about it is if we're successful, he can't report the theft. He can't report someone took his bribe money before he got a chance to launder it."

"Taking a large amount of cash out of the country is illegal. Isn't it?" Phil asked, looking at Ralph.

"Yeah. I looked that up too. You're supposed to report to the authorities if you are taking more than ten thousand in cash out of the country."

"That's wonderful. You're proposing to commit a crime the victim can't report. Very nice. Still, there are problems. Suppose somehow we succeed. You now have Moss's problem. How are we going to convert the cash into some useable form?"

"There are four of us, and we can take our time. Look, eventually I want to get the money to Beth's parents. I haven't thought about it much. Maybe Sherry, given her newfound wealth, would be able to anonymously pay off the Watson's loans. Then over the years we'd make deposits with the cash and pay Sherry back. I'm not sure. The whole idea's new."

Phil steepled his fingers and blew through them as he thought for a minute. Then he spoke up. "That might work. Still, you've got one big problem. How are you going to steal the money?"

Ralph continued his pacing. Finally, he spoke up. "Moss is going to be very nervous when he's transporting the money. But he's got to be vulnerable somehow. It's up to us to figure out how. Right now, my plan is to double up on the surveillance of Moss. We know his flight leaves for the Cayman Islands three weeks from now. We've got some time to gather more evidence. Maybe we can break into his house and take the money. Maybe we can figure out how he's planning to carry the money. Maybe we can switch suitcases with him, or just steal his suitcase at the airport."

"Wow, this seems really risky," Phil said. "I'm not sure we can pull it off."

"Come on, you're the guy who wore disguises and broke into businesses to plant cameras and recording devises. You can't be afraid of a little thievery."

"No, I'm not, but you're missing the critical difference between what we did before and what you're proposing."

"What's that?" Ralph asked, turning and looking Phil in the face.

"As you said, Moss is going to be really nervous. He's going to be very protective of his stash of cash. He'll have it well hidden in his house, probably in a safe. Also, when he's carrying it to the Cayman Islands, he's going to be very cautious. He's won't leave the briefcase, or whatever, out of his sight. In the other cases, our victims weren't trying to be careful. They weren't wary at all. Moss is going to be different."

"Fair enough," Ralph said, turning away. "It just means our surveillance is going to have to be very good. I'm going back to Pittsburgh tomorrow. Jim has agreed to look after the store in the afternoon. He doesn't have any classes. Do you want to come?"

"Sure, I can come," Phil answered. "Is it okay if I talk this over with Sherry? She's been working on ways to get back at Judge Moss, but probably not stealing his money. I'm not sure she'll like this idea."

"Yes, that's fine, talk about it with her."

Just then the bell rang, indicating the arrival of a customer. Phil went to the front and saw Sherry. "What are you doing here?" he asked. "We were just talking about you."

"You don't seem happy it's me, Phil," she said with a smile.

"No, it's not that," Phil stammered. "It's just a surprise. I thought you went to the library this morning."

"They didn't need me. Since I went on the hourly payroll, if I'm not needed, I shouldn't hang around doing busy work. People on the regular payroll are perfectly capable of doing what they had me doing. And I wanted to come here to talk to you two."

"You have an idea of what to do about Judge Moss or the Calcotts?" Phil asked.

"In fact, I do."

"Good, Ralph has an idea too. He's in the back. I'll rustle up another chair, so the three of us can talk."

When the three of them were seated, Phil asked Sherry to explain her idea.

"It's simple," she instructed. "Judges are elected in Pennsylvania, so we just need to feed our information to a newspaper reporter in Pittsburgh. What we have will create a big scandal. It's possible Judge Moss will be impeached based on what we found. It's like impeachment at the federal level. If the state assembly determines an impeachable offense has been committed, then the state senate must find the person guilty by a two-thirds vote. I say we set the wheels in motion. If impeachment doesn't work, the scandal created by the investigation will make it very difficult for Judge Moss to survive the next time he has to face the voters."

"When will that be?" Ralph asked.

"After judges are elected," Sherry responded. "They face an up or down vote to retain their position when they've been in office for ten years. Judge Moss comes up in four years. Anyway, my strategy is to create so much bad publicity that Moss will be impeached, or voted out of office, or maybe he'll resign."

Ralph looked skeptical. "It might be difficult to get a reporter interested without telling them where and how we got the information."

"I'm not so sure," Sherry answered. "At times reporters respond to hints and rumors. We might not have to divulge all our information, or maybe we should send it in confidence. Reporters are really good at protecting sources."

"I guess you're right. I can see how it might work," Ralph concluded.

Phil looked at his watch. "It's time for me to go to my Wednesday lunch. I expect both ideas might work. In fact, the more I think about it, the more I think they could work in sequence. Ralph, why don't you outline your idea to Sherry. We should try it first. If it works, or even if it doesn't, we can move on Sherry's plan. I've got to go now."

CHAPTER EIGHT

PHIL LEFT THE store and headed to Andy's restaurant where his weekly lunch group met. They'd been meeting for lunch on Wednesdays for more than fifteen years. There were seven of them. Phil and his good friend Jeremy Terrell were historians. Jeremy currently served as chair of the Lackey College history department. William Lin taught in the economics department. George Nathan was in political science, and Bob Latham taught math. Bert Holman was in the physics department. The only woman member, Sally Joins, didn't have a college connection. She served as the editor of the local newspaper.

The group met in the back room of Andy's restaurant because they didn't like being subjected to the TV monitors in the main room. Unless an important football game interrupted, the TVs were tuned to a right-wing news channel the Wednesday lunch group abhorred. They found it much more peaceful to meet in the back.

The back room had quite a bit of space. The Rotary Club met there Mondays, and Andy also hosted wedding receptions and other parties at times. The group had the room reserved every Wednesday. They didn't use the whole space, only two big tables pushed together.

Given his choice of news stations, it was surprising that the group got along with Andy. Often before lunch they kidded each other about the difference between what Andy told them real people thought and what egg-headed liberal professors thought. Today, when Phil got there, Andy and George were in an intense conversation. They clearly weren't agreeing. They were an odd-looking pair. Andy stood six-foot-three and towered over the five-eight George.

"What's up, you two?" Phil asked.

"Hi, Phil," George said. "Andy and I were just finishing up. I'll tell the whole group about it. Let's go to the back room."

When everyone got settled and their orders taken, Phil spoke up. "Okay George, tell us what you and Andy were talking about."

"It's weird," George replied. "I got here a little early and told Andy we'd just heard we're going to be grandparents for the first time."

"Congratulations!" William exclaimed. "You'll love it. You can swoop in and enjoy the grandkids. Then you can hand them back. It's great."

Others offered congratulations. After they settled down, George continued. "Andy's like you. He offered congratulations first. Then it got weird. He asked me if Michael and Stephanie were going to have their child immunized. At first, I didn't know what to say. I told him I wasn't sure, but I hoped so."

Bert interrupted. "Oh no! Andy's not one of those anti-vaccers, is he?"

"I'm not sure," George responded. "He said his wife… her name is Valerie."

"Yes, Valerie," Sally broke in. "I've met her."

"Anyway," George continued. "Andy told me Valerie had lots of friends who didn't believe in vaccinating babies. They were convinced vaccinations cause autism. I told him I thought the study showing a link between vaccinations and autism had been debunked. Still, he wanted me to have Michael get in touch with Valerie."

"Wow, finally a topic I know something about," Bert said with a gleam in his eye. "I teach about the anti-vaccination movement in my class about how science works. While I'd rather just teach physics, the dean requires me to teach this freshman seminar every other year. Anyway, I'm aware of the story. This doctor in the UK, Andrew Wakefield, published an article in the Lancet, a respected journal in medicine. He presented evidence showing a link between the measles, mumps, and rubella vaccine and autism. The article appeared in the late 1990s. Later, other researchers found lots of problems with the article. Eventually the journal retracted the article, and Wakefield lost his license to practice medicine in the UK."

"And haven't there been lots of follow-up studies finding no link between vaccinations and autism?" Bob asked.

"You're right," Bert answered. "The issue has been studied numerous times. No one has found support for Wakefield's findings. It turns out to be fairly easy to find comparable populations, some of whom have been vaccinated and others who haven't. Lots of studies have found no difference in the rates of autism between the two groups."

"So why do people still peddle the notion that vaccinations cause autism?" Sally asked. "I'm sure I'd be able to find several people in town who are convinced of a link and other problems too. Their kids aren't vaccinated."

"I wouldn't want any grandkids I might have to be in school sitting next to the kids of those parents," Jeremy said.

"You're not right," Bert responded. "If your grandkid is immunized, he or she's exceedingly unlikely to get the disease even if the unvaccinated kid does. And if a high enough proportion of the kids are vaccinated, there will be herd immunity. Essentially, if about ninety percent of kids are vaccinated, it really reduces the likelihood an unvaccinated kid will run into the bug. That's herd immunity."

"Aren't we losing herd immunity?" Sally asked. "I've heard there are places where the vaccination rates aren't high enough."

"Yes, and some school systems are considering requiring immunizations as a result," Bert added.

"This whole thing brings up an important question," Bob said. "Why do people seem to want to be ignorant of science? Like Bert said, the science is clear. Except for the one discredited study, there is no evidence of a link between vaccinations and autism. And there haven't been widespread problems with other vaccinations. Why do people persist in believing otherwise?"

"You hit on the right word!" Bert interrupted, almost yelling. "Ignorance. People are just not aware of the facts in lots of situations."

"Why?" Bob continued. "This should be a thing parents take seriously. And they should be consulting doctors—pediatricians, I guess."

Jeremy jumped in. "Some of these people are inclined to believe what they read on the internet more than doctors and regular news sources. It's about where you get information."

"That's only part of it; there's more," Phil said. "It's about the power of the anecdote. Lots of these websites peddling this stuff have very powerful anecdotes. For example, they will have a mother telling the story of her perfectly normal child contracting autism right after he got his shots. There's no discussion about whether she's a one in a billion case, or about whether the kid really had autistic tendencies before the shots. All you have is a powerful anecdote—an outraged mother."

"I understand," William said. "The presentation of statistical evidence isn't as convincing as a good anecdote. We've known that for a long time. It's part of one of my lectures in my statistics class. Isn't the anti-vaccination thing also about mistrust of authority? People not trusting scientists, or their doctors for that matter."

"Yes, that's part of it," Bert responded. "I remember lining up to get the sugar cube with the Sabin polio vaccine. Everyone in the school did, and no one thought twice about it. That wouldn't happen today. Too many people would object."

"And even if no one objected, so many kids are homeschooled today, the coverage of the vaccine wouldn't be nearly as high," George added.

"I hadn't thought about homeschooling," Sally said. "Even if vaccinations are required for entry into schools, it wouldn't get every kid. And William's idea about mistrust of authority is part of what's behind homeschooling, too."

"We've talked about this before. Isn't this all evidence of our collective failure?" George said. "I mean, we're educators, and doesn't this unwillingness to trust authorities point to a failure of the educational system? We should be doing a better job of teaching people to evaluate evidence."

"Yeah, but it's K through twelve," Bob said. "We teach at a college, remember."

"Aren't you smug," Sally broke in. "Lots of college graduate are anti-vaccers, Bob. You guys aren't off the hook."

"This is depressing me," Bert lamented. "I'm depressed because you're probably right, Sally. Still, I'm going back to work. At least maybe I can educate a few students. Maybe we can cut into the number of people who don't trust science."

"Yeah, and the wine is gone too, so it's time we went back to work. And we shouldn't be depressing Bert," Jeremy said as he joined Bert standing up.

The group settled the bill by all contributing the same amount as usual. Bob, the mathematician, determined the amount.

As Phil walked home, he wondered why he liked the lunch group so much. Maybe it linked him to his old days as a college professor. Maybe the contrast with the schemes Ralph and Sherry were discussing when he left the store made the group appealing. In any event, even though he didn't contribute much some days, he loved the Wednesday lunch group. The people in the group were great friends and keeping up with them was important to him. He hated having to miss Wednesday lunch when he was out of town.

CHAPTER NINE

PHIL AND RALPH drove to Pittsburgh the next day. The previous evening, Sherry had told Phil about her conversation with Ralph. Essentially, they'd agreed to pursue both approaches. Ralph's attempt to steal the bribe money from Judge Moss seemed like a long shot. Still, Phil could tell it intrigued Sherry. In addition, if they succeeded or not, they would be able to pursue Sherry's suggestion. They felt they had enough evidence to interest a reporter.

Phil filled the silence as they drove. "It surprised me how gung-ho Sherry is about trying to steal Judge Moss's money. We talked about it for quite a while last night. She's got all kinds of crazy ideas."

"Yeah, she seemed to really like the idea when we talked about it. She's particularly intrigued by the notion that the judge wouldn't be able to report the crime. He's not going to tell the authorities 'somebody stole my stash of cash' without generating a lot of questions about where he got it and why he took it out of the country."

"Now all we have to do is figure out how to get our hands on it."

Ralph responded after a brief pause. "Yeah, it might not be easy. Today we'll plant more cameras and listening devices to see what we can learn. This time it'll only be Moss's house. I thought about trying to do his office in the courthouse. I decided it's too risky."

"Good thinking."

A week later, the group gathered at Phil and Sherry's to hear Ralph's report on his additional surveillance of Judge Moss. After they settled in the living room with glasses of wine, Beth put the thumb drive in Phil's computer and did the magic required to show the images on his TV.

Ralph provided the commentary. "This first camera shows the view through the window of Moss's home office. The lighting is bad, so lots of the video is hard to make out. Anyway, we suspected Moss keeps the money in a safe, and we were right. This is Moss putting the money in a big wall safe. It's the money he got from the lawyer we heard on the phone call last time."

"The lawyer's named Jim Simmons," Beth reported. "We heard a phone call from him about a half hour before this video. He just said he was ready to make a delivery, and Judge Moss grumbled something about it being about time."

"How'd you recognize him? The lawyer, I mean," Phil asked.

"We got a good look at him when he knocked on Moss's door. It checked out with a picture of him on his law firm's website," Ralph answered.

"And I thought I recognized his voice from the other time we heard him," Beth added.

"You're right," Sherry agreed. "The video isn't that good. Can you run it in slow motion?"

"Good idea," Beth said.

Halfway through the video, Sherry got up and pointed to the screen. "You're right. Now I see it. Moss's putting a small bag into a safe."

"That's what we thought," Ralph responded. "And the bag would easily hold fifty thousand dollars."

"How do you know how big fifty thousand dollars would be?" Phil asked.

"I did the math. One thousand dollars is ten one hundreds, so fifty times ten is five hundred. Five hundred new bills packed tight would easily fit into a bag the size of the one Moss is handling in the video."

"I understand," Phil said. "I remember he wanted crisp bills. Lots of cash might be difficult to carry. Crisp bills would pack tighter."

Beth jumped in. "We figured out what Moss probably uses to carry the money. We got shots of him coming in and out of his house. One day his car was in the shop, and the repair place had to keep it overnight. We heard several phone calls about the car repair. Anyway, he usually enters and exits through his garage. With no car, he showed up in the videos because he used an Uber to get to work. Look at these two short ones."

"I see it," Sherry said after the first video. "It's the briefcase he's carrying."

"The second video is clearer," Beth added. "Look."

"You're right," Phil concluded. "The briefcase he's carrying is almost a small suitcase. It can hold lots of bags like we saw him putting in the safe."

"And he probably puts other stuff in there with the cash. To disguise it, I mean," Sherry commented.

"That's it." Ralph stood and stretched. "Nothing else useful. There were lots of phone calls, mostly with his girlfriend. Judge Moss wanted Catherine to accompany him on his trip to Grand Cayman, but she turned him down. He seemed a little peeved. After she visited him, he got over it."

"That's good news," Sherry said. "He's most vulnerable when he's traveling. It's better if he doesn't have a traveling companion."

"We thought so, too," Ralph responded. "We focused on the trip, and I'll let Beth tell you what she discovered."

"Okay, I hacked into the computers of the travel agency he uses. I have his entire itinerary—plane flights, complete with seat assignments, rental car information, and hotel." Reaching into a file folder, she gave Sherry and Phil a sheet of paper containing all the information.

"This is great." Phil smiled. "Sherry and I talked about stealing his suitcase. Knowing about this briefcase might make it easier. Can we go back to the videos of him on his front porch when he waited for the Uber? It's our best shot of checking out the suitcase/briefcase thing. Can we zoom in?"

"Sure. Just a second," Beth replied.

She put the video in slow motion until the best shot of Moss's briefcase, then she zoomed in.

Sherry broke in. "Let's get some printouts of those pictures. I can go to a luggage store I know in New York and give them a phony baloney story about my friend losing his favorite briefcase. I'll tell them I want an exact replacement."

"How do you know about luggage stores in New York?" Beth asked.

"I used to work in New York. The luggage store took up the first floor of a building where I worked."

"When I get home, Beth and I will print the best pictures of Moss's briefcase we can," Ralph said.

Phil nodded. "That's great, Ralph. I'm going to study the Cayman Islands airport set up. Our best chance will come there. He'll be tired from the flights, and he might let down his guard. That still brings up a question. Suppose we get his money? How do we get it back into the states?"

"I'm not sure," Sherry answered. "I suppose it depends on how much cash we get our hands on. We're pretty sure it will be fifty thousand. Surely that's a minimum. He should also have the money from the Calcotts. I bet it will be a lot. I wouldn't worry about what to do with it yet."

"I feel a little useless at the moment. I guess I'll Google, 'How do I launder money?'" Phil commented with a twinkle in his eye.

"Bad idea, Phil," Ralph said with a laugh. "Don't do it."

"I guess I'll have to be more subtle."

"Please do," echoed the others.

CHAPTER TEN

ON THE DAY Moss was scheduled to travel, Beth made it through security at the Pittsburgh airport. Her flight was headed to New York and didn't leave for several hours. Instead of finding the gate for her flight, she took a seat in the area for the flight from Pittsburgh to Miami. A half an hour before the scheduled boarding time, Judge Moss took a seat in her row. She texted Ralph, telling him Moss must have checked a bag. He only had the briefcase with him.

Beth had fixed her hair in a ponytail and dressed very casually. She didn't think the judge even looked at her in his courtroom. If he had, there'd be no way he'd recognize her now. Besides, Moss had his head buried in a newspaper. She got a good look at the briefcase. It was identical to the one Sherry bought on her quick trip to New York. After she'd finished her inspection, Beth wheeled her carryon suitcase down the row of seats toward Moss. When she got to him, her suitcase knocked over his briefcase. Beth turned around. "Oh, I'm so sorry." Before Moss reacted, she reached down and uprighted the briefcase.

Beth casually walked away from the gate. When she got around a corner, she extracted her cell phone from her purse and texted Ralph again. "About twenty pounds no luggage tag." Beth felt confident of her guess. She and

Ralph had practiced with the identical briefcase. As a result, Beth had become quite proficient at judging weights. She smiled at herself. She'd pulled off her job, and Moss didn't suspect a thing.

Several hours later, Sherry saw Moss arrive in Miami at the gate for the flight to Grand Cayman. He looked a little disheveled as people changing planes often do. She sat across from him, being sure her blouse was strategically unbuttoned, showing ample cleavage. Her new bra pushed her front up a bit. She felt sure Moss would notice. Also, she'd put a red tint in her hair and wore more make up than usual: bright red lipstick, more eye shadow, and some rouge. She thought she looked a little trampy. Phil and Ralph told her she'd be sure to attract attention anyway. Sure enough, Moss's glance lingered. When she saw she had his attention, she crossed her legs and her already short skirt rode up a little more. She didn't want to seem too obvious, so five minutes later she walked off in search of a cup of coffee.

When she got back to the seating area, her old seat had been taken. She noticed Moss, and a couple of other guys too, followed her with their eyes as she sat down. She got out her magazine and read. Thirty minutes later, the gate attendant called for the flight to board. Pausing strategically, Sherry took a place in the line a few people behind Moss. On the plane, Moss stashed his briefcase under the seat in front of him, not in the overhead bin. Since Moss had the aisle seat, he had to get up when Sherry arrived to claim the window seat. She smiled at him as he let her in. She couldn't help noticing he paid attention to her exposed top as she took her seat. She gave him another bright smile.

Sherry acted friendly during the flight. Having rehearsed her lines with Phil, she was ready. She told Judge Moss she lived in Chicago and worked in sales. She'd previously had a sales job, so she knew what details to include. Moss told her about being a judge in Pittsburgh. He offered to buy her a drink when the flight attendant brought the drink cart. She declined, telling him she just wanted orange juice. Late in the flight, Moss asked her where she planned to stay in Grand Cayman.

"On the beach," she replied with a smile.

"No, I mean which hotel."

Sherry gave him the name of a hotel right across the street from where she knew Moss had booked a room. She commented, "I'm not sure what it'll be like. A friend arranged it all. She's already on the island, and she's sending a driver to pick me up at the airport. It's funny. The easiest way for me to meet my ride is to go to the rental car area."

"I'm going to pick up a rental car," Moss responded. "Maybe we can try to find the rental car pick up together."

"It's a date," Sherry said with a big smile. Then she picked up her magazine and read for the remainder of the flight.

After immigration, Sherry waited at the baggage claim area with Moss, and he let her go first through the customs line after they collected their luggage. The car rental offices were a short walk from the terminal. Moss looked at Sherry's small roller suitcase and said, "You travel light."

"Bikinis don't take up much space," Sherry said, grinning at him. "My friend is sending a driver to the Alamo office. Which agency are you using?"

"Alamo too. What a coincidence. I guess we're destined to be together."

Sherry didn't reply. She just smiled and walked slowly. She didn't want Moss to be first in line when they reached the rental car place.

When they got to Alamo, Sherry looked around as if she were looking for her ride. "I don't spot the car coming to get me. I'll text my friend to tell her I'm waiting. After that, I'll go in and sit down."

After texting Phil, telling him she'd arrived, Sherry went into the rental car office. Their luck held. Moss stood third in the line in front of the counter. Sherry rolled her suitcase to the side and sat beside Ralph. He'd positioned himself behind a big suitcase. After depositing her suitcase, she came up beside Moss. "Here, let me take your bags. I can keep watch on them until my ride shows. My friend told me the driver was running late."

Then Sherry grabbed Moss's roller bag and briefcase, smiled at him, and set both bags beside the seat she'd claimed.

Moss seemed a little disconcerted by what Sherry had done, but he didn't complain. He looked over nervously at her a few times. Each time he looked; Sherry gave him a big smile. When Moss made it to the front of the line and was clearly focused on the rental agent, Ralph exchanged briefcases, always keeping his movements behind the larger suitcase. After switching the briefcases, Ralph got up and left with his big suitcase and Moss's briefcase. Just a few minutes later, a horn honked outside, and Sherry got up. She looked at Moss, who'd turned toward her. "That's my ride. Your stuff's there, safe and sound," she said, pointing. "See you," she added with a wave and another smile.

Sherry barely heard Moss's "I hope so" as she hurried to the car. She saw Ralph lying in the back seat as she got in the front. Phil loaded her suitcase in the back of the SUV and hustled around to the driver's seat.

When they were well away from the airport, Ralph sat up and shouted. "We did it! You wouldn't believe it. Moss hardly took his eyes off Sherry. When he finally had to pay attention to the rental agent guy, we made the switch."

"Did Beth get the weight right?" Phil asked.

Ralph hefted Moss's briefcase. "Yeah. She did a good job. I'm sure we're close enough. It doesn't matter. Even if he figures it out right away, we're out of there. There's no way he can tell what happened. He'll suspect Sherry. He'd do that anyway, even if he doesn't open his briefcase until tomorrow. We're clear."

"Here's your car," Phil said as he pulled into a parking space beside a little sedan. They'd left Ralph's rental car parked at a strip mall when they were on their way to the airport. "You'd better put on your disguise before you get out."

"Okay," Ralph responded as he put on a black wig and changed his shirt. "How do I look?" he asked.

The other two turned around. "There's not much chance you will run into Moss," Sherry said. "Even if you do, there's no way he'll recognize you as the guy sitting behind the big suitcase in the Alamo office."

"You're right. He stared at you the whole time. I'll go back and pick up Beth. Her plane gets in about a half an hour from now. See you at the house."

After Ralph backed out of his parking space, Phil and Sherry made the same maneuver and drove to the townhouse he and Ralph had rented the day before. The townhouse was in a complex at the far west end of the island, far away from the hotel Moss had booked.

Beth and Ralph arrived two hours after Phil and Sherry. Dressed in shorts, Sherry had a towel on her head because she'd washed the red rinse out of her hair. Ralph took Beth's suitcase up to the bedroom they were sharing. A few minutes later they came back down the stairs. They'd both had changed into shorts and t-shirts.

"Let's go over there," Phil said, pointing to the table in the dining area. "We're all set up. Sherry and I have fixed sangria."

The briefcase sat in the middle of the table, and the four of them arranged themselves in the chairs.

"Sherry should do the honors," Ralph announced. "She had to sit beside the guy for a whole plane flight."

Everyone agreed, so Sherry got up and tried to open the briefcase. It clearly had been locked. Ralph handed Sherry the key they'd saved from the identical briefcase. The key went into the briefcase with no problem. Despite considerable effort, the lock wouldn't turn.

"I wonder if Moss's having the same problem?" Beth asked.

"I bet he is," Ralph replied. "I'm going to have to get the big screwdriver I brought. We should be able to pry it open."

When Ralph came back with the screwdriver, he put the briefcase on the living-room floor. Inserting the tip of the screwdriver between the two halves of the briefcase, he pushed down on the screwdriver. The briefcase scooted away from him. "Phil, come and hold this thing," he yelled, a little frustrated.

"Sure," Phil answered. "It appears to be slippery."

Phil positioned himself so he stopped the briefcase from moving as Ralph tried to pry it open. Ralph had become red in the face when the briefcase finally came open. "Wow, that's one powerful lock!" he exclaimed.

"Bring it back to the table, Ralph," Beth commanded. "We all want to be there for the unveiling."

As the other three looked, Ralph opened the briefcase. The top contained spaces for file folders. Inside, they found two large ledger books. Ralph pulled one out and examined it closely. The top of the ledger book pages looked normal, but when Ralph opened the book, he saw most of the pages had been hollowed out to make two places where stacks of hundred-dollar bills sat. The bills fit tightly.

"I bet the guy looking through the scanner would never detect the money, even if he was looking for it," Sherry said.

"Look at the other ledger, Ralph," Beth said eagerly.

Ralph extracted the other ledger and inspected it. "It's identical."

The other side of the briefcase seemed to have personal items: slippers, boxer briefs, socks, pajamas, toiletries, and a couple of paperback novels. Ralph took out one of the slippers and found a roll of bills tucked inside. Upon inspection, all the items had money stashed in them. The paperbacks had been hollowed out like the ledger, the socks had bills inside, and the toiletry bag had quite a large stash. Even the boxer briefs were wrapped around a small stack of bills. When Ralph finished, there were several piles of bills on the table.

"You've got to give him credit," Phil commented. "He's invented an ingenious system. I bet he sails through security."

"Let's count it," Sherry suggested. "I'll get a pencil and some paper. We can split up the money. After you've finished counting a stack, remember the total. I'll add it up when we're through counting."

Silence reigned as the group started. Phil finished his stack of bills, a smaller one. "A hundred and five thousand."

"Be quiet, Phil," Sherry said. "We're trying to count."

After they counted all the money, Sherry used the calculator on her phone to do the addition. "Six hundred and twenty-five thousand," she exclaimed. "Here Beth, you'd better double check. I might have entered one of the numbers wrong."

After a brief pause as the other three watched, Beth looked up. "I got the same thing, six hundred and twenty-five thousand."

As they sat back, looking at the cash, Ralph piped up. "Remember Beth, when we said it looked like crime paid off for Judge Moss. It sure did."

"Yeah," Sherry responded. "Now it's paying off for us."

CHAPTER ELEVEN

BEFORE THE GROUP went out to dinner, Phil and Sherry walked along the beach holding hands. The warm tropical breeze felt great. They were in shorts and sandals.

"I bet this will be a day you remember for a long time," Phil said. "I've lived a lot of days, and I can't remember what happened on most days. On the other hand, some are memorable."

"You're right, Phil. It's not every day I help steal more than half a million dollars. I'll probably remember today vividly."

"So, what do you think about what we've done?"

"It's the kind of question I expect from you, Phil," Sherry replied with a smile.

"That's not an answer."

"Why don't you go first, Phil? What's your opinion?"

"Okay, if that's the way you want it, I'll go first. I'm thrilled. It's not like other things I've done since Mary Jane died, the revenge and our project with the victims of sexual harassment. I did a lot of planning for those and quite a bit of the execution. In this situation, I hardly had a role. It must have been different for you and Ralph. You were the ones who actually did it. And this guy Judge Moss is a big-time crook. Six hundred and twenty-five thousand dollars in bribes. There's no way he deserves the money."

Sherry looked thoughtful. "I can see that. Remember when I hadn't figured out you and Ralph were involved in the poisonings? I thought the poisoner had to be at fault because he took the law in his own hands like a vigilante. Well, aren't we at it again? This time it doesn't bother me at all."

"I'm not sure stealing his money is what a vigilante would do."

"Maybe not," Sherry said. "When we send what we learned to the newspaper, won't we be doing something the authorities should do? Aren't we trying to be the ones to dispense justice?"

Phil nodded. "Yes, it's a kind of vigilante justice. I guess that's true of all my recent activities. While I've resisted thinking of myself that way, unfortunately it fits."

Phil seemed unsettled as he restarted the conversation a few minutes later. "I think we're more like Robin Hood than just a run-of-the-mill vigilante. I like being Robin Hood. Steal from the rich to give to the poor. Isn't that what we're doing? We've got the first part, stealing from the rich. If we can figure out how to get the money to the Watsons, we'll accomplish the second part, giving to the poor."

"Oh Phil, I like it. I like being Robin Hood much more than being an ordinary vigilante. Now we have a problem—how do we get the six hundred and twenty-five thousand dollars back to the States in a useful form? We just can't hand the Watsons bags of cash."

"Ralph and I have been working on that. It's going to take some work and some time. Nevertheless, we think we know how we can get the money laundered."

"Money laundering, that's a crime for sure."

"Yes, it is. If you like being Robin Hood, you've already welcomed a life of crime. Stealing from the rich is clearly a crime. The nice thing about our stealing is that it will most likely never be reported. Stealing from a crook is a special kind of stealing from the rich."

When they reached a grove of palm trees, Sherry spoke again. "We'd better turn around. We don't want to be late."

After they'd turned around and walked a short way, Phil said, "I'm going to be worried about you for a while. You're the one in real jeopardy. If Moss got ahold of the passenger manifest, he might be able find your real name."

"I don't think so. He might try to find Cheryl Masters from Chicago. That's the name I gave him. And there's no way he saw my passport with my real name on it."

"I hope you're right. Still, he's a judge. I bet he has police friends, and they might be able to help him get the passenger manifest. It has your real name on it, doesn't it?"

"Yes, I had to give the airline my real name, date of birth, and passport number. Wouldn't the police have to get a warrant? Getting the passenger information would be a search, and I bet they can't do a search like that without a warrant."

"Yeah, I guess so. I'm just worried."

"Well Phil, I'm not going to ruin our time in this tropical paradise worrying. In fact, I want to change the subject. Remember I said I'd tell you if I had any big ideas about what I'd do with my newfound wealth? I don't mean the money we just took. I mean my share of the money from selling the farm."

"So, you have an idea?"

"Do you like children?" Sherry asked.

"Yes, I do. Mary Jane and I weren't able to have children. Finding out was one of the toughest things we had to adjust to during our marriage. We both wanted children. I liked being an uncle and being around my colleague's children, particularly Jeremy and Linda's. We babysat them a bunch of times. And we spent quite a bit of time with our niece and nephew. Why do you ask?"

Sherry stopped walking and faced Phil. "I like children too. So, what do you say to the notion that we should adopt a child or two? I've got all this money, and it just seems right to use it to help some kids."

"I'm not sure a couple of people living together like us could adopt. We'd have to be married," Phil stammered. "Are you proposing?"

Sherry paused. "Yes, I guess I am."

Phil responded. "I accept. I accept your proposal, both parts of it—the marriage and the idea of adopting."

They embraced and shared a long kiss.

Then Phil stepped back and asked, "Are you sure?"

"Yes, silly, I'm sure," Sherry answered, laughing. "I've never proposed before. It's kinda nice. And I liked your response."

"I've never been proposed to before. I have to say I liked it."

They kissed again.

Breaking out of Phil's embrace, Sherry resumed walking. "I don't want to go making any announcements yet, and I don't want a big wedding. Let's start looking into the adoption business. There are lots of options. We can take care of the marriage any time."

Phil replied, "Your plan makes good sense. We should let Beth and Ralph have the big wedding. It should be their time in the spotlight."

Looking down the beach Sherry said, "That's Beth and Ralph coming now. They look like they're having fun."

"Yeah, that's them. They both really look good. When Ralph started taking off weight… this is going to sound awful. I thought he looked like a fat guy who slimmed down."

"I don't understand."

"I guess he didn't look natural. Maybe it was his clothes, and maybe the weight came off his face after he'd lost it other places. What I'm trying to say is, he's past that phase. He just looks good now. And Beth's there, too."

"She's still wants to lose a little more. You know, then again maybe you don't. Women really want to look good in their wedding dresses."

"Makes sense. I'm sure you'll look good in yours."

After dinner, Ralph explained the plans for laundering the money. "I have an acquaintance back in Ohio I'm relying on. It's Richard Brothers, the son of my boss back at my first job in Youngstown. Richard, actually Dick, was the finance guy in the company. They did a lot of cash business, so they had money they wanted to hide from taxes. When this whole thing came up, I remembered Dick's dad used to take trips to the Cayman Islands."

"Convenient," Beth interrupted.

"Yes, it was. Anyway, the basic idea is to find someone who can take your cash and buy something with it, some real estate for example. They buy it for a corporation, an LLC, you've set up here in the Cayman Islands. A few months later, your agent sells your corporation's property, and distributes the proceeds to you. The check you get is legal, the payment of your corporation's earnings."

"I see it," Sherry said. "How do you find this agent you're talking about?"

"It's best if you use a lawyer," Phil answered. "You need a lawyer to set up the LLC, and one-stop shopping is a good idea."

"Yeah, Dick gave me a list of names. His dad died a couple of years ago, and he's doing the trips here now. Also, Phil and I talked to one of the banks yesterday. They had a list of recommendations too. One guy, Timothy Maurice, was on both lists. We went to Mr. Maurice's office and explained what we wanted to do. He didn't blink once. It was clear this wasn't his first rodeo."

Sherry looked concerned. "Didn't we intercept a phone call between Moss and some lawyer? I don't suppose it's Maurice."

"Good memory Sherry," Phil replied. "No, it's not Maurice. We checked, and Moss's lawyer wasn't on Dick's list."

Beth got up and started pacing. "So, it's all set up. We just hand him the money. You make it sound so simple. How do you know you can trust him?"

"He was on our list and the bank list too," Ralph replied. "Look honey, we just can't take bundles of cash back home. We can't deposit more than ten thousand dollars in a bank each year. Even with four of us, it would take forever."

"It makes me nervous too, Beth," Sherry said. "The whole thing is risky."

"I agree," Ralph commented. "But there's no way to eliminate the risk. I have to admit, I felt good when someone made both Dick's list and the bank's list."

Phil nodded in agreement. "Listen, we shouldn't do anything until Moss is headed home. Right now, even with your red hair gone and your clothes changed, you shouldn't be anywhere near the airport or even drive by Moss's hotel. We have Moss's schedule. He's going to leave day after tomorrow. After we're sure he's gone, you can come out of hiding."

"Phil's going to check at the airport to be sure Moss leaves on time," Ralph said. "After he's gone, we'll visit our lawyer and do the high finance."

Beth was still nervous. "Look guys, I think I want to take some cash home. I'd hate to give all of it to some local lawyer we don't really know."

"Sure." Ralph put his arm around her. "We're all going to take 9,500 dollars with us. We can put that much in the bank with no problem. I should have said that first. I'm sorry."

CHAPTER TWELVE

A WEEK AFTER they'd counted the money, the foursome gathered in the evening at Ralph and Beth's. They had been back from the Cayman Islands for three days.

Sherry hugged Ralph and Beth. "How's your sunburn, Beth?"

"It's getting better. I remember telling you how tough it was to sit on airplanes when your back hurts like mine did."

"I'm so sorry. I'm sure it hurt."

"Like I said, it's getting better. One of my nurse friends gave me a salve. It's really helped. Anyway, if I do peel, I hope it'll be cleared up well before the wedding. That's my big concern."

"It should be just fine by then."

"Let's get down to business," Phil said. "I thought we were going to talk about going after Moss."

"Yes," Sherry said. "My idea is to send a thumb drive to a *Pittsburgh Post-Gazette* reporter. We'd have to write a letter explaining what's on the thumb drive. It should have the recording of the two phone calls and two videos of the people, Calcott and the lawyer, coming to Moss's house. Also, we should include the phone calls between Moss and his travel agent. A trip to Grand Cayman should be very interesting to the reporter. There's enough there to get any self-respecting reporter to start digging."

"So, how do we pick a reporter?" Beth asked.

"We have an idea," Sherry replied. "Phil and I decided we should contact the reporter who wrote the story about the builders, Wilson Enterprises, winning when they were sued by the tenants. The story seemed sympathetic to the tenants who'd lost the case. If you read between the lines, it sounded like the reporter thought the tenants had been screwed."

"So, we write a letter and include the thumb drive?" Ralph asked. "That's fine, and we have to make clear we're only corresponding once. There's no way he, or is it a she?"

"She."

"No way she can get back to us. We should mail the stuff from somewhere obscure and be sure we wipe off any fingerprints."

"Maybe Sherry and I can take a short trip," Phil said.

"Where to?" Beth asked.

"I'm thinking of Cleveland," Phil replied. "It's not far, and there are interesting things we can do there. The Rock and Roll Hall of Fame, for example. I think the downtown has been spiffed up."

"Sounds like fun," replied Sherry.

Phil continued. "We'll go after my Wednesday lunch. Can you have the letter and the thumb drive ready then?"

"I've been drafting the letter in my head since we started talking about it," Sherry said. "It'll be easy for me to type it out tonight. I'll deliver it in an envelope to Ralph tomorrow."

"Good, and Beth and I will get the thumb drive prepared tonight after dinner," Ralph said. "It shouldn't be hard. Like Sherry, I've been thinking how I'd put it all together. I'm going to make it a Power Point document. That way I can embed the videos and the sound, along with the explanation."

The group walked to Andy's restaurant for dinner.

The next morning before Phil went to work at Ralph's store, Sherry gestured to a place next to her on the couch. "Phil, I want to talk about what I've found. I called three adoption agencies. As we expected, all three of them were happy to hear we're getting married. It's not impossible for a single mother to adopt. Still, it's a lot easier for couples. None of them seemed to be concerned about the fact that we won't have been married for long."

"I'm glad because there's nothing we can do about it."

"There might be some waiting no matter what we want. I guess I knew this before, if we're picky about the age of the child, we might have to wait a long time. There are lots of six years old and older kids waiting to be placed. If you want a younger child, it can take longer. Infants, which are what a lot of people prefer, are hardest to come by."

"So, we have to make a decision about the age of the child."

"Yes, we do. While I've always wanted an infant, the waits can be long. It's just that those early years are so important, and with an older kid, you can't tell what happened in the first few years."

"I agree, lots of the older kids are in foster homes, and their early years may well have been really messed up."

"I feel selfish saying this, but with all the drugs and the deaths from overdoses, even fairly young children could have had early experiences that scar them for life. Still, there are more unknowns with older kids. While those kids need a good family, I'm not sure I'm up to providing it. I guess I want an infant, so we have the best chance of avoiding some problems."

"I hear what you're saying. We're both new to this parenting thing. We'd better give ourselves the best chance of succeeding. I agree we'd be better off if we adopted an infant."

"We should get married right away, so we can get the process started."

"You'll get no argument from me," Phil said as he took Sherry in his arms.

<h1 style="text-align:center">CHAPTER THIRTEEN</h1>

PHIL ARRIVED AT Andy's late for Wednesday lunch. Andy manned his normal post, ready to seat people. "The rest of your gang is already here, Phil. They have some hot topic. They're all trying to talk at once. They just barged right by me today."

"I wonder what it is," Phil said.

"Beats me."

The rest of his lunch group were all seated around the table in the back room when Phil arrived. As Andy had suggested, at least two animated conversations were underway. When Phil sat down interrupting the conversations, Jeremy spoke up. "Phil, we already ordered for you. We're eager to find out your opinion."

"About what?" Phil blurted.

"Margaret's plans to resign, what else?" Bert answered.

"What? This is the first I've heard of it. The message must have been on the school email. I don't check it every day. I guess I should. Since I quit, it's become less and less interesting."

"You're right," Bob responded. "The email came this morning. Margaret announced her retirement effective the end of the school year. The announcement was mostly boiler plate. She's enjoyed her tenure as president. She accomplished a great deal. It's time for her to retire. Not much information really, and George wouldn't tell us the inside scoop until we were all assembled. So, George…"

"Okay. I'm on the executive committee of the faculty assembly. Yesterday afternoon we all received a phone call from the president's office about a meeting at nine o'clock this morning—very hush-hush. Actually, nothing particularly unusual. We have a couple of these short-notice, secret meetings each semester. Margaret likes to run ideas by us sometimes, and she likes knowing we won't leak sensitive information."

"It's nice to have you on the inside," Bert interrupted.

"Yes, Bert. While I can't talk about some of the meetings, this one I can. Margaret showed us the email she planned to release right after the meeting. In addition, she authorized us to add some details in our conversations, so here goes. Basically, Margaret wants to scale back. Nathan has a terrible commute, so after she retires, they're going to move closer to his work. Margaret has some friends who work at a consulting firm. They've told her they'd hire her on a project-by-project basis. She'll mostly be able to work from home."

"So basically, she's tired of being president," William commented. "Is that what I'm to take from what you've said?"

George answered. "Yes, that's not a bad summary. The deal about shortening Nathan's commute is part of it. She carries some guilt there. You're right. She's tired. It's not an easy job."

"You're probably right, George," Sally said. "It looks to me like a twenty-four hour a day job. I remember when that student committed suicide three years ago. Margaret had to go tell the family, and then she drove back here to be with students in the dorm. I'm not sure she got any sleep that night. We did a story about the whole thing."

"Yeah, it probably is a twenty-four hour a day job," Jeremy added. "At least you're on call for twenty-four hours. Lots of days nothing happens. On other days it's different. Students get into mischief all the time. At a small place like Lackey, while the student services people take the lead, the president has to be right there."

"And it's not just student mischief," Phil continued. "The hard part of the job is the care and feeding of the board. Let's face it, for the most part the board members are chosen because they have the potential to be big donors. As a result, most of our board members are from the business world—high up in the business world. They're used to being in charge. Lots of those guys can be hard to get along with."

"And the board is going to pick the next president, right?" Bert asked.

"Yes. The board already knew about the announcement, and the board chair knows he should select a search committee soon. Margaret assured us that Bill Josten, the chair of the board, is aware of the importance of including faculty and staff on the search committee."

"Josten's a lawyer," Bob said.

"Yes, he's the managing partner of a big firm in Philadelphia," George responded. "I've met him a few times, and he seems very sensible. I can't say as much for a few of the other board members, Johnson and McNulty, for example."

"I have a question for you all," Sally broke in. "I'm going to have to write a big story about Margaret O'Brien's presidency. For the most part, I have a good idea of the community's opinion of Margaret. They like her. She's done a good job of listening to community input, and the college is generally viewed as a good citizen, wouldn't you say Councilman Terrel?"

"You're right," Jeremy said. "There haven't been any real town and gown dustups during Margaret's tenure. Of course, I'd have to recuse myself from council deliberations if anything came up. I'd say the city government really likes Margaret. She's been willing to work with them."

"I can cover the community," Sally said. "What about the college? How are people at the college going to evaluate Margaret's presidency? You guys are my eyes and ears. What do you say?"

William spoke up first. "Lackey has made lots of progress under Margaret.

Our finances are sound. Sure, we could use a bigger endowment. What school couldn't? Still, our endowment has grown. We discount tuition quite a bit, and like other schools, tuition discounting is growing. We're not unusual there. I'd say the quality of the students has improved recently. The admission person Margaret hired, Avery Randolph, is really good. All things considered, she's been a successful president."

"I agree," Bert added. "She's been good about upholding academic values. That's important to me."

"Wasn't there a big to-do on campus about five years ago?" Sally asked. "I heard a bunch of faculty were mad at Margaret at the time."

"You mean the Ramirez case?" Bob asked.

"Yes, I think that's it," Sally answered.

"I know the details," Bob volunteered. "I served on the tenure and promotion committee when the case came up. So, this guy Juan Ramirez in the geology department came up for tenure. While all the evidence suggested he cleared the teaching hurdle, he appeared to be a complete zero in research. He hadn't even finished his PhD. His department still put him up for tenure. My committee and Margaret turned him down. As you said, Sally, it became a big to-do on campus. Students protested and so did some faculty. Margaret took the flack, and I for one, admired her for doing so."

"Me too," Bert added. "That's what I meant when I said she upheld academic values. We can't tenure people with no PhD. Most of the faculty who were upset with the Ramirez case were older. They were tenured back in the day when a PhD wasn't required. Margaret did the right thing listening to Bob and his committee."

"I remember talking to students who were really upset about Ramirez," Phil said. "I told them I thought he decided not to get tenure. They were shocked. I told them a PhD was a requirement, and Ramirez knew it. If you've been told there's a requirement, and you don't do it, it must be because you decided you don't want whatever it was, tenure in this case."

"I talked to a bunch of students about it too," George commented. "The students I talked to were upset about us losing our only Hispanic faculty member. I sympathized with them. Then I explained affirmative action can only go so far. We can't have lower standards for minority faculty."

"So, you guys supported Margaret in the Ramirez thing," Sally concluded.

"Yes," Jeremy responded. "And if you polled the faculty today, you'd get a big majority on our side. Even in this short time, many of his supporters have retired. The faculty is much stronger as a result. In my opinion, it's one of her big accomplishments."

"This is going to sound funny," Bob said. "As much as I like Margaret, she's stayed longer than a college president should."

"What?" echoed several members of the group.

"College presidents have a dual role. They have to be academic leaders and fundraisers. Most of the time we pick good academics to be presidents. We do it because we want them to run the campus, to be our leader. The other part of their job is to raise money and represent the college in the wider world. They're picked to do one job, but usually not the other half. To be successful in the money raising, a president is required to be comfortable with rich people, and rich people have to be comfortable with the president. To pull this off, it's better if the presidents look rich. As a result, presidents' houses are big and luxurious. The problem is the outside part of the job pulls them away from the inside part of their job. So, after about six or seven years, we need to pick another academic to bring back a balance."

"I don't agree," George said, clearly bothered. "You don't have to sacrifice the fundraising. You can just hire a competent dean and delegate the academic side. Lots of schools have hired presidents without good academic credentials, former senators and congressmen or business leaders. These guys can be good fundraisers, and the academics don't suffer because there is a strong dean who runs the academic side."

"That model doesn't always work," William said. "I know several guys who've been through what you're talking about. Economics departments are often in business schools, and business schools sometimes fall for the fundraiser dean with no academic experience. In a couple of those cases, it backfired on them. Their deans wanted to change the curriculum. You can't really prevent the president from meddling in academics if he or she wants to."

"I also don't agree with Bob," Jeremy added. "Presidential searches are crap shoots. You can't really tell what you're going to get. I say if you have a winner, keep the person as long as you can. I'm really sad Margaret's retiring. She is top notch, and it's too bad to lose her."

"I'm with Jeremy too," Bert said. "I'm going to keep my fingers crossed through this whole search process. Frankly, I don't expect we'll find anyone as good as Margaret. I just hope we come close."

After the lunch broke up, Phil hustled home. He and Sherry wanted to be on their way to Cleveland as soon as possible. While they drove, he filled Sherry in about the lunch group discussion. She said she hadn't been surprised. One of the librarians, a close friend of Margaret's, had hinted Margaret might leave soon.

"Lilian told me specifically not to mention her suspicions," Sherry said.

"Well, it surprised me. I guess my sources aren't as good as yours."

"So, what do you think of our chances of getting a new president as good as Margaret?"

"I'm worried. One of the guys at lunch said presidential searches are a crap shoot. I'm inclined to agree. You don't know what you're going to get."

"So, it's the curse of interesting times," Sherry concluded.

"I guess it is," Phil replied. "Now that I'm retired, it doesn't seem all that important."

CHAPTER FOURTEEN

PHIL AND SHERRY made a quick stop in Henderson on their way to Cleveland. They applied for a marriage license at the courthouse. They enjoyed themselves in Cleveland, a honeymoon before the wedding, and had fun purchasing wedding rings. On Sunday they drove most of the way home. After a short drive on Monday morning, they were first in line to be married by the justice of the peace.

On their way to Henderson, they'd had a discussion about when they should announce their marriage. Sherry started the discussion. "We shouldn't tell anyone until after Beth and Ralph's wedding. It's going to be a big wingding, and it should be. I want them to be in the limelight. Announcing our wedding would get in the way."

"I guess that's okay," Phil responded. "I was thinking we could send out… not a wedding invitation, but maybe a wedding announcement."

"Maybe yes, but actually no. In general, I'm opposed to wedding announcements, particularly for people in our age group. Announcements are a way people troll for gifts, and it's even worse when they register at stores. We don't need or want any wedding gifts. We have too much stuff already. I say we just tell people about our marriage sometime after Ralph and Beth's wedding. When the adoption happens, we'll need stuff for the baby, so we can send out announcements and have a big celebration."

After the ceremony, witnessed by two of the clerks in the justice of the peace's office, they walked out of the courtroom with their arms around each other.

When they were out the front door of the courthouse, Sherry pulled Phil to the side of the building. "Let's find a dark corner where we can kiss."

Phil went with her willingly.

After several long kisses at the back of the building, they broke apart when they heard a car coming.

"Look at us, acting like a couple of teenagers," Phil blurted.

"Yeah. Don't you like it, husband?" Sherry asked with a leer.

"You know I do. I'm incredibly happy."

"Me too."

They wandered around the square in Henderson, doing a little window shopping, and some actual shopping too. At eleven-thirty, they drove to their favorite restaurant for lunch. Once seated, Sherry told Phil how this wedding contrasted with her first wedding. "I wore a gorgeous white gown with a long train. The men were all in tuxedos, and the church, all decorated with flowers, looked great. I knew my parents didn't approve of Joel. They put on a happy face for my sake. The reception was a big bash. Looking back on it, I guess a few people drank too much. It didn't bother me at the time."

"So, this turned out to be a little different. No fancy dress, not that you don't look great, no decorated church, and no reception."

"Unlike my first marriage, this one will last. I was too young for my first marriage. We're solid. Joel and I never were."

"There are lots of other differences."

"Yeah, no nervous parents, no crowd, and no worrying about who would get drunk at the reception," Sherry said. "I hope you're okay with not telling anyone for a while. I feel like I sort of forced that decision."

"No problem. We can tell our friends after Beth and Ralph's wedding."

That same morning, Kristen Fowler walked into the *Pittsburgh Post-Gazette* offices. She arrived a little late because of the doctor's appointment she'd just finished. Every day she feared might be her last. Like almost every other daily, the *Post-Gazette* circulation shrank every year. While she'd survived one round of cuts, she wasn't sure she'd be as lucky the next time. She'd only been with the paper for two years, so she had every right to be nervous.

She cleared her desk every evening, so only this morning's mail cluttered the clean space she'd left the day before. She thumbed through it. No pink slip, thank goodness. The most interesting looking thing turned out to be a small package with a Cleveland postmark. Kristen attacked it with her letter opener and soon had it open. The package contained a thumb drive wrapped in a piece of paper. She smoothed out the paper and read it.

It contained instructions for accessing the thumb drive and a short commentary about the file on the drive. The note was signed XYZ. Whoever they were, they certainly sounded computer savvy. Kristen started up her computer and opened the Power Point file. The first slide contained a copy of a story she'd done on the trial of Wilson Enterprises. She remembered it well. It had been probably her best story. She'd only made the front page one other time. The next slide only said, "Click here to open the audio file of a phone call between Thaddeus Moss and Jim Simmons on September 15." Before clicking on the link, Kristen got her ear buds out of her desk and plugged them in. After a few seconds, she heard:

"Jim, I'm getting antsy, I haven't been contacted by Wilson. I expected him to get to me yesterday. That's what we agreed."

"I'll get right on it. It isn't like Wilson to miss a deadline like that."

"We agreed on fifty K, right? And you know I need it. Tell him he'd better come through."

"He's good for it, Thad. I'll let him know how important this all is."

"You do that."

Kristen sat back, stunned. This call was about a bribe. It had to be. She clicked for the next slide, which showed a video of Jim Simmonds arriving at what she expected might be Judge Moss's house. He carried a briefcase. It wasn't a long visit, and the date and time stamp on the video showed Simmonds had only been in the house for four minutes.

The next slide had another audio file, this time a call between Judge Moss and someone named Quinn Calcott. It appeared to be very similar to the first call. They had to be talking about a bribe. This time the Calcott guy mentioned having cash for the Judge. The next Power Point slide contained a video showing a guy, presumably Calcott, making a short visit to the same house.

The final slide had another audio file. It contained a discussion between Judge Moss and a travel agent. Moss made reservations to go to Grand Cayman for a short stay.

Kristen felt numb. XYZ, whoever he or she was, had to have been eavesdropping on Judge Moss. In addition, they had a video camera on Moss's front door. She grabbed a legal pad from her bottom drawer and started making notes. First, she had to find out Quinn Calcott's identity. Second, she had to figure out the connection between Judge Moss and Calcott. Third, she had to verify that the videos showed the entrance to Moss's house. Finally, she had to figure out how to approach her editor. The evidence she'd received had to have been illegally obtained. She knew she wouldn't be able to use the information directly. Still, she thought she could make a case to start an investigation.

It didn't take Kristen long to find out about Quinn Calcott, the owner of the Diamond Times jewelry stores. She also found a link between Calcott and Judge Moss. Last month, Moss presided in a suit Calcott filed against a Sybil Watson, the owner of a shoe store. Calcott's wife had broken her ankle, so they were suing the shoe store owner, Mrs. Watson. The store owner claimed the accident hadn't been her fault at all. The details of the case made clear the judge had ruled against Watson's lawyer at every turn. As she read the trial transcript, another shoe fell. The Calcott's lawyer, Frank Martin, worked at Johnson, Simms, and Fox, the same law firm as Jim Simmons.

Kristen realized she'd have to dig much harder to find evidence to use in a story. If she pulled it off, the story would be a blockbuster. She had a short story to write before deadline. She needed to get on it. Before she started, she called the editor-in-chief and set up a meeting for the only time slot he had after today's deadline.

In the bathroom where she'd gone to primp before meeting with Mike Felton, she looked at herself in the mirror. At twenty-eight, she thought she still looked good. Her curly brown hair was nicely styled. She'd finally found a guy who did a good job with it. In eighth grade, she'd been one of the tallest girls then she'd stopped growing. She wished she'd grown a couple of inches taller, but no such luck. She worked hard to keep her weight down. All things considered, she felt good about herself, and her boyfriend told her she looked great.

When Kristen walked into editor, Mike Felton's, office, she saw he was in a good mood. She closed his door behind her and sat down. Mike had worked at the paper for a long time. Despite being bald and developing a paunch, he looked younger than he probably was. Kristen often got a crick in her neck when looking at Mike. He stood about six foot three, and she had to admit his size intimidated her a little.

"What can I do for you, Kristen?" Mike asked.

"I have a lead on what might be a blockbuster story. It's complicated."

"So, tell me about it. I like blockbuster stories."

Kristen had her laptop. She'd saved the thumb drive file on it. Before she came, she'd checked to see if everything worked, and it did. "It would be easiest if I showed you. I got this thumb drive in the mail. I've got the file from it up on my laptop. It's short."

Mike looked interested as Kristen put the laptop on his desk and came around behind him to be sure everything worked.

Mike watched and listened intently through the entire Power Point presentation, clicking to advance the slides without any prompting. After he finished, Kristen picked up her computer and went back to the chair facing her editor.

Mike gazed at the ceiling. After a few moments, he looked Kristen in the eyes. "I'll be damned. I'm not sure where to start. So, you don't have any idea who sent this?"

"No, none at all. The package postmark said Cleveland, and the short note accompanying it was signed XYZ. I guess I got it because I wrote the story about the Wilson case. In any event, I've been able to fill in some information. Judge Thaddeus Moss is one of the speakers in both phone calls. Jim Simmons is the other participant in the first call. He represented Wilson Enterprises in the case I covered the first slide. The Calcott guy in the second call owns the Diamond Times jewelry stores, and he and his wife recently won a million-dollar judgment in Thaddeus Moss's courtroom. The house where the guys showed up is Moss's house. There's one more fact. The Calcott's lawyer works at the same law firm as Simmons."

"And the Simmons guy and the Calcott guy are the people seen entering the house?"

"Oh yes, I left that out of my summary. Sorry."

Editor Felton looked at the ceiling again while Kristen sat in nervous silence.

When his gaze settled on Kristen, he finally spoke. "So, tell me what you propose."

"I recognize I can't rely on this information alone. I guess I'd be able to call it an unnamed source. I'm sure I've got to have corroboration. You asked me what I propose. So here goes… I want to be relieved from all other assignments so I can track down information to back up what I just showed you. It looks like we have a crooked judge and a major law firm engaged in unethical behavior. We can't let it go uninvestigated."

"Which law firm is it?"

"Johnson, Simms, and Fox."

"Oh my God." Mike gulped, got up from his chair and started to pace. "I have four good friends who're partners in Johnson, Simms, and Fox. They're major players in the legal community. It will kill them if this comes out."

"I wouldn't be surprised," Kristen commented, swiveling around to face Mike, who, in mid pace, now occupied the far corner of his office.

Mike stopped pacing and sat back down. "Look Kristen, I'm going to go along with what you've suggested. Not surprisingly, I have a few stipulations. First, this has to be completely hush-hush. We can't have any leaks. No one can be aware of what you're working on. I guess I'll tell Barbara I've pulled you off for a special assignment. She doesn't have to know more than that. She can assign other people to the stories you normally cover."

"It shouldn't be too difficult. There's not anything big on my plate right now."

"Okay, second, I want you to work with Franklin Sexton. He's a private detective we use at times. In fact, I'm going to get you an office at his place. It's a couple of blocks away. Sexton can give you a parking place. That way you can avoid any questions from people around here. You can check your phone remotely, can't you?"

"Yes."

"Good. Third, assuming you can substantiate what's on the video, we'll have to bring in the editorial team to decide how to roll this out. This won't be a normal story. I suspect our lawyers will have to weigh in too. I guess that's it for now. Don't come to the office tomorrow. Work from home. It'll take me a day to get things arranged with Sexton."

"Fair enough, boss," Kristen said, thrilled.

"One more thing," Mike added. "I want weekly briefings. Maybe we can do them at my house on Sunday afternoons. This should be the last time we're together for a while."

"That works for me. My boyfriend's face is stuck in front of the football games every Sunday. Usually it's on TV, and every once in a while, he gets Steelers tickets somehow. It'll be just fine to have an excuse to be gone on Sunday afternoon. He won't miss me."

"I've met him. Yes, at the Christmas party. He's a young professor at Pitt, isn't he?"

"Yes, in the economics department. He's an econometrician, whatever that is. We don't talk much about what he does. I do hear about the campus politics."

"Politics of all kinds are probably hard to ignore," Mike said. "I dare say some of your colleagues talk a lot about newspaper politics when they get home."

Kristen laughed. "No Mike, never. That would never happen." Then she got up. She heard, "Good luck," as she walked out the editor's door.

CHAPTER FIFTEEN

BETH FELT NERVOUS as she and Ralph approached her parent's house. The house was new, only two years old, not the house she'd grown up in. Despite being smaller, it sat on a wooded lot in a nice neighborhood. Though she'd been there a few times, it still didn't feel right. While she recognized the paintings on the walls and much of the furniture, the whole thing unsettled her.

Ralph sensed some of Beth's nervousness, but he misdiagnosed the situation. He suspected Beth's mood resulted from the reason they'd come to Pittsburgh. Two things were on the agenda: the wedding and convincing the Watsons to accept the money they'd stolen from Judge Moss. Ralph had no concern about the wedding stuff. The wedding was Beth's deal. He had plenty of practice saying, "Whatever you want, honey." The money wouldn't be as easy. He didn't expect the Watsons would accept charity from them without considerable explanation. They'd checked with Phil and Sherry who'd reluctantly okayed giving the Watson's the details. Still, Ralph hoped they wouldn't have to reveal too much.

Sybil greeted them at the door, giving Beth a big hug and Ralph a decidedly smaller, awkward one. "Your father is running late at the shop. He should be here in twenty minutes."

"That's all right, Mom," Beth responded as she and Ralph sat on the couch.

"Yeah," Ralph commented. "Beth wants to talk to you about wedding details. I doubt Dave would be very interested."

"Are you, Ralph?" Sybil asked.

"Not as much as Beth."

"Fair enough. The wedding's only a week and a half away. What do you have for me, darling?" Sybil asked, pointing to the large folder in Beth's lap.

"It's the wedding plans. Here, why don't you trade places with Ralph. That'll make it easier to show you the pictures."

After Sybil and Ralph switched seats, Beth opened her folder and showed her mom a picture. "That's the dress. Not surprisingly, it looks gorgeous on the model. I've gone to two fittings, and it looks good on me too. I pick it up next Monday."

"It looks fabulous. I can pick out just the shoes to wear with it," Sybil responded with a smile. "It looks expensive. I hope it doesn't cost as much as it looks like it does. You shouldn't blow all your money on a wedding."

"Don't worry, Mom. The dress is reasonable, and we can afford it." Looking at Ralph, she added, "Ralph wouldn't let me break the bank on a wedding dress."

"No ma'am," Ralph said. "I want her to have what she wants, and I also want to have some money left over."

"Good for you, Ralph."

"Moving right along," Beth continued. "This is the country club in Henderson. It's where we're going to have the rehearsal dinner. Don't worry about the expense there. Our friends Phil and Sherry are hosting the dinner. She's come into a lot of money because her family sold their farm to an oil company—one of the ones that does fracking."

"That's real nice of your friends."

"I guess the rehearsal dinner is usually the responsibility of the groom's parents. However, my folks can't afford anything," Ralph said. "Like you said, it's awfully nice of Phil and Sherry to offer. Actually, they both have quite a bit of money."

"Must be nice," Sybil said wistfully.

Beth turned the page. "This is the hall where we're going to hold the reception. It's at a winery about ten miles out of town. It's fairly new, and we were able to get their hall at a reasonable rate."

"Before you go on," Sybil interrupted. "Let's talk. Are you sure you are all right with the seating arrangement I sent you by email last week? I've heard the seating chart for any dinner is often the hardest thing."

"Yes mom, your seating arrangement is okay with me. As you might expect, I'm not thrilled at having Carl and his plus one at our table. Since he's my brother, I guess it would be a big slap to have him anywhere else."

"I know you two don't get along. I hope he doesn't cause a fuss somehow. He promised he'd tell me who he planned to bring to the wedding. I haven't heard yet. I'll bug him again tomorrow. I don't approve of the kind of women he tends to go out with. On this occasion, there's no way around letting him have a date."

"It's my day, and even he couldn't ruin it."

"That's a great attitude, darling. Now let's get back to your pictures."

After looking at the picture of the winery hall, Sybil said, "I like the idea of the hall at the winery. This picture doesn't really show much detail."

At that point, they heard Dave Watson drive into the garage. When he came in the kitchen door, Sybil yelled, "Wash your hands, Dear, and then come and greet the young ones."

"Yes, Dear," came from the kitchen.

After Dave joined the group, they quickly brought him up to date on the wedding details. He clearly became uncomfortable with what he saw. Finally, he spoke up. He looked straight at Beth. "I don't want to burst your bubble, Honey. This looks way too expensive. You know our financial position took a big hit recently."

"Dave, the kids have told us from the start they can cover it, and their rich friends are going to take care of the rehearsal dinner. I'm nervous, too. It turns out these two are in the driver's seat. There doesn't appear to be any way to stop them."

"It just seems excessive." Focusing on Ralph, he continued. "I thought you weren't in favor of a big splashy wedding. What happened to you?"

Ralph sighed, looked at Beth. "Is it time to change the subject?"

"Yes, I guess it is. Why don't you start."

"Okay. It left a bad taste in my mouth when you guys lost the court case. From my vantage point, it looked as if the judge always ruled in favor of the Calcotts. I'll just say it. I thought the trial had been rigged. And to make a long story short, I turned out to be right. The Calcotts bribed Judge Moss."

"Wait a minute, boy. Back up," Dave interrupted, holding up his hands. "How the heck do you know that?"

Ralph sighed again and looked to Beth for support.

Beth jumped in to help. "Mom and Dad, you guys have to assure us that nothing Ralph's about to tell you will ever be repeated. Okay?"

Dave and Sybil looked startled. Finally, they nodded in agreement.

"I put up surveillance equipment at Moss's house and Calcott's house and office," Ralph said. "We intercepted a phone call between Calcott and Moss. Without outright saying it, the conversation concerned a bribe. Then we saw Quinn Calcott show up at Moss's house."

"Oh, my goodness!" Sybil blurted.

"I thought something must have been phony," Dave added.

"What are we going to do about it?" Sybil asked.

"Mom, that's what we want to explain next," Beth responded.

Ralph nodded. "You continue the story, Beth."

"Okay. We learned Judge Moss has taken bribes in other trials. As a result, he's collected lots of cash."

Dave interrupted. "I guess you can't write a check and put 'judge's bribe' in the comment line."

Everyone laughed. "No," Beth continued. "Judge Moss has a lot of cash he has to launder. Our phone intercept told us the judge had a trip to the Cayman Islands planned. Let me cut to the chase. We went to the Cayman Islands and managed to switch briefcases with the judge. We've got his stash of cash, and he can't report the theft. He can't go and say, 'Someone's taken the cash I got illegally.' As a result, we got a lot of cash, over six hundred thousand dollars. Just like the judge, we've had to launder it. Eventually we'll get it back in useable form."

"Holy cow!" Dave exclaimed. "I understand why you two wanted us to promise to keep quiet. And the big wedding expenses make sense, too."

"There's one more thing, Mister Watson," Ralph added. "We want to use most of the money to make you whole. Like Beth said, we're in the process of laundering the money, so it's not in the states yet. Eventually, we'll have enough to replace the savings you guys lost. There isn't a better use for Judge Moss's ill-gotten gains."

Neither Sybil nor Dave responded.

"Mom and Dad, it's a lot to spring on you, right now. You've got to accept what we did. We hope it's okay with you."

"So, you're telling me my daughter's a crook, and you want me to be okay with it!" Sybil exclaimed.

"Wait a minute, Honey. Don't be mad at the kids. Yes, I guess some of what they did turns out to be illegal. I'm thinking of their motive. They wanted to help us, and they wanted to punish a crooked judge. Frankly, I'm overwhelmed. Look at them. No offense, but you two don't look like international crooks."

"No offense taken, Dad," Beth commented, smiling. "Being ordinary looking is probably one of the secrets to our being successful. Anyway, we've gotten away with it so far."

"What about Judge Moss?" Dave asked.

"We've sent our information to a *Post-Gazette* reporter. Not the stuff about us robbing him on Grand Cayman, the stuff about the bribes. If the reporter's any good, she'll follow up. We hope Judge Moss will be the subject of a big exposé sometime soon. We can't tell if it will work. The way we figure, if they do a good job, the paper will get a big scoop. Papers like this kind of stuff, uncovering corruption."

"I'm flabbergasted," Dave concluded. "What about you, Sybil? Would you like to be out of debt again?"

"Well sure, but I'm worried about the kids. I don't want them to get in trouble."

"They seem awfully crafty to me. You shouldn't worry. I want to hear how they did it. Can you tell me the details, Ralph?"

"Sure."

Ralph and Beth accompanied Dave and Sybil to a local restaurant for dinner. Sybil had agreed to put what she had fixed in the freezer, so they could celebrate.

By the end of dinner in a booth well away from other diners, the elder Watsons had the full picture of the activities in Pittsburgh and the Cayman Islands. As they said goodbye to Beth and Ralph, it was clear they were happy with the way everything turned out.

CHAPTER SIXTEEN

KRISTEN FOWLER WALKED into the office at the detective agency. The quietness of the place bothered her. It lacked the hustle and bustle of the newspaper. She wasn't looking forward to her day. She had a lot of work to do, and she feared it might be a waste of time.

When she'd arrived at the detective agency three days ago, she'd met Franklin Sexton and showed him the evidence on the thumb drive. After a lengthy discussion, they'd decided on a plan of attack. Since Franklin was busy with another project, he gave the thumb drive to one of his techs to see what secrets it would reveal. After he finished his other work, he volunteered to compile dossiers on Moss, Simmons, and Calcott. Kristen's assignment came down to trying to figure out if any of the other lawyers at Johnson, Simms, and Fox were involved.

Court records were available online, so Kristen had no difficulty scooping up a lot of information. She'd busily taken notes for most of two days. At this point, she seemed to be drowning in information. She needed a way to organize what she'd found. She had two major results. First, Jim Simmons, the lawyer for Wilson Enterprises, hadn't lost a case in Judge Moss's court in the past three years. Kristen had the data to track back further if necessary. She hoped three years would be enough. Also, Frank

Martin, the Calcott's lawyer, had only lost one case in Moss's court. It happened three years ago. Since that one loss, he had an impressive string of victories.

Kristen realized she'd been spinning her wheels for the last hour. Finally, she decided to call her boyfriend, Gilbert Vorhees. He did lots of work with data. He'd probably be able to help her. Luckily, she reached Gil at work. She invited him for dinner and alluded to other benefits.

When Gil arrived at her apartment at five o'clock, Kristen welcomed him with a big kiss. When he tried to continue the process, Kristen wriggled away. "Gil, I need your help. We can get to what you want later."

"Okay. What's up?" he asked with a disappointed look on his face.

Kristen swore Gil to secrecy and then explained her project. She even showed him the slides from the thumb drive.

"Wow," Gil said after he'd viewed the presentation. "This is big. Really big. If you can crack this, it'll be front-page stuff. People get Pulitzers for this kind of reporting."

"Don't get ahead of things, Gil. We can't really use the information I just showed you. It wasn't obtained legally. Whoever did it violated a bunch of laws. You can't tap people's phones. And it's just one source. For me to have a story, I have to have multiple sources."

"So, what you have to do is follow up the leads you have. Is that it?"

"Yes. I'm working with a private detective. The editor and chief of the paper, Mike Felton, you met him at the Christmas party, is helping me."

"I'm sorry, I don't remember many names from that Christmas party."

"Well, anyway, he remembers you. Or at least he remembers you were a professor at Pitt."

"So, what can I do to help?"

Kristen pointed to her three-ring binder. "I've got three years of information from the court docket of Judge Moss. Moss handles civil suits, someone suing someone else. I've compiled information on the cases, the lawyers involved, and the outcome of the case. It's too much information. I haven't the faintest idea how to organize it. You're a data guy. Can you help?"

"What did you do with the cases settled out of court?"

"Good question. At this point, I used a rule of thumb. If the settlement amounted to eighty percent or more of the original amount, I called it a win for the plaintiff's lawyer. Less than eighty, I called it a win for the defense's lawyer. I recognize it's arbitrary. I had to use something."

"Let me look at the binder."

After Gil paged through the binder, he concluded, "You need to get this information into an Excel spreadsheet. One of the things you're trying to find out is whether other lawyers at this firm are involved, right?"

"Correct."

"You aren't sure there's only one firm's lawyers involved. You need to get all this information in a file. Let's go to your laptop. I'll show you how to do it."

When he opened Kristen's laptop, Gil fired up Excel and put Kristen's binder beside the computer. "We'll put the lawyer's name, the law firm's name, the date of the case, the name of the case, and the outcome."

After typing a line in the spreadsheet, he showed it to Kristen and asked, "Is there any more information you have on each case?"

"No, there's nothing more."

"All right, it works best if one of us types and the other one calls out the information. After we get the information in, we can figure out what it's telling us."

"Thanks so much, Gil. I wouldn't have known how to do this."

A half an hour after they started, they switched places, Gil calling out the information and Kristen typing. After another half hour, Kristen got up to fix dinner. Gil continued doing both jobs.

When she started dinner and set the table, Kristen asked, "Do you want wine with dinner? I have a nice Malbec. It's your favorite."

"Just give me a half glass with dinner. I need to be clear headed to finish the data entry. I can work on the bottle more seriously when we get to the analysis. A little buzz can help creativity," he commented, smiling.

"Fair enough. Let's not get too creative. Anyway, dinner will be ready in five minutes."

When Kristen called him, Gil got up from the computer, and stretching, came to the table. "Looks good. Thanks for cooking."

During dinner, the discussion avoided the current project. They focused on weekend plans and gossip about their friends. Kristen felt like she only had about half of Gil's attention. Finally, she said, "You seem preoccupied."

"Sorry, I can't help wondering what we're going to do with the data we're compiling. When I have a project, particularly a new one, part of my mind is working on it all the time. Usually it's subconscious, but sometimes it makes its way into my conscious mind. I should be better at paying attention to you."

"Don't worry. If it's my project you're thinking about, you are paying attention to me."

The remainder of the dinner passed in silence.

Leaving the dishes in the sink, the two of them polished off the data entry in another twenty minutes. When they'd finished, Gil spoke up. "I've got ideas. While some are probably bad, a few might be good."

"I've got no ideas, so you're ahead of me. Tell me what you've got."

"So, it's easy to determine winning percentages. Here, let me show you."

Gil created another column in the spreadsheet and filled it with a formula Kristen didn't understand. After he finished, he copied the formula into the other cells in the column, and the result showed winning percentages.

"Here, the lawyer is Simmons, and his winning percentage is one hundred," Gil commented, pointing to one of the entries on the spreadsheet. "That's a result you already have."

"I understand. And there are other one hundreds, too."

"You have to be careful. It looks to me as if a bunch of those one hundreds are for lawyers who've only been in the data once. They won the only case they had in Moss's court. It's not strong evidence. Here, let's look at the lawyers who've got one hundreds for at least four cases."

Gil went back to the spreadsheet and highlighted the three one hundreds meeting his criteria.

"So those are the ones I should look at?"

"At least they're strong suspects. Wait, you said one of the other guys you know is crooked lost one case early."

"Yes, Frank Martin. Let me see," she said taking the laptop from Gil. "Here he is, his winning percentage is eighty-three and a third, if my arithmetic is correct. He's won five out of the six cases, and he only lost in the first year. Let's check for any more like him."

"There's one more, Phillip Gestner," added Gil, looking over Kristen's shoulder. "He got the same eighty-three and a third with the same pattern."

"And he works for Johnson, Simms, and Fox too."

"This is not scientific at all, but it's sensible," Gil concluded. "It highlighted five lawyers, two you knew were crooked."

"Yes. Should I check out the other three?"

"At the moment, yes. Unfortunately, you aren't through gathering data like this. You have a problem, one that is rampant in bad social science. You don't have a control group. You need to look at some other judges' data."

"Why? I don't really suspect they're taking bribes like Judge Moss."

"Let me put it to you this way. Suppose I got heads six times in a row with a coin flip. You'd call it fairly amazing, and it is a low probability event. A coin flip is supposedly fair. Heads and tails are each supposed to come up half the time. Now, what if one lawyer is a lot better than his opponents? The likelihood of him winning a case would be much higher than one half. Winning six times in a row might not be that unlikely for him. Or suppose a lawyer wasn't great in the courtroom, but he decided to be very choosy in the cases he took. You'd get the same result."

"I see," Kristen responded. "In what we've done, maybe we picked out the really good lawyers, or like your second example, the guys who only take slam-dunk cases."

"Precisely. It's nice to work with smart people. I only wish all my students at Pitt picked things up as fast as you do."

"So, how do I get around the problem?"

"You need to look at a lot more data sets like this one. It's possible you'll find one hundred percent winning percentages are rare. That would strongly suggest Judge Moss is up to something. It's also possible the lawyers who excel in Moss's court turn out to be mediocre when they're before other judges. That would also suggest they are in cahoots with Moss."

"So, I've got to do all this a bunch more times?"

"I'm sorry, yes. While this much identified your targets, you haven't really proved anything. And, while you can't actually prove anything with more data, you can really strengthen your case."

"Ugh."

"Honey, I'd plead for a research assistant. Maybe the paper could get you one, or maybe the detective agency. They wouldn't have to know the subject of the story, and they wouldn't be working with Moss's docket. You have a very straightforward job for someone to do. It's the kind of thing we have our bright seniors, or even not so bright first-year graduate students, do."

Kristen turned and hugged Gil. "You've been fantastic. I'll probably call you again to do the formula thing. That's all for tonight."

"No problem with the formula," Gil said, pulling her closer. "But that's not all for tonight."

CHAPTER SEVENTEEN

A WEEK AFTER Kristen started work, Beth and Ralph went over to Phil and Sherry's for dinner. As they were enjoying their drinks before dinner, Ralph asked Phil if he'd heard anything more from their lawyer in Grand Cayman.

"Nothing I haven't already told you about. A couple of days after we got back, he sent a letter telling me about the property he'd purchased on behalf of our LLC. I don't expect we'll hear anything else for quite a while."

"The whole thing makes me a little nervous," Beth commented. "I just wish it was all finished."

"Me too," Sherry agreed. "But I've started to think about what we'll do when we get the money. I know the bulk of it is going to your folks, Beth, but there should be some left over. We've got to figure out what we'll do with the rest of our dough."

"Some of it is going to pay the bills from the Williams – Watson wedding, if I'm not mistaken," Phil broke in. "It's this weekend. We used some of the cash we brought back as the down payment for the rehearsal dinner this Friday night."

"Yes, only four more days of the single life," Beth said, smiling. "The wedding actually won't take much more money. We've also used cash to make a large down payment on the reception stuff. I still think we have to decide what to do with the money."

Sherry responded, "We should make some contributions with the money. Do you guys have favorite charities?"

"If I had my way," Beth piped in, "I'd give it to Planned Parenthood. They offer lots of valuable services to women, and they get attacked all the time by groups worried about abortions, which they really don't do that much. They'd get my vote."

"I'd have no problem with that choice," Phil commented. "My vote would go for the Nature Conservancy. I like the way they use capitalism to fight the excesses of capitalism. They buy land and then don't develop it. They don't try to stop development by changing laws people claim take away their property rights. They're different."

"I'm going to have to ponder the whole thing," Sherry responded. "Actually, I've been thinking about it a great deal now that I've come into all this money. I already make contributions to several charities, and it bothers me how many of them sell their donor lists to other charities. It's disgusting how much junk mail I get now."

"And if you start giving much larger donations, it'll only get worse," Phil warned. "As it is, since Sherry moved in, my mailbox is fuller than it's ever been."

"I bet when you start giving larger donations, you'll be on their lists for phone calls," Ralph said.

"It might get worse than that," Phil said. "The College makes annual in-person visits to big donors and even to alumni with potential who haven't donated. Sherry, whether you like it or not, you just moved into the group with significant potential."

"I guess people look at those property transfers in the paper," Sherry commented wistfully. "I've noticed some people are treating me differently. I'm not sure I like it."

"Let's all feel sorry for the poor little rich girl," Ralph said, laughing.

Sherry reached across the table and slapped him on the arm. "Shush, child. I know I'm really fortunate. Still, my new status does come with some worries."

Beth got up and started pacing. "Let's change the subject. I'm frustrated. There's been no evidence of anything from the *Post-Gazette*. How long does it take for them to break a story? It's been more than a week since they got our package."

"I've been wondering about it," Ralph added. "We put them in a tough spot. Obviously from the information we provided, there is something to be investigated. The problem is they can't just go with a sensational story based on one source."

"You're right, Ralph," Phil said. "And it might be more complicated because the source used illegal means to gather evidence. They can't directly use what we found out. Even if they find evidence to corroborate what we provided them, I'm not sure they can go directly to print. They may have to go to the authorities. They can arrange to have an exclusive when the police pounce. Before that, I'm not sure they can just publish."

"What about the *Washington Post* and Watergate and Deep Throat?" Sherry asked. "They wrote their stories without involving the authorities."

"While you're right, that was different," Phil responded. "It involved the President and the White House. Who would they go to? Our case is different. A charge against a local judge, some local lawyers, and some of their clients is different."

"Another thing I'd investigate if I'd received our package is the clients," Ralph commented. "I'd want to try to find out if the clients always knew about the bribes. In the two examples we sent them, the clients knew about it. Heck, Calcott actually paid it. In other cases, the lawyers may have paid the bribe without telling the clients."

"Oh, I get it," Beth said. "You're telling me it's complicated, so I shouldn't expect anything very soon."

"Yeah, I guess you've given a good summary," Phil concluded. "Let's move into the kitchen. Sherry's prepared what we need for 'make your own pizzas.'"

"I made a salad, too. Phil, you cool your heels. You get the last shot at the pizza stuff anyway. Come on, you two."

CHAPTER EIGHTEEN

KRISTEN AND LLOYD, the assistant assigned to her by the detective agency, worked at the court dockets on the two desks the detective agency placed at Kristen's disposal. They'd been at it for two days. Though it had been tedious work, Kristen had become convinced they had to do it. Based on her experience with Gil, she skipped a step. She and Lloyd, a long-haired twenty something who wore black clothes all the time, were entering their findings directly into Excel spreadsheets. While it had been a great deal slower than taking notes, in the end it would be faster. Gil had agreed to come to her apartment at three, so she and Lloyd hurried. She found it a little weird working with Lloyd. She'd decided not to outline the project to him. Mike advised her to keep the group in the know as small as possible. As far as Lloyd knew, he had a short-term assignment combing through the records for the interactions between lawyers and judges.

Kristen hustled to her apartment from the detective agency at two forty-five. She quickly changed clothes. She didn't need her work attire for her meeting with Gil. She retrieved some pretzels from her cupboard and put them in a bowl.

At five after three, Kristen started to pace. She'd already checked the front window twice looking for Gil. Two minutes later, her cell phone buzzed—a text message from Gil. He was stuck with a colleague and wouldn't be there until four.

Kristen didn't know whether to be mad or relieved. Gil knew how much this project meant to her, so he should have arrived at three. He should have been able to avoid his colleague. Maybe she was being too harsh. At least he'd sent the text message. He hadn't blown her off completely. Kristen decided to open a beer and calm down.

Gil finally arrived at five after four, full of apologies.

Somewhat mollified, Kristen led Gil to the computer and showed him the new files she and Lloyd had compiled. After she filled him in on the details, Gil happily consented to her offer of a beer and went to work.

After a few minutes, he cursed. When she hurried to see what was going on, he reported, "The formula I'm trying isn't able to work. It says that the data are alphanumeric, when they shouldn't be."

"Alphanumeric?"

"Yes. Oh, I guess it's computer jargon. It means the data are a mix of letters and numbers. The formula I'm trying to use will only work if all the data are numbers."

As Kristen leaned in, Gil pointed to a column. "All these entries should be numbers, right?"

"Yes."

After a few minutes, Gil shouted, "I found it. This is a lower case el, not a one. That's the problem. It usually doesn't make a difference. In this case, the formula can't work with the data as it is. I bet I can fix it in a hurry."

"I wonder why they don't make computers smart enough to avoid that kind of thing," Kristen remarked. "You and I—well, at least you, can tell what's going on."

"Right now computers aren't that smart. They're very literal. They will do what you tell them to. If you tell them to do something they can't, they balk. In this case, I tried to do a numerical calculation with a letter, and the computer told me it couldn't do it. I've got it fixed now."

Gil went back to work while Kristen paced. She knew better than to interrupt him as he did whatever he did. While she'd had patience entering the data, she found it difficult to wait now. She thought, *When I was entering the data, I knew how much I had to do. I could see the end. Now I can't tell if it's going to take him another minute or another hour. This is frustrating.*

Thirty minutes after he started, Gil pushed his chair back from the desk. "I've got some results for you. I've been able to clean up the data, and I've computed winning percentages for the lawyers in other courtrooms."

Kristen, who'd wandered into her bedroom, came running out and pulled up a chair. "What do you have for me?" she asked excitedly.

"First, let's look at the two you know are crooked.

"Simmons, who always wins in Judge Moss's court, turns out to be mediocre in other judges' courts. I combined his cases in the three other judges' courts, and his winning percentage is only fifty-seven percent. He won four of seven cases."

"So, he's not nearly as successful as he is when he's before Judge Moss."

"Bingo. I'd say this evidence clearly supports the notion that he and Moss are in cahoots."

"What about Martin?"

"You get a similar result. Martin had a string of five wins in a row in Moss's court, if I remember correctly."

"Right," Kristen piped in.

"He too is mediocre in the other judge's courts. He shows up ten times in the data, with only four wins. It's the same with Simmons. He and Moss seem to be in cahoots."

"What about the other big winners in the data from Moss's court?"

"The other one from the same law firm, Phillip Gestner, looks the same. While he did very well in Moss's court, he's really very bad in the other courts. His winning percentage is twenty-two percent, only two wins in nine appearances. I'd put him in the same group as Simmons and Martin."

"Sounds reasonable."

"That's about it. The other two guys, Buckner and Lawler, who had good records in Moss's court, had great records in the rest of the data."

"So, they're just good lawyers."

"Or they just take on slam-dunk cases. Maybe it's part of being a good lawyer."

"Yeah, I guess so. Anyway, you've been wonderful, Gil," Kristen said, coming over and plopping in his lap.

After a long kiss, Gill pushed Kristen off. "There's one more thing I can do for you, and it's important."

Kristen straightened her clothes. "What's that?"

"It shouldn't take long. We need to determine just how unusual it is for a lawyer to have a long win streak in any one court. It's still possible our findings aren't unusual. It's possible that other lawyer-judge combinations produce records like the ones we've seen in Moss's court."

"Okay. How hard will that be to do?"

"It shouldn't take long. All the data are here. I just have to rearrange things."

"Thanks so much, Gil."

"Keep those thoughts for the acceptance speech when you win the Pulitzer."

"I might just have a more immediate way to manifest my gratitude," Kristen smirked, giving Gil a wink. "Do you want another beer?"

"Both things you're offering sound great," Gil answered.

After half an hour, Gil got up and went to the refrigerator to get a third beer.

Kristen, who'd started to get up, slumped back on the couch and went back to the magazine she'd been reading.

Twenty minutes later, Gil got up again. "I'm finished."

Kristen went to Gil and hugged him from the back. "What did you learn?"

"Here, I put it in graph form. It shows the winning percentages of lawyer-judge combinations for lawyers and judges who had at least four interactions. On the right-hand edge of the graph is the one-hundred percent for the Simmons-Moss combination. There are five other lawyer-judge combinations with one-hundreds. I checked them out. Those lawyers did well with other judges, too."

"So, Simmons is really unusual in the data."

"Spoken like a sensible social scientist, Kristen. I'm impressed."

"What about Martin and Gestner?"

"It's a little messier with them. They won five of the six cases in Moss's court, for eighty-three and a third percent. There are more lawyer judge combinations in that range, but not too many. I checked the lawyers out, and they tended to do well with other judges. In some instances, it's not as neat as you might want it. Still, basically Simmons, Martin, and Gestner stand out."

"And they are all in the same law firm. That's strong evidence too."

"Sure, and it might be easy to find out whether they are about the same age, and maybe whether they hang together."

Kristen grabbed the computer and opened the internet. "It should be easy to check out their ages. The law firm's website will have pictures."

When the pictures appeared, Kristen looked at Gil, and reported, "Well, we struck out there. Simmons looks to be about twenty or so years older than the other two. He's probably in his mid-sixties. Martin and Gestner might be about the same age. Somewhere in their forties."

"Maybe the younger ones worked with Simmons before they made partner. The connection doesn't have to be age," Gil suggested.

"I guess a reporter will have to do some work."

"I think she'd better."

CHAPTER NINETEEN

THE CURRENT FACULTY members in Phil's Wednesday lunch group trailed in later than expected. Phil and Sally had been waiting for five minutes.

"What's up?" Sally asked. "You're all together and late."

"We just came from a faculty meeting. Well, Bert wasn't there," George answered.

"No, you're wrong," Bert declared. "I had to teach, but I ran to catch the last little bit of the meeting."

"Wow!" Phil exclaimed. "Let me just say things have changed since I retired. As I remember it, it's like pulling teeth to get the faculty to come to meetings. And isn't it unusual to have a meeting late in the morning? I can't remember ever having a faculty meeting that didn't start at three-thirty or four."

"You're right, Phil. This special meeting at an unusual time broke all the rules," George said. "We had to accommodate the Board Chair's timing. Actually, he appeared on a video link. The meeting focused on the search."

"Yeah, they announced the presidential search committee, and George is on it," Bert said.

"Who else is on it?" Phil asked.

"It's a real rogues' gallery, if you ask me," Bert answered. "Oh, with the exception of George, of course."

"Calm down, Bert. It's not a bad committee," Jeremy interjected.

"So, who's on it?" Phil asked again.

George answered, "The majority of the committee is from the board, mostly guys who've been on the board for a while. The faculty are: Lydia Armento, who teaches Spanish, Bill Clemmons from classics, Frank Jenkins from English, and me. The staff people are: the head librarian, William Sturgis and Billy Suggs, from athletics."

"What did I tell you?" Bert blurted out. "Not a scientist on the committee. I can't understand how you can have a committee without a single person from math or any of the sciences."

"I agree," Bob commented.

"It does look odd," Phil responded, glad he wasn't really involved.

"Actually, I brought it up with Josten, the board chair, when he called me about being on the committee," George reported. "He told me two of the board members had strong science backgrounds. Though I'm sure you're not mollified, Bert, at least he'd thought about it."

"Still, it's a slight," Bert said, scowling.

"I have to agree with Bert on this one," Bob said. "Again, excepting George, the faculty on the committee don't have a quantitative bone in their bodies."

"Is it really important who's on the search committee?" Sally asked. "The whole process is weird if you ask me. Why doesn't the board just ask for applications and hire who they want? That's the way it would work in business."

"Faculty and staff at a place like Lackey, and most other small colleges too, are used to what's called shared governance," Phil answered. "The administration and the board govern for the most part. When it comes to the curriculum and other academic matters, the faculty is in charge. So, we aren't just employees like people who work in business. And with tenure, we can't just be fired. Faculty members are part of the governance structure."

"Phil's right," Bob said. "But we aren't so special in this case, however. As I understand it, the search committee, which already has a majority from the board, is charged to provide an unranked list of three potential presidents to the board. The board picks the president, the search committee doesn't."

"Okay. While I understand how it makes sense, it's still weird," Sally commented.

William spoke up. "I'm surprised we've made it this far without anyone mentioning the really important part of the meeting."

"The closed search?" George asked.

"You're right, George," William answered. "It's a big change. Lots of other colleges and universities are moving in that direction. I'd hoped we'd be different."

"You guys are speaking in code again," Sally grumbled. "What's a closed search?"

"I'm surprised," Phil said. "Last time we had an open search. Let me explain, Sally. Most of the people who apply for a college presidency have responsible positions, and some of them don't want it known they're looking to move. Maybe they're a college president somewhere else. You don't want people to be aware you're applying to other schools. So, at the start, the list of applicants is kept secret—it's closed. However, when you whittle down the list to three or four finalists, you open up, you announce who they are, and bring them to campus for a round of interviews. In the end, the process is open. Everyone who's interested can have a list of the finalists."

"That's an open search, right? So how does a closed search work?" Sally asked.

"The last step Phil outlined doesn't happen," Bob responded. "The search is closed all the way. The idea is that you'll get better applicants with a closed search. Lots of good candidates will not apply to open searches because they don't want to take the chance of coming in second. In an open search, you run the risk of making the top three but not number one. In that case everyone where you currently work will know you're looking, which you might not want, and they'll also find out you ended up second or third, which you don't want either."

"Yeah, that's the supposed up-side," Bert said. "Better applicants. The down-side is the campus doesn't get to comment on the candidates. I want that chance. When I learned who the finalists were the last time, I called people I knew in the physics departments where the finalists taught. Though none of the finalists were physicists, they all had reputations on their campuses. I got good information, and I passed it on to the search committee."

"I remember," Phil declared. "I sat on that search committee, and several faculty members did what Bert did. The committee used the information in its final deliberations. Letters of recommendation are often not useful. Lots of people have friends who are willing to write nice letters about them. The kind of information Bert got was less likely to be biased. As I remember it, despite the fact she's a sociologist, the physicists you talked to liked Margaret."

"Yes, they did," Bert replied. "With a closed search we lose a potentially good source of information. George, can you try to get them to change their decision? I hate to have the community removed from the process this way."

"No. The horse is out of the barn. I guess they talked about it before you got there. Josten put the *Chronicle of Higher Education* ad up for us all to read. It's already been submitted. It'll be out in two days. The ad explicitly mentions we're conducting a closed search."

"Yeah, we were all blindsided by the change," Jeremy griped. "This is the kind of thing the campus community should have been consulted on. I'm sure Margaret wouldn't have done it without consultation."

Bob interrupted. "This is not Margaret's deal. I bet she's staying away from the details about her replacement. This is the board's doing. Nevertheless, George's right. There is nothing we can do about it."

Phil spoke up. "Can I change the subject?"

"Yeah. Go ahead," Bert said. "We've run into a dead end here. No scientists on the committee and a closed search. Two bad decisions. What do you have?"

"I just wanted to remind you all of Ralph's wedding this Saturday. He and Beth wanted me to be sure to remind you."

"I'm certainly going," Jeremy said.

"Me too," echoed the others.

"The reception's at that new winery, right?" Bob asked.

"I heard their wine isn't very good," William commented. "Geoff from our department went to some group's fundraiser there, and he wasn't impressed."

"I'm not the one to ask about the wine," Phil said. "I'm not a connoisseur by any means. I can tell red wine from white wine most of the time, and I distinguish between beer and wine every time. Beyond that I'm lost."

Everyone laughed.

Still laughing, Jeremy said, "Phil's right, he can't tell one kind of wine from another. It's not about the wine. We've all used Ralph to fix our computers. He's a wizard, as far as I can tell. I'm glad he's found someone. It can't be easy in a small town like Lackey."

CHAPTER TWENTY

ALL OF THE out-of-town guests were invited to the rehearsal dinner on Friday night. Thirty people sent back the RSVP cards saying they were coming. The four parents were there and several aunts, uncles, and cousins from both families. Some of Beth's friends from Pittsburgh and a couple of Ralph's high school buddies filled out the group. They appeared to Sherry to be mixing well. Both families were middle class, and they were a little awed by the fancy restaurant.

Phil came over to Sherry. "I count twenty-eight. Who's missing?"

"Yeah. It's Beth's brother Carl and his plus one. While Beth didn't want to invite him, Sybil leaned on her, and she relented."

"I haven't heard much about Carl."

"He's Beth's older brother, and apparently he pestered his sister all the time. She doesn't like him. He's a clerk at an auto parts store. Beth told me he runs around with a bad crowd and drinks too much. She's afraid of who he'll bring. She's never liked any of his girlfriends."

Looking at the door, Phil said, "He's here."

"Whoa. Look at that sports coat," Sherry declared. "It's magenta."

"It's loud, whatever it is," Phil replied. "And look at what she's wearing."

"Don't stare, Phil. It's totally inappropriate to wear something that low cut to an event like this. She actually might be a fairly good-looking girl, but what she's wearing—that top, the short skirt, the spike heels, and all that makeup just aren't the right thing."

"She's certainly got the attention of one of Ralph's cousins. Look at that one, Chad, the teenager. He's about to drool."

"Beth and Ralph are coming up to them," Phil said. "I hope they can keep their cool. Carl's giving Beth a hug. She looks a little stiff, but she seems to be handling it well. Oh gosh. Ralph is pointing at us. Here they come."

Phil and Sherry watched Carl and the girl heading their way. When they got to them, Phil took the initiative, sticking out his hand to Carl. "You must be Beth's brother Carl. I'm Phil Philemon, and this is Sherry Ahearn."

Carl shook Phil's and Sherry's hands. "You're right, I'm Carl." Turning to his date who had stepped back a little, he continued, "This is Amanda Ripple. I heard you two were responsible for this dinner. Sis told me I should thank you, so thank you."

"You're welcome, Carl. I'm happy you made it," Phil responded.

Sherry looked up and saw Beth's mother, Sybil, headed toward them with steam coming out her ears. Quickly, Sherry moved to intercept Sybil. "Sybil, all the guests are here. We can ask the restaurant people to start serving in maybe fifteen minutes. Okay with you?"

Sybil was clearly distracted. "Oh, I guess so. I want to talk to my son. I'm beyond upset with him. How could he imagine his date's outfit is acceptable?"

"While I understand you're upset, talking to him should wait," Sherry said, relieved Phil had the good sense to maneuver Carl and Amanda out of Sybil's range by taking them to the drink table.

Sybil wasn't placated. "The outfit on that girl is awful. She had to know that dress is not the appropriate thing to wear. I have half a mind to kick the both of them out."

"It's best to ignore them," Sherry responded. "I agree. The outfit's awful. I suspect Carl had her wear it just to get a rise out of you, Beth, and Dave. Making a fuss about it would be playing right into his hands. She's clearly the kind of girl who doesn't want to be ignored. I say ignoring her is the best option. After the event, you can give Carl an earful. My advice now is to cool it."

Sybil turned, watching Carl and his date get their drinks. "I'm not sure I can control myself. I saw red when I got a look at that outfit. I'm afraid her boobs are going to pop out at any minute."

"I worry about that too. Still, creating a scene would just make things worse. Please alert your family members to play it cool and ignore Carl. That would be the best way to handle things."

"I guess you're right, Sherry. Carl is clearly trying to get a rise out of me. I'm ashamed now. He sure came close to getting the reaction he'd planned on." She took a deep breath and walked to her husband and the group of Watson relatives surrounding him.

Two minutes later, Beth came up beside Sherry. "Thanks for calming my mom down. It's just like Carl to bring a floozy like that here. He always wants to hog the attention. Now that I'm calmed down some, I like your idea. Ignoring him will be the biggest punishment. Ralph is telling his relatives how we want this to go."

"I'm glad you like my idea. If we can just get through this without one of them creating a scene, it'll be a victory. I'm keeping my fingers crossed."

After the dinner, which went incredibly smoothly, Ralph and Beth got up and thanked all the guests for coming, and Phil and Sherry each gave toasts. After Phil's toast, he saw Carl preparing to stand, so he quickly announced, "That's it for tonight. We look forward to seeing you all at the ceremony and the reception tomorrow." Dave and Sybil stood up in a hurry, as did Ralph's parents. Carl looked angry, but clearly everyone had started to leave, so he wasn't able to offer his toast or whatever. One of the cousins on his side grabbed him for a conversation while the rest of the guests were leaving. Amanda looked peeved. No one paid any attention to her.

Phil and Sherry stayed back to settle with the restaurant people.

"We dodged a bullet at the end there," Sherry said. "It looked to me like Carl intended to make a toast, at least I thought so."

"Yeah, I cut things off sort of abruptly at the end, and both sets of parents jumped right up. They suspected Carl was about to do something dumb. I say we succeeded. Ignoring Carl and his girlfriend turned out to be a great strategy. I'm not sure anyone talked to them during the entire dinner, and even Chad kept from staring at Amanda, at least most of the time."

"I'm a little afraid of what might happen tomorrow."

"I wonder what she's going to wear."

"There's no telling. I bet they're steamed about how they were treated tonight. They might try to cause trouble tomorrow, maybe at the reception."

"I've been wondering about the reception," Phil commented. "I'm going to ask William to latch on to Carl and keep him out of trouble. William played on the defensive line in college. He should be able to keep Carl under control."

"Thinking ahead, are you?" Sherry gave Phil a big hug. "It's one of the things I like about you."

The wedding the next day was well attended. As Phil looked at the audience, he wondered if the main street stores were closed that Saturday. All Ralph's fellow store owners were at the wedding. He and Ralph were already standing in front of the church waiting for the wedding procession to start when Carl and Amanda made their entrance. Phil thought, *I guess there's no chance of her boobs falling out of this outfit. It's a skin-tight jump suit. I wonder what she could be thinking?* He looked at Ralph, who just rolled his eyes.

All thoughts of Carl and Amanda disappeared when Sherry and the other attendant, Beth's cousin April, started down the aisle followed by Beth on her father's arm. As often is the case, despite all the build-up, the wedding ceremony itself didn't last long. Beth and Ralph had written their own vows, and everyone approved.

After the ceremony, as they gathered for the photo session, Sybil came up to Beth and hugged her. "That turned out lovely, darling. I'm so glad you found Ralph. You two make a great couple."

"Thanks Mom," Beth said, blushing a little.

Sybil glanced over to where Carl and Amanda were standing and announced, "What was that girl was thinking? Wearing a skin-tight outfit like that is totally inappropriate. It so tight, it might cut off her circulation."

"I can see Mom. I've decided I'm not going to let Carl ruin my special day."

"Good for you. I've decided I'm not letting her in any of the family photos. It's bad enough to have to have Carl in his red sports coat."

"It's magenta, Mom."

"Whatever."

After the photos, the wedding party joined the reception at the winery. The large room had no trouble holding the crowd. When Carl and Amanda arrived a little after the rest of the family members who'd been at the photos, Phil's strategy was working. He saw William intercept Carl and Amanda at the door to the room for the reception.

Everyone at the reception seemed to be having a good time, particularly Beth and Ralph. Phil and Sherry had a large number of friends in common with the couple, so they had no trouble mixing. Phil kept an eye on Carl and Amanda. When they finally broke away from William, Linda, Jeremy Terrell's' wife, and Margaret O'Brien, came up to Amanda and took her aside. Phil had no way of hearing what they were discussing. After a few minutes it looked as if Amanda had been crying. She grabbed Carl's hand and dragged him toward the door.

Phil walked up to Linda, who'd rejoined Jeremy. "What did you and

Margaret say to that girl?"

"No problem. We just told her she had on the trashiest outfit we'd ever seen at a wedding, and Margaret and I told her we were going to drag her out of the building if she didn't go peaceably. Margaret is fairly imposing, so she could tell we were serious."

"What gave you the guts to do something like that?"

"William told us about what you asked him to do while we were waiting for things to start, and it horrified me when she walked into the ceremony. There's nothing to do at that point, so we waited until it looked like William's efforts ran out of gas. Then we pounced."

Margaret had joined the conversation, so Phil repeated, "Thanks so much, both of you."

"I don't know what kind of repercussions will occur in the Watson family," Margaret said. "The girl in the hideous outfit was Beth's brother's date."

"It should be okay. Beth doesn't interact with Carl, the brother, very often," Phil answered. "And her mother can handle him. I'm just glad Beth's mom didn't have to deal with him this afternoon. We had to calm her down last night. She came close to attacking that girl. If it's possible, she had on a worse outfit last night."

"That's hard to believe," Linda said.

The remainder of the reception passed uneventfully, and the crowd threw bird seed at the couple as they left for their trip to Pittsburgh. They'd planned a delayed honeymoon. They were just taking a short trip to Pittsburgh this weekend. Beth wasn't able to schedule anything longer because of some conflict at the hospital. The actual honeymoon would be in the Virgin Islands.

CHAPTER TWENTY-ONE

THE NEXT WEDNESDAY, Phil waited impatiently for Ralph to return from running errands. Ralph knew he had to make it back in time for Phil to go to his lunch group. Ralph finally showed up full of apologies, and Phil hurried to Andy's. He breathed a sigh of relief when he saw Bob and Sally talking to Andy.

As Phil approached the group, two of the others came in the door. The five of them bid goodbye to Andy and made their way into the back room. The missing members of the group showed up a few minutes later.

Phil was eager to tell his lunch group about his marriage. He and Sherry had told Beth and Ralph the night before, and Sherry was going into the library to tell her friends there. Phil was sure the news would travel fast after a few people knew. Lackey was a small town.

"Before you all get started with something at the college, I have some news," Phil said, holding up his ring for them to see.

"When?"

"It was a couple of weeks ago. We didn't want to cause a fuss of any kind. We wanted Beth and Ralph in the limelight, so we're starting to tell people now."

"Congratulations." Jeremy got up and hugged Phil.

The others got up too, but mostly they gave high fives.

After they settled down, Phil explained, "We're going to try to adopt a child, and we thought it would look better if we were married."

"Yeah, it doesn't look good if you put 'living in sin' on the blank for marital status," Bert said.

Everyone laughed.

"Enough about me," Phil said. "What else is going on?"

After a pause, Bob started the discussion. "My news isn't as momentous, but my nephew just got a football scholarship offer from the University of Cincinnati. They're a division one school, so it's a full ride. I'm going to have to eat crow. I told his father he should be saving for the kid's college expenses. He didn't listen. He assured me the boy would get a scholarship. It's turned out his way."

"You're right, though," George commented. "Banking on a full scholarship is a risky proposition. The kid might get injured. What position does he play?"

"He played linebacker and fullback in high school, but he's been recruited to play defense. He'll be a linebacker."

"That's great for your brother. It's the younger one, Jim, right?"

"Yes, it's Jim's boy, Eric, who's getting the scholarship."

"Does he want to go to Cincinnati?" William asked.

"I'm not sure," Bob answered. "His dad's convinced he'll get more offers before he has to decide. No matter what, I can tell he's elated with this offer. He's not going to have to pay for the kid's college. His other child is a girl. She's talented enough, but no jock. He'll probably have to pay for her."

"I don't know how those guys do it," Phil said. "Playing division one football is like a full-time job. Lackey's football players are students, maybe not great ones. Nevertheless, they go to classes and have real majors. Division one players hardly have time to be students."

"Phil's right," William commented. "I played football in college, only division three. Still, it took a lot of time. I signed up for a light class load each fall semester. I took an overload second semester to compensate. With spring football in division one, it's harder to do that."

"I bet Eric will be red-shirted," Jeremy said. "He'll probably go to summer school each summer on top of that. With the summers, it should be easy for him to graduate. If he's a good student, he might even be able to get a graduate degree before he's finished."

"I don't think he's a good student," Bob added. "At least every time I've been with him, all he wants to talk about is football."

Bert, who'd been trying to break into the conversation, finally did. "I don't understand why colleges have football teams. We're just about the only country where anything like that happens. Oxford and Cambridge have crew teams, but sports like football and basketball are the only big-money college sports anywhere in the world. It's outrageous."

"I have to agree with Bert," Sally said. "The amount of money involved is unconscionable. If you look at the list of the highest paid public employees by state, a football or a basketball coach tops the list in most states. It's the Penn State football coach in Pennsylvania. While there are a few college presidents and medical school people, it's mostly coaches."

Bert continued. "I've seen those lists. They astound me. Lots of those coaches make more than a million dollars, and some of them make several million."

"Bert, you have to take into consideration how much money the coaches bring in," Jeremy said. "The revenue from football is enormous at some schools. You've got the gate receipts, including the luxury boxes, and television revenues. Football and basketball make a profit, and those profits support the rest of the athletic program. Women's sports and sports like tennis, golf, and track and cross country don't earn any revenue."

"Even with those enormous revenues from football and basketball, there aren't very many schools whose athletic departments break even," William responded. "Really, it's only a handful. Economists have studied these things, and almost all athletic departments get subsidies from the rest of the university. Often there's an explicit student fee covering the athletic department's losses."

"That doesn't make athletics different from the library," Phil said. "Though the library makes some money from fines, it isn't enough to cover cost of running a library. The vast majority of their money comes from tuition students pay."

"You have a phony analogy there," Bert argued. "You can't have a college without a library. I maintain you can have a college without an athletic department. And you certainly can have a college without big-time sports."

"Some schools claim big-time sports pay for themselves through donations," George answered. "The sports program connects the alumni to the school, and it attracts some donors who aren't alumni. If you're looking for a mention of your alma mater in the newspaper, you're most likely to find it on the sports page."

"George, economists have studied that too, and the findings are fairly clear," William said. "Extra donations aren't enough to justify the expenses associated with big-time sports."

"What about a school like Lackey?" Sally asked. "You guys have a football team and offer lots of sports. But with your small stadium and low-cost tickets, you can't make much money."

"The way I understand it, athletics have a different role at a school like Lackey," Bob answered. "Athletics are part of our recruiting strategy. Take football. Lots of high school teams won't have anyone recruited by a big-time school. Each year there are a bunch of guys on the team who won't get scholarships. Some of them still want to play, even though they weren't high school stars. We get lots of students who come to Lackey because we give them a chance to continue a sport they're passionate about."

"Bob's right," George added. "And it's not just football. It's sports like field hockey, lacrosse, swimming, track, and tennis. A large percentage of our students play some varsity sport. I doubt we'd be able to recruit a full class without our athletic offerings."

Phil joined in. "Yes, the athletes at a big school like Penn State are a small fraction of the student body. They're a drop in the bucket. It's ironic. The small schools don't have big-time athletics. Still, in crucial ways, athletics are more important for them."

"So, it's really a United States thing, not a college thing," Bert asked.

"Yes, it looks that way," Jeremy replied.

"Look what time it is," Bob suddenly announced. "We've got to get back to work. We'll never figure out the reason sports are so popular at colleges, or in the US for that matter."

As they got up, Phil thanked them all for coming to Ralph and Beth's wedding.

Jeremy responded, "I enjoyed it, and Linda particularly liked having a chance to get that girl to leave. The outfit she had on shouldn't be worn in public, and Linda loved having the chance to tell her."

"Yes," Phil said. "And I'm not sure I thanked Linda enough for her role. Carl, Beth's brother, brought that girl. He and Beth haven't been on the best of terms for some time. In my opinion, he tried to use the girl to cause a scene. I'm really grateful Linda and Margaret headed her off before it happened."

CHAPTER TWENTY-TWO

KRISTEN ARRIVED AT her editor, Mike Felton's, house at four on Sunday afternoon. While the house looked big, it wasn't as big as some of the other houses on the block. Kristen guessed it would be normal for the editor to have a nice house. She should have expected it.

Much to her surprise, Mike opened the door in a track suit. She'd never seen him in anything other than the coat and tie he wore to the office every day. She realized she'd dressed up too much for the meeting, but she couldn't do anything about it. The house furnishings were impressive, lots of antiques.

"I bet you have something to show me in that folder," Mike said in greeting. "Let's go to the dining room table so we can spread them out. Clara is off on her weekend grocery shopping trip, so we should have a while to use the table. If we hear her coming, we'll have to move to the living room. I haven't a notion why she's so particular about the table, but she is."

"Okay, I can show you what I have," Kristen said as she walked toward the table. She sat at one end, and Mike pulled a side chair next to her.

Kristen opened her folder. "First, I tried to get a handle on the size of the problem."

"I don't understand."

"Let me be more specific. I wanted to find out how many lawyers were involved."

"Okay, I get it. How did you go about it?"

"I looked at all the lawyers who were in Judge Moss's court room. He almost exclusively handles civil suits. I knew two of the names involved, so I checked them out first. Jim Simmons, who handled one of the cases, won all six of his cases in Moss's courtroom in the last three years." Pointing to the entry in the spreadsheet, she showed Mike the one hundred percent in the winning percentage column.

"I'm going to have some questions later. Go on for now."

"The other lawyer, Frank Martin, won five of the six cases. There, the eighty-three and a third for Martin," she commented, pointing again.

After Mike nodded, she continued. "Looking more closely at his record, the one loss happened the first time he faced Judge Moss. After that loss, he had five straight victories. The point I'm making is that this technique shows the two lawyers we're sure look suspicious."

"Looking at your numbers, there are several others who have really good winning percentages in Moss's court."

"Yes, they do. It's possible they're just good lawyers, not cheaters. Recognizing that, we had to gather more data. Basically, if the lawyer did well in Moss's court and also did well in other judge's courts, he or she just might be really good. On the other hand, if a lawyer did exceedingly well in Moss's court, but only average in other judge's courts, he might well be a cheater."

"Makes sense. So you had to collect the same data from the other judges."

"Yes, and it was tedious. Anyway, let me cut to the chase. I only found one other lawyer who appears to be a good suspect. Like Simmons and Martin, Phillip Gestner had an extremely good record in Moss's court and a thoroughly mediocre one in the other courts I checked. The other lawyers who did well in Moss's court also did well in the other judges' courts. And the clincher for me is that Simmons, Martin, and Gestner all work in the same law firm."

"Johnson, Sims, and Fox, right?" Mike asked.

"Right."

"This is really impressive stuff, Kristen. I pretty much understand it. My only question is about cases settled out of court. The judge has to approve the settlements, so he's involved. Still, his involvement is much less than if there is a hearing or a trial. Does your analysis ignore out-of-court settlements?"

"No, I don't ignore them. Here's what I did. I used a rule of thumb. If the settlement amounted to eighty percent or more of the original amount, I called it a win for the plaintiff's lawyer. If less than eighty, I called it a win for the defense's lawyer. It's arbitrary, but it's not sensible to ignore those cases."

"What made you use eighty percent?"

"I had to use something, and Gil, my boyfriend, told me it might be a weakness in my analysis. I had to do what he called sensitivity analysis. In that analysis, I tried sixty and seventy percent. Luckily for me it didn't change the results. The same three lawyers were standouts. They did really well in Moss's court, and they were average or worse in the other judges' courts."

"That sounds very sensible. I'll have to thank your boyfriend when I see him next."

"Okay, I have to have two sources before I can write the story. Does this analysis count as a source? I mean, I've got the recordings and the video from the package I got, and now I have this analysis. Is this enough?"

Mike pushed his chair back and exhaled loudly. "I'm going to have to think about it. Let's pick up these papers and go back to the living room."

In the living room, Kristen sat on the couch and Mike in a chair opposite her. After he settled into his chair, Mike turned silent. After five minutes, Kristen started to squirm. Finally, Mike spoke. "Two things bother me.

First, I'm not sure we can use the information in the package you got. Clearly, whoever sent it obtained it illegally. Second, even if we could use it, and I let you use the analysis I just saw, and I'm not saying I will, you only have two sources on two of the lawyers. All you have on the third lawyer…"

"Gestner, Phillip Gestner."

"Yes, Gestner. All you have on him is the statistical analysis."

"Fair enough, I don't have much on him. Actually, I'm stymied now. It's difficult to go up to a lawyer and ask whether his coworkers are cheats. I guess I might be able to look at the possessions of these three lawyers. I can find out if they drive flashier cars than the other lawyers or live in bigger houses. Still, that wouldn't prove anything. The analysis shows they've won a lot of cases. Maybe it would be better to look at Moss, he's the one getting the bribes. Frank is collecting information on Moss and the lawyers."

"You're barking up the wrong tree. You shouldn't go after the lawyers or the judge. It's better to go after the people who hired those lawyers. In the information you were given, one of the bribes came from the plaintiff. What's his name?" Mike asked.

"Calcott."

"That's right, and in the other case the lawyer actually paid the bribe with money from the client."

"So you're saying the clients might be the right ones to investigate?"

"Yes. The lawyers are going to have been very careful. At least if they play to type. I'm not sure about the clients. Some of them may not have been as careful. They had to come up with a load of cash. That's probably not too difficult for the guy who runs a string of jewelry stores. It might not have been as easy for some of the others. If I'm right, you might be able to make some progress there."

"Thanks, Mike. Now I feel like a fool. I should have thought about that angle. I guess I got too wrapped up in my statistical investigation of the lawyers. I'm sorry."

"You shouldn't feel sorry. What you did might turn out to be critical. It's quite possible the client who's willing to talk to you will be one of the Gestner's clients. If you hadn't done the analysis you showed me, we would never have found him. You should be proud of what you discovered. It looks like it took a lot of work."

"Thanks. I already feel like I've put in a lot of work, and I can foresee more work. I've got sixteen clients to check out, if I just focus on the ones in the last three years."

"That's a great place to start. Be careful as you approach these people. I'm not sure how I'd go about it."

"I'll figure out something. We can talk it over in a week. Before I go, I have a question. Suppose we find evidence nailing Moss. In that case, what is our responsibility with the police? Don't we have to go to them before we publish?"

"No, we don't. The only situation in which we'd have to get them involved is if publishing the story would put somebody in jeopardy of bodily harm. No problem in this case. Maybe we would give them a heads up the night before the story. I'm not even sure about that."

"Okay. That makes sense. What if I can't uncover anything? I can't tap phones or offer a reluctant witness immunity for their testimony. It might turn out that we can't find more evidence. Do we tell the police about the information in the package I received?"

"I'll have to think about it. Don't be so defeatist. You've got a good chance of finding something out. If we can't find anything, we'll cross that bridge when we have to."

As Kristen drove away from Mike's house, she wondered how to approach the clients. She knew she should reveal her connection to the newspaper. Ethics demanded it. The tricky part is how she'd describe the story. She wouldn't tell them she was working on a case about bribery in the courts. As she drove, she mulled over the possibilities.

CHAPTER TWENTY-THREE

THAT SAME SUNDAY morning, Thaddeus Moss and his girlfriend Catherine Forbes were enjoying a long, leisurely breakfast reading the Sunday paper. While Thad possessed few kitchen skills, he had the ability to make omelets and bacon. Catherine enjoyed staying Saturday nights because she liked the Sunday morning ritual. The meal tasted great, and she enjoyed slowly reading the paper. Like a lot of guys, Thad started the paper with the sports section. Catherine started with the front section. When they'd finished their first sections of the paper, Thad took the front section. Catherine had no interest in sports, so she grabbed the society news.

As they did every Sunday, they moved from the breakfast table to the couch to read their new sections. Thad sat on one end of the couch, and Catherine laid down on the rest of the couch with her head on a pillow she placed next to Thad. Her feet dangled over the other end. When they finished their respective sections of the paper, Catherine shifted position, and they finished their ritual by reading the comics together. About ten minutes into their couch time, Thad glanced at Catherine's paper and exclaimed, "Let me see that!"

"What?" Catherine seemed surprised.

"I want to look at that page," Thad replied.

"It's just a bunch of wedding pictures. I'm shocked. Why would you be interested in wedding pictures?"

"I might have recognized one of the people."

Catherine sat up and handed the paper to Thad. She asked, "Which one is it?"

"Here." Thad pointed to a picture of four people.

"It's a bride and groom and their attendants," Catherine said. "The wedding took place in Lackey, wherever that is."

"Yeah, I can read." Judge Moss sounded a little annoyed. "I've seen one of the women somewhere, not the bride. I guess it's the maid of honor."

"She's pretty. I'm not surprised you remember her. Where did you run into her?"

Thad paused. "Let me look at that picture again."

After looking at the picture closely, Thad added, "No, I don't know her. She looks a little like one of the flight attendants on my recent flight to Miami."

"So, you pay attention to the flight attendants," Catherine asked in a teasing voice.

"I guess I do. None of them are ever invited for Sunday breakfast, just you."

"Not to mention Saturday night," Catherine added with a twinkle in her eye. Thad looked a little distracted, so Catherine opened the front of her robe. Thad wasn't that distracted. He reached in and stroked her breast as he leaned over to kiss her. Catherine deepened the kiss. *She wouldn't let any flight attendant get in the way of the good thing she had going with Thad.*

Thad waved goodbye to Catherine late that morning. After her car headed down the street, he hurried back to the paper. It had scattered on the floor during their surprise quickie. Thad had no idea what it had been all about, but he liked it. He found the wedding picture after a bit of a search. The woman in the picture was the babe who'd led him on during his flight to Grand Cayman. He knew for sure. And she had to have been part of the group who switched briefcases. It still made him angry when he thought about being robbed. The caption listed her as Sherry Ahearn. He felt good to have a name. He'd call Carl Henson to find out what a private detective could discover about her.

Carl Henson ran a small detective agency in Pittsburgh, and business hadn't been booming. He'd been glad to get a call from Thaddeus Moss. He'd done some work for Moss a few years earlier. Moss's son had some difficulty with a young girl who claimed the boy had gotten her pregnant. Carl helped determine the young woman had been with lots of boys, a real slut. The case hadn't gotten anywhere near a courtroom after Carl made his report to the girl's attorney. Thad Moss had been grateful. He paid top dollar and didn't complain. Carl needed more clients who paid top dollar and didn't complain.

Carl's first act was Google. He found he was able to get a surprising amount of information on the internet. Carl typed in "Sherry Ahearn, Lackey, PA." With very little trouble, he found quite a bit about Ms. Ahearn. He found she worked in the Lackey College library. Also, she'd been mentioned in a long article about an interesting case. Several months ago, she'd witnessed a killing and then faked her death so the killers wouldn't come after her. She and her mother spent some time in FBI witness protection. When the case broke, she'd come back to Lackey. While Carl remembered the big case, the take down of a human trafficking ring, he didn't remember anything about Sherry Ahearn's part of the story.

The next mention of Sherry Ahearn came from the same paper as the story about the faked death. She came up in the listings of property transfers. A couple of months ago, it appears the Ahearns, Gladys, Sherry, and Richard, sold what must have been a bunch of acreage to the Premium

Oil Company for ten million dollars. Carl couldn't quite tell how big the farm had been. It appeared to be big. Fracking made lots of those farms valuable.

After those three hits, Carl basically drew a blank. There were some other mentions of Sherry Ahearn from a while back. He wasn't sure it was the same Sherry Ahearn. He wound up with no address and no phone number, and he'd wasted some of Thad Moss's money looking for them. He looked at the picture of Sherry. She appeared to be a foxy looking chick, so maybe he didn't feel too bad about having to go look for her. And the land sale made her rich, or at least part of a rich family. It should be easy to find information about a rich, good-looking woman in a small town.

Carl's six-foot four-inch height caused problems for him as a private detective. Being so tall made it difficult in small towns. For the most part, except at night, he had to stay in his car to do any surveillance. Also, he found it difficult to walk into bars and ask questions without standing out. As well as being big, he looked a little rough. He had unruly black curly hair that often didn't look good, and he'd broken his nose several times in fights with other big guys. One time the fight involved a little guy. Still, he ended up with a broken nose. The little guy hit him with a beer bottle. Being big and a little nasty looking worked to his advantage at times, but not always. Moss had asked him to try to keep a low profile. Moss didn't want this Ahearn woman to be aware she was being watched.

After driving to Lackey Monday afternoon, Henson parked his old BMW three series across from the Lackey library. He decided he'd stay until closing time and slouched down in the seat. He put a magazine in front of his face and looked bored. He figured he looked like a dad waiting for his son or daughter to show up or a husband waiting for his wife. He saw surprisingly little activity on this part of the college campus. The library remained open past what he figured would be closing time. Maybe college libraries didn't close. He wasn't sure. He'd never been in the library during his two years in college. He waited until the library finally closed at midnight, but Sherry Ahearn wasn't among the three staff members who walked out.

Carl had eaten the sandwich he'd brought, so he wasn't hungry. He decided to drive around Lackey. The place turned out to be tiny. It contained only one main street, and as far as Carl saw, there were only two restaurants. One, a Chinese place called Chin's, closed at eleven according to the sign on the door, and the other called Andy's closed at midnight. Absolutely nothing appeared to be going on. Carl had struck out.

His search the next morning was just as frustrating. He didn't catch Ahearn coming to work at the library when it opened at seven, and she didn't come in the rest of the morning. He decided to go to Andy's for lunch. There wouldn't be anything out of the ordinary for an out-of-towner to go to a local restaurant. He'd already concocted a story. He decided he'd be a computer programmer looking for a place to live away from city traffic and noise. He could do his work anywhere with a computer hookup and good Wi-Fi, so he wanted to check out small towns. Lackey had appealed because of the college.

At Andy's, the buzz among the locals focused on the basketball game that night. It was the first game of the season and everyone seemed excited. The people he overheard in Andy's expected Lackey to have a great season. Someone asked him if he'd played basketball in his youth. Carl had heard the question many times. "Too uncoordinated for basketball. I played football. I'm big, and as an offensive lineman I just leaned on people." He always got a laugh, and it worked at Andy's too. His basketball story turned out to be easy to tell because basically it jibed with his experience. While he'd been asked to come out for basketball by the high school coach, he hadn't made the final cut. Still, he liked to watch basketball, so he decided to go to the game. Maybe Ahearn would be a basketball fan. From the discussion at Andy's, it sounded like everyone in town loved the sport.

In the afternoon, Carl walked around the residential streets. He figured he'd use his cover story if anyone stopped him. No one did. There were some nice, newer houses on the outskirts. Most of the houses closer to town were older and smaller. It looked like a nice, quiet little town. Some of the houses were apparently rented out to college students. They had several cars parked in their driveways, and the lawns weren't very well kept up. He hoped he'd spot Sherry Ahearn raking leaves or something, but he had no such luck. This whole case had become frustrating.

Carl showed up at the gymnasium at six thirty-five for the seven o'clock game. After he purchased his ticket, he found a surprisingly large number of people already in the stands. He took a seat near mid-court in the next-to-last row and scanned the crowd—no Sherry Ahearn. After coming up empty, Carl focused on the two entrances to the gymnasium.

Just his luck, one of the guys he'd bantered with at the restaurant at noon spied him and came up to sit beside him. "Decided to take in the basketball game," the guy commented.

"Yeah," Carl answered. He stuck out his hand and shook with the guy saying, "Carl Elliott." Carl never used his real last name. He felt better using his first name. That way, if he ran into anyone he knew, he'd be able to respond when they called him Carl.

"Nice to meet you, Carl. I'm Billy Yoder."

"This place is filling up fast," Carl said refocusing on the entries.

"Yeah. It might be a sellout."

Suddenly Carl saw Sherry Ahearn enter and walk toward the other side of the gym. She came in with some guy. Taking a chance, Carl asked Billy, "Who's that chick, the one in the red top and white pants? She's really hot."

"Oh, that's Sherry Ahearn. You're right. She's really hot."

"That her husband?"

"No, it's Phil Philemon. He used to teach here. Now that you ask, I don't know what their status is. I heard a rumor that they might be married, but I'm not sure of my source. In any event, Philemon and Ahearn are living together. Yeah, I know that because her farmhouse burned down, part of that big FBI deal—the human trafficking bust. She moved in with Philemon after that. The arrests and the FBI and all woke up this sleepy little town for a while."

The two teams came onto the floor for the start of the game, interrupting Billy's description of the events surrounding the human trafficking case. Carl felt just as happy not to have to listen to Billy.

When the game started, Carl sneaked looks at Sherry Ahearn and Phil Philemon to memorize their faces. The game didn't turn out to be very interesting. Lackey dominated. They had a very good big guy, and the other team didn't match either his size or ability. At halftime, Carl asked Billy, "What's the deal with this guy Nate Smith? He's really good. Why isn't he at a bigger-time school?"

"The way I heard it, we recruited him as a six two guard coming out of high school. Over the summer before last year, he grew six inches, so he comes here at six eight. And the amazing thing is: he's still coordinated. While people around here were worried he'd transfer after last year, he's still here."

"I guess he won't play much in the second half. He's already got eighteen points, and Lackey has a twenty-point lead."

"Yeah, Coach Mc Sweeny doesn't like to run up the score, and besides, he wants to get an idea of what some of the freshmen can do. The new guard, Billings, may turn out to be a good player. He's quick, sometimes too quick for his own good. Right now, it looks as if he's committing too many turnovers."

"Young players can improve, and you're right, he's quick. It helps him on the defensive end."

Halfway through the second half, Carl waved goodbye to Billy. "I'm going to beat the traffic," he said as he started down the bleachers. He exited the door he'd seen Ahearn enter. When he got outside the gym, he looked for a place where he would be inconspicuous as he waited to follow Ahearn and this guy Philemon after the game. If things worked out right, he should be able to spot the car they were driving. If his luck held, he could follow them home. He found a parking place near the exit and backed his car in. That way he'd be in position to follow a car out of the parking lot. After he parked, he hustled back to his spot just outside the gym.

A trickle of fans started to leave because the outcome wasn't in doubt. Only the final score had yet to be determined. Carl heard the final buzzer because a group of fans had the door open when it sounded. A rush of fans came out after that; clearly some were hustling to get to their cars to beat the traffic. Others were students who didn't head for the parking lot. Five minutes later, he spotted Ahearn and the guy. They didn't seem to be in a hurry. They were talking to some other fans. Finally, they broke away and headed to the parking lot. Carl followed them, letting them get about thirty yards ahead. He'd wanted to be able to locate the car they were driving and then run back to get his car. To his surprise, they didn't get into a car at all. They walked through the parking lot and went onto a path leading off campus.

Okay, Carl thought, *I can follow you on foot.* Luckily for him, there were a couple of other groups who'd taken the same path. He kept a group between Ahearn and himself. The path let out on the neighborhood streets. The group behind Ahearn and the guy turned on the first cross street, so, worried about being exposed, Carl slowed to let the couple get farther ahead. They turned left on the next street. Carl sped up and hid behind a tree. He saw Ahearn and the guy, Philemon, opening the door of the house across the street from where he hid. Carl took out his notebook and wrote down the address of the house. He only had two entries for his two days of work: *Phil Philemon and 102 Quincy Street.* Two entries felt like very little. Still, he didn't need much more. He'd take some pictures of the house in the morning. Then he'd see what there was to learn about Phil Philemon. If he had any luck investigating Philemon, he'd go home and prepare his report for Moss. He figured he'd be ready to give his report to Moss the next evening.

CHAPTER TWENTY-FOUR

PHIL'S ARRIVAL AT Andy's for Wednesday lunch completed the group.

"Ah, Phil, you're late. It's unusual. You're usually one of the first to arrive. Were you newlyweds up too late celebrating the basketball team's success?" Bob asked.

"You're a funny guy, Bob. No, we weren't. The time just got away from me. Still, I have to admit, we looked good, especially for a first game."

"As you're aware, Phil, I made the game too," Jeremy commented. "Nate Smith is so good. The other team can't guard him, but I found myself most impressed by the freshmen: the guard, Billings, and the forward, Billchek."

"The two Bills. Is that it?" William interrupted.

"Okay, the two Bills," Jeremy responded with a chuckle. "Anyway, when Nate Smith went to the bench, those two guys carried the team, and we actually expanded our lead. By the end of the season, when they have more experience, we'll be a powerhouse."

"Wow, Jeremy, you sound like Phil," Bob said. "I didn't know you were a such a big fan."

"You're right. I haven't been such a big fan in the past. I guess I got hooked last year. And Wilson Billchek is one of my freshman advisees.

He's a good kid. Unlike many of our athletes, he's really interested in academics. He's going to be a history major."

"Enough about basketball already," George declared after they were interrupted by the waitress taking their orders. "I want to return to one of our earlier discussions. Remember when we talked about the split in the country being driven by how well people deal with change?"

Several people nodded, and Bob spoke up. "Yeah, Sally's idea, if I'm not mistaken."

"Right," George responded. "I've been looking at the political science literature, and I would like to amend the conclusion to say it's about the fear of change, and I'd put the equal emphasis on the word 'fear' and the word 'change.' There's lots of psychological research that's been picked up in political science showing conservatives are more likely to be motivated by fear than liberals."

"What kind of research?" Bert asked. "I'm not sure I put much stock in a lot of the psychological research I've seen. Rats running around mazes."

"Yeah," William added. "I've heard experimental psychologists called 'rat-running psychologist.' The Lackey department is split down the middle between the rat runners and couch guys—the counseling ones."

"This is not about rats," George responded. "Let me explain. One of the studies used a set of interviews to classify the subjects as either conservatives or liberals. Then they showed the subjects pictures on a computer screen. Some of the pictures were pleasant: cute puppies or people putting their arms around each other; others were unpleasant: car wrecks or spiders on faces. The experimenters monitored the eye movements of the people. They found the liberals spent more time looking at the positive images and the conservatives spent more time on the negative images."

"Interesting," Phil said skeptically. "I'm not sure I get the connection."

"Other studies make the connection," George said. "Take immigration. If you're attracted to negative images like the conservatives in the study I just mentioned, you'll connect immigration to stories you hear about immigrants who've committed crimes. On the other hand, if you're like the liberals in the study, you'll focus on William and all the other immigrants who've added so much to our country."

"I get it," Bob declared. "The reason Sally's change idea works is that conservatives react to change, like lots of immigrants, as something to fear. Liberals on the other hand put a positive spin on the changes."

"That's a good summary," George commented. "Actually, there's more to it. It turns out that whether you are motivated by fear or not, whether you are conservative or liberal, is at least partially an inherited trait. People have always thought that political beliefs were inherited from parents, but they mean since you grew up around your parents you tended to think like them. The more recent research says it's not just that. It's genetic too."

"What?" Bert asked. "I find that hard to believe."

"I'm not sure I quite believe it either, Bert," George replied. "The studies use sophisticated statistical techniques, the kind of thing they didn't teach when I went to grad school, so I don't fully understand the analysis. Still, the studies are compelling to the experts in the field. There are large samples of people who are twins, and this helps them to separate nature from nurture."

"I guess those poor identical twins who were separated at birth have been poked and prodded all their lives," Sally said.

"They have sure been used in lots of studies," Phil added.

"George, how do these studies account for the other political differences in the country?" Sally asked. "I mean, there's a pronounced urban/rural split and a coastal/non-coastal split. How is that genetic?"

"Great question, Sally. There are two parts to the answer. First, it's not all genetic. Most of the research would say genetics only accounts for thirty or forty percent of the observed difference. The environment is clearly important, too. Second, if we assume people like to live near people with similar views, migration patterns might be responsible for some of the differences we were talking about."

"Ah," Bert said. "I knew I've always been right. When anyone asked me why people behave in any particular way, I have a ready answer and I'm always correct. The answer is: it's either genetics or environment or some combination. I'm always right."

"Cute, Bert," Jeremy commented. "The research George is talking about is interesting. If you'd asked me whether genetics had anything to do with political attitudes, I'd have said no. I would have attributed the similarity in family attitudes to shared environment, not shared genes. Apparently, I'm wrong."

"Well said," Phil added. "I'm in the same boat. It makes me wonder if other attitudes are inherited in the genetic sense. If we'd had the right twin studies in the past, we might have been able to figure out more about history."

"Let me be an optimist," George commented. "This research about the differences between liberals and conservatives should help us understand each other. If we can understand each other better, maybe we can have better conversations. If you're aware of what's motivating someone you're arguing with, you've got a better chance of coming up with a compelling counter to his or her point of view."

"Yeah, maybe," Bob said. "Maybe, we've just learned it's not useful to even engage in an argument. According to this research, the other guy's views are baked in. They're in his genes. No amount of argument is going to dislodge him from his viewpoint."

"No, Bob. You are being too extreme," George declared. "The research says both genetic and environmental factors are important. Recognizing the existence of the genetic component might help us to manipulate the environment in a productive way."

"I've reached my level of tolerance for social science today," Bert concluded as he got up. "It's time for me to get back to my office."

CHAPTER TWENTY-FIVE

CARL HENSON MET with Thaddeus Moss at Moss's house on Wednesday evening. He liked going to Moss's place because he knew he'd get good Scotch. Moss gave him a choice, and he picked the Oban. The two of them settled in the living room with their drinks.

Carl opened his file to review his outline. "I located Sherry Ahearn in Lackey. It turned out to be difficult. She's not in the phone book, so I didn't have an address. I learned her house burned down relatively recently, and she moved in with her boyfriend. Maybe he's more than a boyfriend. The guy I talked to thought they might be recently married. While the Lackey College website lists her as working in the library, she didn't show up there on either of the days I checked. I finally spotted her at a Lackey College basketball game and followed her home. Here's a picture of the house."

Moss took the picture. "It doesn't look like much."

"No, it's nothing special. A two-bedroom bungalow."

"Did you learn anything else?"

"Two more things. First, Ahearn got mixed up in the human trafficking case the FBI busted last summer. She witnessed a shooting near the farm where she lived with her mother. The guys who did the shooting came to the house, barricaded it, and set it on fire. Ahearn and her elderly mother managed to escape. For some reason, the FBI didn't want them to testify right away, so they told the local fire department to report they'd found two bodies in the burned farmhouse. Meanwhile, Ahearn and her mother were taken out of town and put in witness protection. It caused quite a stir when the human trafficking case broke, and she showed up in town alive and well."

"Sounds like quite a story. Anything more?"

"Yeah. The second part is related. Since their farmhouse burned down, apparently Ahearn and her mother decided to sell the farm. There's a brother involved, too. Anyway, like quite a few farmers in the area, they cashed in big time. They sold to an oil company involved in fracking. Ahearn, her mother, and her brother sold the farm for ten million."

"So, the family's rich. That's very interesting," Thaddeus Moss commented as he leaned back on the couch and stared at the ceiling.

"Yes, they're rich. I didn't catch any indicators of the newfound wealth. No fancy cars in the driveway or any talk about it in town."

Moss sat silently, and Carl didn't have anything else to say, so silence prevailed. Eventually, Carl got uncomfortable. Still, he kept quiet.

Finally, Moss spoke up. "I'm wondering what I might want you to do next. Is that all you found out?"

"I have the rundown on the guy she's living with. His name is Phil Philemon, actually it's Milton Philemon; everyone calls him Phil. He used to be a history professor at Lackey, but he quit a couple of years ago. The only thing he does is help out a friend who runs a computer repair business in Lackey. A guy I talked to said Philemon seemed to travel a lot. Also, his wife died in a traffic accident. When I got home, I Googled Philemon. I found out quite a bit about him. He had been a big deal at the College, full professor, former chair of the history department, and on lots of committees. I also found a story about the traffic accident involving his wife. A drunk driver ran into her. The guy wasn't charged with much of a crime because the police mucked up the investigation. They gathered evidence in the guy's house without a warrant."

Moss didn't look like he cared much while Carl had been talking. Finally, he snapped out of his daze. "I have an idea about what I want you to do next," he said. "I want you to find out all you can about the mother and the brother. Where does she live now? The farmhouse is gone. Does she live with her daughter and this guy Philemon? I doubt it. The house looks small. And what about the brother? Where does he live and what does he do?"

"Okay, will do. I don't know if either of them live close. The story about Ahearn faking her death mentioned the other two. It's possible they aren't in Pennsylvania anymore."

"Travel if you have to. It's no problem. The more I think about it, the more I need to have information about the other two family members."

Though Carl wondered why Moss expressed so much interest in the Ahearn family, he knew he'd better not ask.

Moss interrupted his thoughts. "Send me a bill for the work you've done so far. It's been excellent. I appreciate how fast you were able to find her. The information is fascinating."

"I'll try to be as quick with the rest of the information," Carl added as he and Moss got out of their seats and went to the front door.

"Thanks for the scotch," Carl said at the door. "It'll keep me coming back." He left smiling.

CHAPTER TWENTY-SIX

KRISTEN FOWLER HADN'T had any luck interviewing the clients of the lawyers she thought were bribing Judge Moss. She decided to tell them she had been assigned a story about satisfaction with the court system. She concocted a short questionnaire for them and followed up with open-ended questions. Two of the first people she contacted turned her down. They weren't interested in helping her. The three she had been able to interview were very satisfied. As Kristen left the third house, she recognized her approach must be all wrong. The people who won their cases because of bribes were likely to be satisfied and wouldn't be willing to admit to bribing the judge. She decided to switch to the people who'd lost their cases.

The first person she contacted was Vernon Hughes, Frank Martin's client in the only case Martin lost in Judge Moss's court. Hughes, a sixty-year-old man who lived in a middle-class neighborhood, didn't seem happy about talking to a reporter. The interior of his house felt odd to Kristen. Feminine touches were everywhere—frilly curtains and little knickknacks. Still, the house was filthy. There were dust bunnies in the corners and dishes piled up in the kitchen sink. Hughes had to move a pile of newspapers from a chair before she could sit down.

Hughes didn't show any signs of interest when she outlined her project. He was nice enough to fill out her questionnaire. The answers on Hughes' questionnaire indicated that he'd been dissatisfied with his interaction with the court system. Kristen started her questions by asking whether his dissatisfaction stemmed from his interactions with his lawyer or with the Judge.

"Both."

"Can you give more details?" Kristen asked.

"Well, the judge seemed to rule against us all the time, and my lawyer, Frank Martin, didn't appear to be trying very hard."

"That's odd," Kristen prodded. "I thought lawyers always tried hard. Wouldn't the lawyer get a third of the judgement if you won? That should have given him plenty of incentive to work hard for you."

"Yeah, that's what I thought. Martin and I didn't get along. Before the trial started, he told me he had a way to guarantee we'd win. Unfortunately, in the end, we didn't agree on a strategy. While I guess I should have looked for another lawyer at that point, I didn't have the good sense to do it."

Kristen got really excited, though she tried to hide it. "Guarantee a win? Can you give me more details?"

Hughes demurred. "I'd rather not say."

"Isn't that unusual? I mean, wasn't it odd for him to offer a guaranteed way to win? He hadn't suggested anything illegal, had he?"

"No, nothing like that. I don't want to talk about. It's in the past, and that's where I want to keep it. I've moved on."

Though Kristen knew Hughes had lied to her, she knew enough not to push. Mr. Hughes wouldn't reveal anything in his current mood, and it didn't make sense to antagonize him. "Okay, thanks for your participation," she said as she got up and put his survey and her notebook in a briefcase. "I'll put you down as someone who didn't have a good experience with the court system."

"That's clearly true."

Kristen shook Mr. Hughes' hand and walked out the front door. When she got to her car, she felt discouraged. She could tell she was close before he clammed up. She knew Martin had suggested a bribe to him. Still, Kristen was convinced Hughes wouldn't tell her about it, at least right now. She scanned her list of people to interview. Her only other option was the Poseys, Mildred and Alan. They were Phillip Gestner's clients in the one case he'd lost in Judge Moss's court. Maybe they'd also turned down the idea of a bribe.

Kristen called the Posey's number and got Mrs. Posey, Mildred. She said she'd be happy to participate in Kristen's study, and she was available right away. Kristen liked to play a game with herself after she'd talked to people on the phone. She liked to describe them to herself—general appearance, things like height, weight, hair color, and age. She'd been dead wrong with Mr. Hughes. Based on his voice on the phone, she'd envisioned him as slim with a beard. He'd turned out to be a bit overweight, clean shaven, and completely bald. She pegged Mildred Posey as about fifty-five years old, blonde, and tall.

The Mildred Posey who answered the door turned out to be at least seventy with gray hair and only five one or five two. Kristen smiled as she introduced herself. She couldn't have been more wrong about Mrs. Posey. Much to Kristen's delight, Mrs. Posey asked if she wanted coffee. "No, thank you. I'm a tea drinker," she responded.

"Oh, good," Mrs. Posey said with a smile. "I drink tea too. I'll fix a pot. It'll just take a minute."

Kristen looked around the living room as Mrs. Posey scurried out. The small room had a crowd of what were probably family pictures on the mantle above the fireplace. Mrs. Posey caught Kristen looking at the pictures when she returned with a tea pot and two cups. She put the teapot and cups down on a small table and came up beside Kristen.

"That's my Alan in his Army uniform," she commented, pointing to one of the pictures. "He served in the Viet Nam War and won a bronze star. I didn't have such a good time when he went away. We'd just been married two years, and Buster'd only turned one. It's a lot of work taking care of a little one, particularly a long way from home. We'd moved to Oklahoma, Fort Sill. Alan's assignment was in the artillery."

"That must have been tough. Your husband was very good looking."

"Thanks for saying that. I had a hard time—him being gone and in a war. I thought of taking Buster, actually it's Alan Junior. We always called him Buster. Anyway, I considered bringing him back here and moving in with my parents, but I didn't. That's Buster in his football uniform. And those are my grandchildren, Sally and Jimmy. They live fairly close. It's been great to have them since Alan died last year."

"I'm so sorry," Kristen said. "I didn't know your husband had died."

"I'm all alone now. People tell me I should move into one of those senior citizen places. Not yet. I'm not ready to leave my house. Enough about me. Take a seat and I'll pour the tea. You have some questions about courts?"

Weird, Kristen thought. *People are different. While Hughes had been so close-mouthed, Mrs. Posey is a chatterbox.* "Thank you," Kristen said as she accepted the proffered teacup. "Yes, I'm a newspaper reporter, and I'm working on a project about people's satisfaction with their experiences in the courts. My records indicate you and your husband were involved in a court case a few years ago."

As Kristen reached for her questionnaire, Mrs. Posey spoke up. "Yes, and I can tell you we didn't like our experience at all. A guy had run a red light, and Alan didn't have time to avoid him. Even though he'd been at fault, the guy sued Alan for a ton of money. Since we were innocent, we resisted the insurance company's idea that we should settle. Alan didn't do anything wrong, and we thought we'd get justice."

Kristen sensed Mrs. Posey's emotions come to the surface when she talked about the lawsuit. She knew it was no time for a questionnaire. She wanted Mrs. Posey to continue. "You lost the suit."

"Yes, we did. Our lawyer turned out to be a no good. The whole thing took a toll on Alan. To this day, I believe it's the reason he passed. He felt really down after we lost in court. And paying the judgement wiped out a great deal of our savings. His health got worse after that. He'd been injured in the war, and he suffered off and on. In the end, he wasn't able to shake the last bug he caught. While I'm not sure it's fair, I blame the court case."

"You didn't like your lawyer. Why?"

"He's a crook, plain and simple, a crook."

Kristen got excited. "Why do you say that?"

"Alan wouldn't like me saying this. Oh, what the heck. He's not here anymore," Mrs. Posey declared, then she paused. Kristen thought she teared up.

After a minute, Mrs. Posey continued. "Sorry, it's still hard sometimes. Anyway, our lawyer, Mr. Gestner, told us he had a fool proof way to deal with our case. He told us we should offer a bribe to the judge. He knew the judge would take the bribe. He must have been a crook too."

Kristen suppressed a triumphant smile. "Judge Moss, right?"

"Yes, Judge Moss. Alan didn't do it. He'd never do anything like that. He'd always been an honorable man. He'd rather lose the case than cheat. We didn't even discuss it when Gestner made the offer. Alan just looked and me and shook his head. We both grew up better than that. I guess we should have dropped Mr. Gestner then and there. For some reason, I can't even remember, we didn't."

Kristen paused then she took out her laptop. "Mrs. Posey, I've got something to show you. A couple of weeks ago I got a package at the newspaper. I have no idea who sent it to me. I want to show you what's on the thumb drive in the package. It will show you what you experienced is still going on."

"I don't understand," Mrs. Posey said with a puzzled look on her face.

"Just watch, and I'll explain." Kristen started the Power Point presentation.

The first slide had her story about the Wilson Enterprise trial. "I wrote that story," she added.

When she'd finished, Mrs. Posey looked at Kristen. "The next file is a conversation between Judge Moss and the Wilson Enterprise's lawyers, Jim Simmons," Kristen said. The volume blared, so she quickly adjusted it.

"They're talking about a bribe!" Mrs. Posey exclaimed.

"Yes," Kristen agreed as she moved to the next slide. "And this is a video of the lawyer Simmons showing up at Judge Moss's house. We think he's making the payment they talked about in the phone conversation."

Mrs. Posey looked at Kristen with big eyes. "This is fascinating."

"The next slide has a phone call between Moss and Quinn Calcott. He'd just won a case in Moss's court."

After Mrs. Posey listened to the phone conversation. "Another bribe!"

"Yes, and this is Calcott showing up at Moss's house to make the payment."

Kristen didn't think she needed to have Mrs. Posey hear the phone call between Moss and his travel agent, so she shut down the program. "There are a few more details. First, the lawyers involved, the guy Simmons, and a Frank Martin, Calcott's lawyer, and your lawyer, Gestner, all work at the same law firm. Second, the people who provided the thumb drive to me broke a lot of laws to obtain the information you just saw. Because they obtained it illegally, the evidence can't be used in court. Also, my editor won't let me use it as my only source for a story. That makes your experience incredibly important, Mrs. Posey."

"We didn't bribe anyone. We turned him down flat."

"Doesn't matter. You were offered the opportunity to bribe the judge. And you are a separate source from the information in the package I received. If you'll give me permission to include your story in an article, I can publish. It's important to stop what's happening in Moss's court."

"Well, if you write a story, it's going to be a big deal."

"Yes, it'll be a major story. And I'm asking a really big favor. If you agree to let me use your information in the story, it would be better if I can use your name. And if I use your name, the police will probably want to talk to you. There's no way my story won't lead to a police investigation. While I can use you as an unnamed source, I'd rather not."

Mrs. Posey looked at Kristen for a long time. Then she smiled. "Heck, what does someone like me have to contribute anymore? At the time Alan didn't want anyone to know about us turning down the chance to bribe the judge. Even then I didn't agree. I went along with it because he asked me to. Now you're giving me a chance to set things right. It'll be good to leave a little mark before I go. Use me as a source. And tell the police who I am."

Overjoyed, Kristen hugged Mrs. Posey. "This is wonderful. I really wanted you to agree to be a source. Now if you've got some more time, I need to do an in-depth interview. If it doesn't work for you right now, I can come back. Whatever's convenient for you."

"I don't have to be anywhere for a couple of hours. I'm ready for your questions. We'd better get some more tea."

"Good idea. This might take a while."

CHAPTER TWENTY-SEVEN

CARL HENSEN DIDN'T have any difficulty tracking down Richard Ahearn, who was the head of county police in Beaufort County, South Carolina. The county included Hilton Head, so Carl figured Richard must work on a lot of cases involving stolen golf clubs. He also tracked Richard, who apparently went by the nickname Trick, back to his days as a football star. Trick made the all-state team in high school. He received a scholarship to play football at the University of South Carolina. For some reason, his football career didn't continue at South Carolina. Carl wondered why but figured it didn't matter, so he didn't pursue it. He had all the information he needed.

He didn't find anything on Gladys Ahearn; she turned out to be almost a complete enigma on the internet. Her only two mentions were in things he'd found before: the story about Sherry faking her death and coming back to testify in the human trafficking case and the listing of the property transfer. He found nothing about where she currently lived. While Carl thought she probably moved away from Lackey, he had no sense where she might be living.

He decided he'd go down to South Carolina to find out more about Richard "Trick" Ahearn. It should be easy to gather information on him.

A county police chief is a public figure. The locals might even know something about where his mother lived.

Carl flew to Savannah and picked up a rental car. He splurged and rented an SUV. *What the heck, Moss pays the bills.* As he drove around, he congratulated himself on his choice. SUV's outnumbered sedans by a considerable margin. In fact, maybe pickups outnumbered sedans too. Anyway, his vehicle didn't stand out, and it drove nicely. He wanted to find where the locals hung out. It had been easy in Lackey. There were only two restaurants, and one of them, Chin's, didn't seem likely. Hilton Head didn't offer the same easy choice.

Carl checked into a Hampton Inn and told the clerk there he might move down south from his home in upstate New York. "The winters are getting too cold for me."

"I hear you. You wouldn't be the first."

"Say," Carl asked. "Where would you recommend I go to get the real skivvy about living here? Where do the real locals hang out? I don't want to go to a real estate agent. They put a positive spin on everything, and I can find out how much houses cost on the internet. I want to find out what it's really like to live down here."

"Lots of the people you run into around here are newcomers. I guess I'd go to Willy's. It's kind of a bar restaurant. Golfers go there for lunch after their morning round of golf. Most of them have moved here from somewhere else, a long time ago in some cases. Also, you might run into a real native or two. Here, I can give you the address."

Carl checked into his room and went out to drive around. There didn't appear to be much going on. He had done his research on Hilton Head. It had been a really sleepy joint until a bridge connected the island to the mainland in the mid-1950s. Large developments: resorts, golf courses, and housing developments followed later. As a result, an old historic section didn't exist. Things were spread out, and for the most part modern. After the light started to fade, Carl headed for Willy's. He didn't expect to find anyone to talk to. Willy's, actually Willy's Seafood and Raw Bar, looked like a nice place. He saw why the locals would gather there for lunch after golf. Carl enjoyed his meal, the red snapper. He went back to the hotel satisfied with himself.

The next morning, Carl drove around Hilton Head. The most productive part of his morning happened when he parked a block away from the county police office. He walked by the building and took a good look at the parking lot. Behind the building, he found a parking spot reserved for the chief. The car in the spot, an unimpressive Hyundai sedan, seemed appropriate for a small-town police chief. Its bright blue paint job would make it easy to follow. Carl wrote down the license number and scoped out a place where he'd be in position to follow the chief home.

The rest of the morning passed uneventfully, so he showed up at Willy's at eleven-thirty. The place didn't look busy yet, and he grabbed a stool at the end of the bar. He sat fairly close to one of the round tables, just the kind of place a large group of golfers might pick for lunch. He ordered some local beer the bartender recommended. Carl preferred dark beer, and he liked what he got. After a few sips, he asked the bartender what kind of beer he had.

"I didn't catch the name," he said.

"Precocious Pelican," the bartender answered as he came over to Carl. "It's a local microbrew, and lots of my regulars like it. I don't know the guys who brew it."

Carl liked having the bartender come over. It gave him an opportunity to start his story. "Look, I'm planning on moving further south. I'm tired of snowy cold winters. I don't want to talk to a real estate agent. If I want to move here, I can find houses online. I need to talk to someone who's local. Someone who's lived her for a long time. Not someone like you. What are you, twenty-two?"

"Good guess. I'm actually twenty-four."

"Anyway, can you introduce me to someone who's local? There must be a bunch of locals who come in here for lunch. My name's Carl Elliott. I'm from upstate New York, near Ithaca. I'd really appreciate it if you'd introduce me to someone who can tell me what it's like to live here."

"I'm Bruce Anthony, Carl, and I'd be happy to introduce you to someone. There's a guy who comes in most every day. He's been living around here for a long time. His name's Max. It's funny, I'm not sure of Max's last name. There's a bunch of people I know only by their first names. While people tell bartenders all kinds of crazy things, they almost never give their last names. Max comes in about ten minutes from now and sits at the bar like you. I'd be happy to introduce you."

At that point a customer came in and sat at the other end of the bar. Bruce went to serve him. The restaurant started to fill up, and sure enough there were several groups who looked like they'd just come off the golf course. Carl didn't like golf. Still, he knew enough to understand some of what they were talking about. He heard complaints about the new bunker on number seven and the tree on number twelve. Carl found it funny. These guys seemed to be reliving their good shots and their bad shots in equal number. Carl marveled at their ability to be so into what he saw as a stupid game. It didn't even involve much exercise. *There must be something to it I don't understand*, he thought.

Five minutes after a third group of golfers filled a table, Carl saw a guy in his late fifties walk in. Unlike the golfers, he dressed in jeans and a scruffy looking shirt, no polyester. He had a gray beard and messy looking hair down over his ears. *That has to be Max.*

Bruce, the bartender, met the guy at the bar. After a brief conversation, Bruce guided the guy to the bar stool next to Carl.

"Carl, this is Max. I'm sure he'd be willing to fill you in on what it's like to live here."

Carl put out his hand. "Carl Elliott from upstate New York."

"Max Granger," Max responded, shaking Carl's hand. "So, Bruce told me you want to learn what it's like to live around here."

"That's right, Max." Carl always tried to use people's names early in a conversation. It helped him remember the names. "Here's the deal. My dad's older brother, my uncle, never married, and he just died of cancer. While I knew he'd had a good career with some insurance company, you could have pushed me over with a feather when I learned he left me a couple million dollars. I looked at my situation, and I figured I didn't have any reason to work anymore."

"And I guess you figured you didn't have any reason to live in upstate New York anymore either," Max commented with a smile.

"After last winter, yeah, you're right," Carl said. At that point, Bruce reappeared with Max's beer.

"Let's order lunch," Max suggested. "I guess you probably need a menu even if I don't. Bruce, why don't you get my new friend Carl a menu?"

"Sure, Boss," Bruce said as he scurried away.

"I usually have the fish and chips," Max announced. "I understand a bunch of the stuff's good. I don't eat here for dinner. Too pricy. The lunches are reasonable. I eat here most days."

After briefly scanning the menu, Carl said, "I'll have the crab cake sandwich. It ought to be good."

"I've never had it. You can tell me what it's like." Then Max signaled Bruce, who took their orders.

Max asked, "What did you do before you came into the big inheritance?"

"I was on the police force, just a patrolman. I made it to lieutenant once. Then I got busted for being drunk on the job. A big mix up—I thought I had the day off. I didn't. One of my friends called me, so I put on my uniform and got there fast. Making a long story short, they knew I'd been drinking. Luckily, it turned out I got to keep the job. The reduction in pay hurt, but I hung on to get the retirement. Now with the inheritance, I have no problem living with the reduced retirement." He paused. He was sure Max bought his story. He started up again. "When did you move to Hilton Head?"

"I've been here for thirty-five years. My folks were killed in a car crash in my third year of college. A lawyer called my older sister, and we sued the hell out of the people who ran into my folks. I got a trust fund out of the deal. I dropped out of college and decided I'd be a golf pro. This seemed like a good place to learn the game. Problem turned out—I'm no good. I hate the game now. Haven't played for more than fifteen years. I liked it here. I hooked up with a great gal who ran a beauty parlor. I did some odd jobs when I got bored. Mostly I just hung out and did a lot of fishing. The girl's gone now, cancer, so I just fish and gossip. I guess that's why Bruce figured I'd be a good one to talk to you about living here."

Their food arrived at that point, so the conversation paused. When Carl finished, he declared the crab cake sandwich to be excellent. Max commented, "No offense. I don't like the look of it, all that lettuce and tomato. I try not to eat vegetables. That's why I like the fish and chips, and don't tell me the French fries are vegetables. Everyone always says that. I'm not buying it."

After their plates were cleared, Carl plied Max with questions about Hilton Head, and Max supplied detailed answers. Max liked to talk, and Carl was good at keeping people talking. It was a skill that worked out well for a private detective.

After half an hour, Carl guided the conversation toward Richard Ahearn. "It's not clear the stock market is going to hold up. If it does, I'm set. If it doesn't, I might be interested in doing some part-time police work when there's a big event. I guess around here it would be a golf tournament. Anyway, they might hire on some extra guys. What can you tell me about the local police?"

Max replied, "Luckily I haven't had any run-ins with them. Most people seem to get along with them okay. This is not a high crime area. A couple of years ago, a poisoning happened in Billington, just off the island. It made the national news as part of the Z deal. They never solved that one. That's about as exciting as it gets. Most of the stuff they deal with is theft."

"What about the chief? While I can look him up, it would be nice to find out the scoop from a local."

"His name is Trick Ahearn. Actually, his name isn't Trick. It's something else. Everyone calls him Trick. He played big-time football at South Carolina. I guess that's wrong; he was just a big-time recruit. He got hurt in his first game. I know some guys who hang with him. They seem to like him."

"That sounds good. Does he live on the island? Sometimes places like this don't pay enough, so a policeman, even a chief, can't afford to live where they work."

"I don't know where he lives, but he's not going to be living there long. I heard he put his house up for sale. His family sold their farm up in Pennsylvania to one of those oil companies. They made a bundle, and Trick is using some of his money to get a bigger house for his family. He's got a couple of kids."

Carl figured he wouldn't get any more details out of Max, so he changed the subject. "Enough about that. I just have one more question. You've told me about where you'd live if you moved here now. You haven't told me about any places to avoid. Are there places you would avoid?"

That topic got Max going, and Carl listened for another twenty minutes before looking at his watch and saying he had somewhere to be. He thanked Max profusely and took his phone number, saying he'd give him a call if he thought of any more questions.

He took in some scenery in the afternoon, and he even went by some of the condo developments Max had recommended. While he had no interest in moving just yet, he did dream of retiring some time. At four forty-five, he drove into position near the parking lot behind the police station.

The chief got into his car a little after five, and Carl pulled in two cars behind him. Carl had lots of experience trailing people. He'd followed a lot of unfaithful husbands and wives in his time. He figured he'd have to be careful with a police chief. It turned out to be easy to keep several cars between the chief and him. The chief made it off the island and turned into a housing development. The houses weren't as big as those on the island, but it looked nice enough. Carl kept driving after he saw the chief pull up to a small house. Sure enough, Max had given him good information. A for-sale sign stood in the front yard. Two blocks later, Carl pulled over and wrote down the address.

While tailing the chief, Carl finally figured out how to find the mother. Originally, he figured he'd wait around here to see if the police chief guy went to visit her. He didn't really like that strategy. It was a long shot. She could even live with him now. Maybe that explained why he wanted a larger house. In any event, he'd probably spin his wheels most of a week and not find out anything. He decided it would be much easier to go to the farms close to the Ahearn farm in Pennsylvania. He'd say he had some legal papers for Mrs. Ahearn and needed an address. Someone there would probably be able to help him.

CHAPTER TWENTY-EIGHT

PHIL'S WEDNESDAY LUNCH group appeared to be in an uproar. When Phil got there, he learned someone on the board had leaked the list of candidates scheduled for interviews at the Hilton near the Pittsburgh airport. The list had spread rapidly, and William had a copy he brought to lunch.

"Let's hold our comments until everyone has seen the list," Phil suggested. He hadn't heard anything about any list.

The others nodded. After Phil finished with the list, he spoke up. "Let's get this part over with. George, you can neither confirm nor deny that this list is accurate. Right?"

"Certainly," George replied. "I can't say anything about the accuracy of this list. What I can say is I'm not the source of any list. It's terribly unprofessional to leak like this, accurate or not."

"Okay, okay," Bert broke in. "I for one am terribly disappointed in the list. My understanding is that the only sitting college president on the list has a bad record where he is. He's clearly a rat trying to leave a sinking ship. None of the others have much experience. They're mostly deans or provosts at lesser schools."

"I'm disappointed too," Bob declared. "Somebody sent a copy to Tracy in our department last night. She's a hard worker, and she looked all of them up. According to her, the list is full of people too old to take on a presidency or too inexperienced for us to have any idea how they'd do. And there are four businessmen in the group. She couldn't find much about them. You'd think we'd be able to attract some better candidates."

"Tracy's sources are better than mine," William said. "I only got the list two hours ago. In any event, I have to agree with the basic sentiment around the table. I'm underwhelmed."

"You should withhold judgement," Phil commented. "The last time, the airport-interview list wasn't very impressive. If I remember right, we didn't interview any sitting college presidents. Most of them were deans or provosts. And Margaret didn't jump off the page at this point. She looked like the other deans or provosts. She had good recommendations. Several others did too. We only really got interested in her after the interview. I'd withhold judgement."

"Yeah, Phil," Bert said. "I bet you guys didn't interview any businessmen last time. You had the good sense to stick to academics."

"That bothers me too," Jeremy added. "Having a president who doesn't have any academic leadership credentials is a bad idea."

"I may be about to get in deep water here," Sally said. "Just for the sake of argument, isn't it possible someone with business experience might be good? You guys keep telling me fundraising is such an important part of the job. A business guy might have been on a college board and gained a lot of good experience."

"That's all true," Bert argued. "It might work out with a business person. Still, aren't most of the business types from a command-and-control background? The boss gives the orders, and everyone obeys. I've heard some horror stories from people who work at schools with military men, generals and admirals, as presidents. It took them a long time to learn the faculty wouldn't salute him."

"Bert's right," Jeremy said. "And he's put his finger on the likely problem.

College governance is unusual. I'm not going to say unique, only unusual. There may be some businesses in which the leader has to be a consensus builder. Anyway, a college president shares the leadership with the board and with the faculty. The president isn't a dictator."

"The more I look at the list, the more I agree with Phil," William commented. "It's what we ought to expect. We have to recognize where we stand on the academic ladder. Sure, we're pretty good. Still, we're not on the top academic rung. If you look at *US News and World Report*, and you can bet anyone interested in a college presidency has, you'll find us in the bottom half of the second hundred liberal arts colleges. Unfortunately, to anyone who doesn't know us, we look mediocre. We're fooling ourselves if we think we're going to get a list of candidates who look great at this point."

Phil nodded in agreement. "And it's quite possible one of them will be good. That's the second half of what I said. We all agree Margaret turned out to be a great president. It's thoroughly possible one of these people who doesn't impress us now will be good too."

"I can't talk about the candidates," George said. "I want to comment on something William just mentioned—US News's rankings. In my opinion, they're terrible. I've been at a board meeting where board members asked Margaret very pointed questions about why our US News ranking is so low. I bet that happens at lots of college board meetings. Those rankings get way too much weight in the minds of everyone."

"Yeah," Bert jumped in. "I agree. If you look closely at those rankings, money drives most of them. Actually, it's money and age. If you spend a great deal, you'll get a good ranking. To spend a great deal, you have to have lots of money. The older schools with the big endowments can spend more."

"You're right," George said. "And if you get great students, you'll get a better ranking too. It's circular. Getting a good ranking gets you good students, and getting good students gets you a good ranking. That makes it very hard to move up the rankings. If you look at the rankings, they're very stable over time. The same schools are at the top. Sure, there are some changes, only minor ones."

"The thing I don't like about the rankings is the emphasis they put on graduation rates," Bob declared. "You're right George, getting good students helps in the rankings, particularly in the graduation rate part. If you get good students, they'll graduate. If you don't, they won't. And there's another factor. If you take chances on good students who come from poor families, they might run into financial trouble and be forced to drop out. So, the key is to attract rich good students."

"Yes, and like George mentioned, it's circular," Jeremy said. "What you've just added is the insight that the ranking doesn't reward risk taking. The school that takes a chance on a student with promise, who doesn't do well on the SATs, is likely to lose in the ranking game. Similarly, the school attracting some good students who happen to be poor is taking a chance in the rankings. The rankings just reinforce the status quo in the country. The rich and talented go to the richest schools, and those schools get rewarded by *US News*."

"We sure are a 'woe is me group' today," Bert announced. "It's usually me who's down. I'm not going to complain about the *US News* rankings, and I guess I'm not going to be gloomy about the list of candidates. I going to hang on to Phil's suggestion. He told us Margaret didn't jump off the page at this point."

"I'm glad to hear you turn out a little positive, Bert," Sally added. "Most of you sound like a bunch of complainers. It's not like you. I hope you wind up liking the new president. I understand how important it is to you."

"Yes, Sally," George agreed. "It's extraordinarily important at a small college like Lackey. And, as a member of the committee I can't say anything, but you should take note—I didn't join in the group badmouthing the candidates."

After George's comment cut off the talk about the presidential search, the discussion turned to more mundane topics. The group broke up twenty minutes later.

CHAPTER TWENTY-NINE

KRISTEN FELT BETRAYED by her editor, Mike, as she left the bar close to the Pitt campus. She had been so excited about finding Mrs. Posey. She'd worked hard on the write up of her part of the story. At their impromptu meeting at the bar, Mike told her he wouldn't be willing to publish it. As he explained, even if he allowed her to use the information on the thumb drive as a source, she only had one source on Gestner. She had to have two sources on at least one of the lawyers involved. In addition, he wasn't sure the legal folks would agree to letting them publish anything based on the statistical information. While he tried to be encouraging, it sounded hollow to Kristen.

She walked to Gil's office to commiserate. He didn't look busy, or at least she didn't see anyone else in his office. He asked, "What's up?"

"I'm bummed. Mike won't let me go with the story based on Mrs. Posey's information. I guess I should have thought of it. The information on the thumb drive only covers Simmons and Martin. It didn't mention Gestner. The statistical work you helped me with uncovered Gestner. As a result, I don't have two sources on any one lawyer. I only heard one positive thing. Mike told me the legal guys might let me use the information from the wiretaps and the videos."

"How did you get Mrs. Posey to cooperate? Tell me again. I was too busy trying to get in your pants to take in all the details."

"I thought you weren't paying enough attention," Kristen said, smiling despite thinking she shouldn't.

"I'm paying attention now."

"I showed her the information I got in the package. I made her understand what happened to her had happened to other people—people who weren't as honest as she and her husband. She seemed really steamed when she saw the videos."

"Use that same tactic with the other guy. You have another guy who turned down the bribe, don't you?"

"Mr. Hughes doesn't like me. He's a real hard ass. He clammed up fast. I'm not sure he'd talk to me again if I asked."

"Don't ask, just show up at his door. And wait a minute, what if you took Mrs. Posey along? She'd be able to explain her situation, and she could say she'd be the star of the show. He'd only be a backup. You can promise that, I bet."

"Yeah, it'd be no problem. So, you want me to show Hughes the stuff I got?"

"Yes, treat him the same way you treated Mrs. Posey, and take her along. It's hard for a guy to turn down two women. I believe it's your best bet. Look honey, you're almost there. If you can get Hughes to cooperate, you'll have a big story."

Kristen called Mildred Posey, who seemed happy to hear from her. After she explained the situation, Mrs. Posey told her she'd be happy to help. She sounded very concerned when Kristen told her the story might not be able to proceed. They agreed Kristen would pick her up at one-thirty the next day.

When they knocked on Vernon Hughes's door, he came after a bit of a wait. Hughes didn't look at all friendly. He stood in the door, blocking their entry.

"You again. What do you want? I told you I didn't want to talk about what happened in the courtroom."

Kristen plowed ahead. "Mr. Hughes, this is Mildred Posey. I'd like you to meet her. She had the same experience you did. And we've got something to show you."

At that point Mrs. Posey stepped forward and thrust out her hand. "I'm Mildred Posey, Mr. Hughes. You ought to watch what Kristen has to show you. Please let us in."

Mr. Hughes finally took Mildred's hand and gave it a brief shake. "Come in if you must. I can't take long."

Hughes scurried around clearing off two chairs for the women. After taking her seat, Kristen took out her laptop and started in. "As I told you before, Mr. Hughes, I'm a newspaper reporter. I'm going to cut to the chase. I want to show you a short video I got from an anonymous source."

Clearly annoyed, Mr. Hughes relented anyway. "Okay, if it's short."

Kristen went to Mr. Hughes and handed him the laptop. Mrs. Posey came too. Both of them looked over his shoulder as the video started. Kristen provided commentary and pushed the enter key to move the Power Point slides.

Mr. Hughes remained silent throughout the presentation. When the women got back to their seats, Mildred spoke up. "What she's just shown you is evidence of bribery, plain and simple. And I know about it because a lawyer in the same law firm as these guys tried to get us to bribe Judge Moss, and we turned him down."

Mr. Hughes didn't respond.

Kristen jumped in. "Mr. Hughes, when I came here before, you indicated you had a disagreement with your attorney, Frank Martin. Frank Martin's the attorney involved in one of the two cases on that video. He arranged for his client, Quinn Calcott, to bribe judge Moss, and Calcott won his case. Did Frank Martin suggest you bribe the judge?"

Mr. Hughes looked concerned, but he didn't respond.

After a couple of minutes, Mrs. Posey filled the silence. "Look, you should cooperate with Kristen. We can't have corruption in our courts. What Judge Moss and these lawyers are doing is wrong. It ought to be stopped."

Finally, Mr. Hughes spoke up. "I don't want to be involved in any newspaper story."

"We're right, aren't we," Kristen pressed.

Mr. Hughes didn't respond.

"I won't have to mention your name. Please tell us what happened?"

After another long pause, Mr. Hughes choked up. Instinctively Mildred jumped up and patted his shoulder. "Please tell us," she pleaded. "It'll be good to get it out in the open."

Mr. Hughes shook his head and then started crying in earnest, hiding his face with his hand. Finally, he spoke through his tears. "You're right. Martin told us we'd win if we bribed the judge. Judy wouldn't have anything to do with it."

"Judy?" Kristen blurted.

Hughes looked up, his face tear stained. "Yes, my wife. Now she's my ex-wife. I guess the bribe thing is when things started to fall apart. While I have to admit I wanted to do what Martin asked, she wouldn't have anything to do with it. We had a big argument. She told me she'd divorce me if I did it, so I didn't. Then she divorced me anyway." Hughes broke down again.

Kristen sat there feeling sorry for Mr. Hughes and triumphant at the same time. Mildred went back to him and tried to provide comfort.

After Mr. Hughes got control of himself, Kristen said, "Mr. Hughes, I'm so sorry this brings up bad memories. I understand why you don't want to talk, and why the notion of being on record is unsettling to you. I have a suggestion. I'm sure you have Judy's contact information, and it sounds like she might be willing to be a source for us."

Hughes looked a little confused, and then he seemed to understand.

"Yeah, sure I have her contact information. I bet she'd be willing to talk to you. It would be just like her to want to be in the newspaper."

Mildred added, "That's our solution. It should work. I'm sorry we made this so hard on you. I hope your ex-wife's being in the paper won't be difficult."

"Actually, you'd be amazed," Kristen commented. "Even the biggest stories blow over fairly quickly. People are front-page news one day, and a week later, very few people remember anything about them."

Mildred added, "The police might want to talk to you. You've got nothing to worry about there. You didn't bribe the judge. Kristen's right. Whatever happens, it will blow over very rapidly."

Mr. Hughes brightened a little. "I sure hope you're right."

Kristen took down the contact information for Judy Hughes, and she and Mildred said goodbye to Mr. Hughes. Kristen almost skipped down his sidewalk on her way to the car. She had the critical second source she needed.

CHAPTER THIRTY

CARL HENSEN SAT back on Thaddeus Moss's couch with his Scotch. He'd just given Moss the address of Gladys Ahearn. As he'd suspected, he had no trouble getting the information from one of her old neighbors. He went to the farmhouse just down the road from the burned spot where the Ahearn house had been. The woman there had kept a card Mrs. Ahearn sent out announcing her move to a retirement community in South Carolina. The woman had been happy to help Carl out.

Carl scoped out the retirement community on the internet. It looked like a nice enough place. Still, retirement communities gave him the willies. All those old people and lots of funerals. The place turned out to be close to her son, which Carl guessed was why Gladys chose it.

After Moss put down the paper, he asked, "What about the son?"

"No problem tracking him down. I went to Hilton Head. He's the chief of the county police down there, so he's a well-known guy. I followed him to his home, which is outside of Hilton Head. I have the address. It won't be good much longer. The house is on the market. The way I see it, the family came into quite a bit of money by selling the land in Pennsylvania, so the guy's upgrading."

Moss appeared to be deep in thought, so he didn't respond right away.

Finally, he spoke up. "You've done great work, Carl. I might need you again. I'm not sure. You probably have a bill for me now."

"You have me figured out." Carl pulled an envelope out of the folder he brought.

Moss took the envelope and opened it. "This is very reasonable. I can give you a cash payment before you leave. I trust you remember how important it is for you to keep all of our interactions confidential."

"Yes. No one will ever hear a word about this work. You can count on it."

While they finished their drinks, the conversation turned to the Steelers. They both knew that in order to avoid talking about a topic, changing the subject to the Steelers would work. After they'd finished their drinks, Carl got up. "I'm sure you've got other stuff to do, Judge Moss."

"Just a minute, Carl. I'll go to my office and get your payment."

Moss walked to the back of the house. Carl figured he had an office there. Carl hadn't ever been in any room other than the living room. As he looked around, he recognized the judge must make a good living. The house looked very impressive. Maybe he came from money. Carl wasn't sure. In any event, Moss came into the living room a few minutes later with a handful of cash.

Carl felt a little crude counting the money in front of the judge. Nevertheless, he'd learned to be sure about things involving money. When he finished his count, he tried to hand a hundred-dollar bill back to Moss. "You must have miscounted. You're over by a hundred."

"No, I didn't miscount. I believe in rewarding good work, and you did good work, Carl."

"Thanks Judge." Carl put the money in his wallet and walked to the door. The two of them shook hands, and Carl went out.

After walking Carl Hensen to the door, Thaddeus Moss picked up the papers he'd received and went back to his office. There he unlocked his middle desk drawer and took out the folder on Sherry Ahearn and her family. He'd been doing some research of his own. Fairly adept with his computer, he'd found pictures of Sherry Ahearn, Trick Ahearn, and the guy Sherry lived with, Phil Philemon. Hensen had provided a picture of their house and the address. Gladys Ahearn's phone number finished the information he needed.

As he sat there, Thad made up his mind to contact his son Christopher. He knew he'd also have to involve Chris's girlfriend Samantha. Chris and Samantha were an odd pair. They'd met in college on the track team. They couldn't have been more different. Chris had been a long-distance runner, mostly the five thousand meters, and Samantha, who actually went by Sam, a shot putter and discus thrower. Sam looked as wide as Chris did slim. They got together after Chris's stint in the Air Force. Chris looked like he was getting closer to Sam's girth as he aged, but he hadn't caught up yet. The more he thought about it, the more Thad realized Sam's strength might come in handy.

Thad punched in the numbers for Chris's cell. He chuckled because lots of people would call it dialing Chris's cell. No one had a dial phone anymore.

Chris answered, "Chris Moss here."

"It's your Dad. I've got two things for you. First, can I reserve the plane, the big one, for the weekend after next? I want to fly out to Arizona—Show Low."

"Why're you going to Show Low this time of year?"

"I want to tell you about that. Why don't you and Sam come for dinner tomorrow? I'll give you an idea of what I'm planning. How about it? I can guarantee I'll have a better meal for you than you'll get at home."

"So, it's nothing you want to discuss on the phone?"

"No, it's just I have a proposition for both you and Sam. I'm sure there will be lots of questions. It will be better to have the discussion in person. And you haven't been over in a month or so."

"Okay. When did you say dinner would be?"

"Seven, I'll order from Mario's. You'll like it."

"No way you'll keep me away."

CHAPTER THIRTY-ONE

THE NEXT EVENING, Moss got home with his takeout order, set the table, and opened some red wine to breathe. While doing this busy work, he mentally reviewed how to present his proposal to Chris and Sam. He figured he would have to offer them a big cut of the proceeds. He'd be asking them to take a huge risk.

The doorbell rang at five to seven, and Thad welcomed Sam and Chris. As they were getting settled on the couch in front of the breadsticks, he recognized just how unappealing he found Samantha. First, her big body didn't appeal. Second, the tattoos covering her arms and God knows where else, weren't his cup of tea. Finally, her overall sloppy appearance didn't help the whole look. She didn't seem to do anything with her hair, a tangled mess. And she wore sloppy clothes all the time. Chris, on the other hand, looked pretty good. He must have come right from work, because he still had on his uniform from the charter company. Thad envied his youth, his height, a little more than six foot, and his great looking blond hair. He figured Chris should be able to land someone more appealing than Samantha.

They made small talk for a while, covering the weather, Chris's most recent flights, Sam's job at an old-folks home, and Thad's most recent cases. After those topics were covered, they moved to the table for the meal. Thad had asked for enough veal scaloppini for five. He knew Chris would like it. Also, though he'd met Sam several times, this was the first time they'd eaten together. He figured she probably ate a great deal of anything. As he watched her shovel the food down, he knew he wouldn't have leftovers.

After the tiramisu, which everyone enjoyed, they went back to the couch, and Chris said, "Great meal, Dad. Still, I know this isn't simply a social call. What do you want?"

"You're right. I have a proposition for you two. It's going to take a while to explain. Chris, I expect you remember I have bank accounts in the Cayman Islands. The last time I went down there, this nice-looking chick started coming on to me on the plane. To make a long story short, she had me quite distracted. We both went to the Alamo office. She told me her ride would be picking her up there, and I had to get my rental car. She told me she'd guard my luggage while she waited for her ride and I dealt with the paperwork. Somehow, she switched briefcases with me. When I got to the hotel, my key didn't work in the briefcase. I finally had to get a pry bar from the hotel to open it, and it turned to be full of wads of paper and a couple of rocks. She stole my money."

"Unbelievable!" Chris declared. "How much money did she get?"

"A little over six hundred thousand."

"Thad, I'm impressed," Sam commented. "You had a big chunk of change."

"Yeah, but I don't anymore."

"Let me guess," Chris said. "You found this chick's identity, and now you want to get your money back."

"Bingo. You're right on track. I did find out who she is. I had Carl Hensen track her down. He also got good information on her and the rest of her family. Her name's Sherry Ahearn. She lives in Lackey, where that Podunk college is. Anyway, it turns out she's rich. She and the rest of her family recently sold their farm to some oil company. They got ten million."

"Carl found all that?" Chris asked. "I always liked him. How's he doing?"

"He seemed fine last night when he slurped up my scotch. He does good work."

"How do you want to get your money back?" Sam asked.

"I took the money to the Caymans in cash. Now I bet Ms. Ahearn has it in accounts, either on the island or back here somewhere or both. A simple burglary wouldn't get us much. My idea is to kidnap her and demand ransom. I'm planning on asking for a million and a half. That'll give me say eight hundred thousand, and the two of you can split seven hundred thousand. It should be easy."

The other two were stunned and sat in silence.

After a few minutes, Chris said, "Dad, you can't think kidnapping will be easy. It's a federal offense. The FBI will get involved right away."

"Listen, Chris. I've thought this out. Grabbing her in Lackey is the only risky part. After that, we'll use your plane to take her to the cabin in Arizona. We can keep her blindfolded the whole time. She'll never have any way of seeing who we are. We'll instruct them to drop the money at the dock on the lake. We'll pick it up in the boat, and we won't release her until the day after we've received the money. That will give us a lot of time to get away."

"You know, Sam," Chris mused. "It might work. The lake Dad's talking about has a real narrow channel across from the dock. Suppose the FBI has the dock under surveillance, if we pick up the cash, hightail it across the lake, and get in the channel, we can get away."

"Don't you like the way the boy's mind works, Sam? Yes, that's exactly my plan. I even think we might have to sacrifice the speed boat. If we sink it after we get off in the middle of the channel, it might look like we've completely disappeared. After we have our money, we can release Ms. Ahearn. We ought to take her to Albuquerque or Phoenix to release her. We should be safe if the release point is somewhere far away from

Show Low. Since she'll be blindfolded the whole time, there's no way she can be aware of where she's been kept."

"So, what's my role in all this?" Sam asked. "You need Chris for the plane. What do you want me to do?"

"We need you for the initial capture. It might take three of us, and I wondered if you could take a couple of weeks off from your job. We will need people in Pennsylvania and in Arizona. Chris and I will have to be in the boat picking up the money. I planned on you babysitting our captive in Arizona. She'll need to eat, and so on. You'd wear a mask anytime you deal with her, and she'll be blindfolded. She's tiny compared to you. You can manhandle her, if she tries to do anything."

"It should be easy, Honey, and you've never seen the Arizona place. It should be reasonable weather out there. The cabin is fairly high, so it will be cold at night. My bet is that it'll be nice during the day. It's a beautiful spot."

"Okay. My job doesn't sound too difficult. We'll have to have a way to communicate."

"Yes, I'm planning to buy a bunch of phones. They call them burner phones. The kind you use then throw away. We'll all have each other's numbers. I guess there shouldn't be much reason to talk. We'll all go out to Arizona to get you set up with Ms. Ahearn. When we have the money, we'll call you on one of your phones, and you can do the release. Chris will be at some airport near the release city to pick you up."

"Sounds like you got this figured out, Dad," Chris said. Then he looked at Sam and asked, "What do you say?"

"I've got one more question," Samantha answered. "Seven hundred thousand dollars would go a long way for us, and eight hundred thousand would more than recoup your losses. Still, why not ask for more?"

"Good question," Thad responded. "The biggest mistake crooks make is being too greedy. It shouldn't be too difficult for Ahearn's mother to get ahold of a million and a half. Still, that's a lot in cash. Any more might be difficult. You're right. I want to recoup my money and a little more, and I wanted to make it worth your while. It's a mistake to ask for more."

Chris looked at Sam, who gave an affirmative nod to his implied question. He looked back at his dad. "We're in, at least for the time being. We may want to back out after we've seen all the details. Give us more."

"Great, I've got a bunch of pictures of Ahearn, her house, and her family."

The threesome went into Thad's office and studied the pictures. After a little search, Thad found some pictures of the cabin in Arizona to show Samantha. Next, they decided to review the kidnapping plot step by step, and Sam kept notes of what they might need. After they'd reviewed the plot in detail, they took turns taking the role of the skeptic. They wanted to be sure they'd thought of everything. When they ran out of possibilities, they looked at their phones—eleven-thirty, time to go home. They agreed to continue to review the plan in their minds. As Sam and Chris were leaving, they decided to meet again in two days.

CHAPTER THIRTY-TWO

KRISTEN FOWLER KNOCKED on Judy Hughes's apartment door for the second time the third day she'd tried to locate her. She'd left two phone messages and received no answers. As she headed down the stairs, she almost bumped into a woman coming up. Kristen hesitated to let her pass and brightened seeing her approach the door across the hall from Judy's apartment.

"Excuse me," Kristen said. "I'm looking for Judy Hughes. She lives in apartment six D, across the hall from you. Do you know how I can find her?"

"Yeah, she's on vacation, a cruise. I'm feeding her cat. She'll be back Sunday after next. Her plane gets in late. She usually gets back from work at five thirty. She'll have to work on that Monday. She told me she's taking every day of her vacation for this trip. If it's real important, I bet she'd be available on Monday evening."

"Thank you so much," Kristen said. She took out a business card and handed it to the woman. "Please give her this if you see her before I get ahold of her."

After a quick peek at the card, the woman commented, "You're a newspaper reporter. What do you want Judy for?"

"I'd rather not say. All I can say is I'm pretty sure Judy will want to talk to me, and it's important. Thanks for your help."

"No problem."

Disappointed, Kristen walked down the stairs. She wanted to interview Judy Hughes so badly. She could be the source she needed. At least she finally knew why she hadn't been able to reach her. She found it small consolation. She had to wait more than a week. She felt frustrated to be so close to breaking through and not being able to get what she wanted. Although she would have a good report to Mike during their Sunday meeting, she didn't have it all. She'd tell him about Judy and the likelihood they'd have just what they needed, but she wasn't sure.

At least she'd report on what she'd learned about Judge Moss. Investigations of his spending habits showed he lived high on the hog. He'd moved into an enormous house, and he took very expensive vacations. She hadn't yet uncovered any big cases he'd won while in private practice. She wasn't through digging, so she might still find something. A big win back then might explain the money. Also, she still needed to find out about his parents. He could have inherited money. She had plenty to do.

Phil and Sherry spent a long time filling out the forms for the adoption agency they'd chosen. They huddled around the computer for most of an afternoon. It reminded Phil of applying to graduate schools. The extensive questionnaire required them to give some long answers, not just yes or no. When they were finished, they thought they looked like excellent prospective parents.

"I guess the biggest strike against us is our age," Sherry lamented. "I bet we're among the older couples who are filling out these applications."

"I expect you're right. The people you talked to didn't balk at our ages, did they?"

"No, and I asked them specifically. They told me there were no age restrictions."

"Good. I expect the information about assets should make us look good. We own the house free and clear. We look quite well-to-do."

Sherry got up from the computer and walked back toward the spare room, the room they'd use for the nursery if things went the way they wanted. "We've got to start working on this room. If everything goes well, the adoption agency will want to come here to do an interview and a walk through the house."

"Okay. What color should we use? It's chancy to use pink or blue. We just agreed we'd take either a boy or a girl. What do we do, green or yellow?"

"I'm not sure. Let's go to the hardware store and look at the color options. We don't want anything too bright. We want this to be a place where the baby can sleep."

"They didn't have anywhere on that form to specify we wanted a baby who would sleep through the night. That's important to me. Is there is no way to get that information across?"

"Very funny. No, there wasn't, Phil, and if you make that request during the home interview, your wife will be very unhappy."

"I guess you can't count on these people having a sense of humor."

"No, you can't."

CHAPTER THIRTY-THREE

CHRISTOPHER MOSS AND his girlfriend Samantha showed up at his father's house for another dinner and planning session. After dinner, Thad showed them some plans he'd drawn up. The first part of the plot involved the abduction of Sherry Ahearn. The more Thad thought about it, the more he figured it best to do the deed at night. He'd printed pictures of the house Ahearn was living in from Google Maps. He had a close-up view and a wider view.

Thad showed Chris and Sam the escape route he'd planned for them after they nabbed their victim. "We can park on the street beside the house," he said. "That way we can take her out the back door, and we won't be exposed carrying a body for very long. She'll go limp, I bet. We'll be able to cover her with a blanket when we carry her out. After that, it's a right turn in a block, a left turn on the main street, and straight on to the interstate." Thad marked the escape route on the overhead picture of the streets in Lackey.

"That looks fine," Chris commented. "I've got one problem. Doesn't she live with some guy?"

"We might have to take him too," Thad replied.

"You mean kidnap two people?" Sam asked.

"It's like everything else in life. There are pros and cons. It would be easier to just take one person. To do that, we'd have to find Sherry Ahearn alone. I had Hensen trail her for the last two days, and I got his report by phone before you came. She doesn't follow any pattern. One day her boyfriend or whatever, this Phil Philemon, walked home with her after she went to work, and the next day she didn't leave the house until after dark. The guy Philemon was with her every night, even when she went out tonight. Hensen told me about it when he called."

Chris interrupted. "I agree. There are pros and cons. A daytime abduction is the only way we might limit it to one person. Doing the snatch in the daytime is dangerous. In addition, she doesn't follow any pattern we can determine. So night is better. As a result, we'll have to take two people."

"Yes, you understand. Things aren't so bad. We caught a break. Ahearn and her gentleman friend are basketball fans. They go to all the Lackey College basketball games. That's where Hensen first found them. They live close enough to walk to. Anyway, that gives us a great opportunity. We can break into the house and be waiting for them when they return. There's a game this Saturday night, and it gets better. Saturday night is a new moon. We won't have to worry about moonlight."

"Okay. The plane can hold two bodies. This sedative you're talking about will keep them under for how long?" Chris asked.

"I'll have to check. It depends on the dose, I'm sure. And we can give them another shot if we have to. We can stash them in the plane at night after we have them, right?"

"Yes, I'll have the plane we're going to use in the hangar. I'll take out the third-row seats, so we can put them there and cover them with a tarp. Even if they wake up, they won't be able to go anywhere. They'll be tied up, I assume."

"Yes, we'll tie them up. The transfer to the plane should be easy."

Samantha jumped in. "It should be no sweat. I've been there. You can drive right up inside the hangar."

"The money pickup is the real difficulty," Thad said. "Here, I have pictures of the lake." He took out several pictures, including closeups of the dock and the narrow channel across the lake. "Look at this picture from across the lake. We have to assume the FBI will be trying to see who comes to make the pickup. Even if we do it at night, they will have night vision goggles. They can use a car in the parking lot, or they can hide in the trees across from the dock."

"Yeah, and they might commandeer the Merton's house," Chris commented. "It's going to be tricky."

"Why are you smiling, Thad?" Sam asked.

"I'm smiling because I've figured out how to deal with them. We need to set off a diversion. And our diversion has to be one that will throw off any surveillance they have set up. We should do the pickup at night. If we're lucky, it will be cloudy. Anyway, we need to figure out a way to start big fires right in front of them—between them and the dock. A bright light is going to blind the guys trying to look through night vision goggles. Chris, you liked to fool around with fireworks. Can you set up something? Something that will burn bright for about three minutes? That should be all it will take."

"Wow Dad. You've really thought this through. I should be able to set up something and rig it so we can detonate it remotely. Still, I'm afraid it's a two-edged sword. Won't the fire expose us?"

"The element of surprise will be on our side. If we do it right, they won't be able to get a good view of us until we're headed across the lake toward the channel."

Thad showed a picture of the channel to Chris and Sam. "When we get to the channel, we'll ditch the boat and hop on the old dock. We can have a car ready and be out of there in nothing flat."

Chris spoke up at this point. "Dad, I've got an idea. Before we strike, let's fly a drone around the lake as a diversion. They might think we're going to pick up the package by drone. It would throw them off."

"Isn't it possible to pick up the package by drone?" Sam asked. "That seems like a better idea than using a boat. What if they have someone watching the dock in the channel?"

"I like the drone idea too," Thad added.

"I bet it's possible," Chris said. "I've only played around with drones a few times. I heard Amazon's planning to deliver packages by drone, so there must be a way of picking them up. I can find out fast. It would still be good to use the lake. There aren't any flying hazards over the lake. Heck, the drone would be capable of taking the package a long way from where we pick it up at the lake. If it works, it's a great idea."

"Okay, I like it. That's why it's good for there to be three of us. Talking together we came up with a better plan than I did on my own. Sam, you and I can have a drink while Chris hits the internet to look up drones picking up packages."

"I like that idea, Thad."

Twenty minutes later, Chris joined the two drinkers. "I'm pretty sure we can do it. We'd need a fairly expensive drone. Dad, if you can advance about five thousand, I can get the drone tomorrow. I'd like to be able to do a lot of practice. And we'll have to specify the size of the box holding the money. Maybe we can tell them to put it in a shoe box or something like that."

"Great son. A shoe box should be big enough. In a minute I'll go back to my office and get five thousand for you. It's best to make this a cash transaction."

"Yeah, that makes sense," Chris said. Looking at Samantha he asked, "What are we drinking?"

CHAPTER THIRTY-FOUR

THE WEDNESDAY LUNCH group straggled into the back room, with Bob coming last. Often late, he took quite a bit of ribbing about his tardiness. When they were finally all seated, Phil started the conversation. "What do we hear about the new president?"

"Nothing," William answered. "They did the airport interviews a couple of weeks ago, and as far as I'm aware, they're not doing any on-campus interviews."

"As you all know, I don't like how this is going," Bert said. "I want a chance to look at them, and if I was considering being president, I'd want a chance to learn about us. Wouldn't you want a chance to talk to the current set of administrators and faculty leaders if you were going to become their president?"

"Yeah, George, how's it all going to work?" Jeremy asked. "Bert has a good point. What if the candidate wants to interview people on campus?"

"That's above my pay grade," George replied. "I can tell you what the search committee is going to do, or already has done. We will send, or have sent, an unranked list of candidates to the full board. What they do after that is out of our hands."

"So, you won't tell us if you've reported to the board yet?" Jeremy asked.

"I can't. We had stern instructions not to say anything. Let me tell you those instructions were emphasized after the leaking of the list of airport interviews. A lot of board members were really steamed."

"We're not going to get anything out of him, guys," Bert advised. "I've been trying every time I ran across him on campus. Let's change the subject. I want to tell you a fable."

"A fable?" Bob asked. "How can we distinguish that from what you usually say?"

"Very funny, Bob. No, this is a story my mother heard from her mother. I just heard it repeated on the radio. I never thought of it with a modern interpretation. I think it's worth listening to."

"Let's hear it," Sally said. "I like the idea of a scientist telling us a fable and admitting he's doing it."

"Everyone is a comic," Bert lamented amidst the laughter.

"Go ahead, Bert," Sally coaxed. "While I was about to say I'm sorry, honestly I'm not."

"Okay," Bert said. "Can I finally start?"

Everyone nodded.

"The story is about a woman who makes a pact with the devil. The devil tells her she can have everything she wants if she promises to give him her first born. She can fly across the ocean. She can get anywhere she wants rapidly. She can have raspberries in the winter and winter squash in the summer. She can have a warm house in the winter and a cool house in the summer. The woman decides to take the deal and enjoys her life immensely. When she gets pregnant, she tries to renegotiate with the devil, but he won't deal, making the woman very miserable."

"I like it," Sally commented. "Like many fables, the moral is very clear."

William broke in before Sally could continue. "I get it, Bert. It's about us, and the devil is the fossil fuel industry. Fossil fuels have given us the ability to fly across the oceans and get where we want very rapidly. Fossil fuels have made it possible to have fruit in the winter, too. A great deal of stuff in the supermarket is grown in the southern hemisphere, and it gets to us by plane or on ships powered by fossil fuels. Climate change is coming to bedevil our children."

Phil jumped in. "Wow, an economist is able to decode the fable. I thought you guys were only good with numbers."

"And he worked 'bedevil' into his summary," George commented. "Very classy."

"Bert's fable is good," Sally concluded. "It could be the basis of a really good editorial. Can you get me a reference? Which Nordic country is it from?"

"I can try," Bert said. "As you know, my mother's still alive, but she's in her nineties and her memory's faded a little."

"I bet Mr. Google will be able to help you out, Sally," Bob added. "Don't you have a youngster working at the paper who you could set to work on finding the background?"

"Yes, I do. My plan now is to assign him the task of getting me the latest data on climate change—how much has sea level risen, how much has the average global temperature risen, and how many people live less than twenty feet above sea level, which cities are in the biggest trouble—stuff like that."

"I can tell you the cities in the biggest trouble," George said. "In the US it'll be New Orleans and Norfolk, Virginia. Parts of New Orleans are already below the Mississippi River, and it's a double whammy in Norfolk. Sea level is rising, and Norfolk is sinking. I'm almost positive those cities are in the biggest near-term danger."

"You're right," Bert commented. "They're in the most immediate danger in the U.S. Venice is in big trouble too, and I bet there are others."

"The statistics of the number of people who live close to the ocean are alarming," Phil said. "As the oceans get higher, lots and lots of people are in danger of flooding from storm surges. I like what William said—climate change is going to bedevil our children."

When they were filing out of the restaurant, Jeremy approached Phil. "What's on your hands? Are you painting?"

Phil looked at his hands and spotted some paint he's missed. "Shucks, I thought I got it all. Yeah, we're painting the guest room. Sherry wants to redo a bunch of stuff in the house. It's a little hard on her living in another woman's house."

"So, she's put you to work."

"Both of us are hard at it. She's better at the detail, so she does the outlining. I fill in the big spaces. While I guess I put on more paint, she does more work."

CHAPTER THIRTY-FIVE

PHIL AND SHERRY made it to the basketball game earlier than usual. It turned out to be necessary. The team had already recorded five wins, including three on the road, so they were stirring quite a bit of enthusiasm on campus and in town. Despite an early arrival, they were lucky to sit near their normal seats. The opponent looked to be the first big challenge of the season, and the game was close for most of the first half. Things changed when Lackey closed the half with a run of eight straight points, so they were ahead by twelve at the half. Phil and Sherry went out to the lobby to talk to their friends.

Jeremy and Linda were there, as were William and Joyce. "It looks like we're seriously good," Phil said. "Wilson should be challenging us, and we're up by twelve."

William responded, "I bet they come back at us hard in the second half. That run we went on to end the half isn't something we're likely to keep up."

"You're right," Jeremy said. "In my view, it will only be because McSweeny doesn't play those freshmen enough. The two new guys, Billings and Billchek, sparked that run at the end of the half. I don't know why they don't play more. Nate Smith played a lot as a freshman. I don't know why they don't start."

"It's tricky," Sherry concluded. "I guess those two are a little better than the seniors who start—only by a small margin, not by a lot. With Smith last year, the coach made an exception. Smith's so good, he didn't want to keep him off the starting five. He's the exception to the rule you reward seniors by starting them. I like the coach doing that."

"Me too," Phil added. "As the season progresses, I bet you find Billings and Billchek playing more minutes than the starters. It's the minutes that matter more than who starts."

As they headed back to their seats, Phil and Sherry greeted more friends. It seemed like the whole town attended the game. As they shuffled to their seats, Phil commented, "It's great to live in a small town like this. We've got a lot of wonderful friends."

Sherry gave him a quick, chaste hug. "Yeah, it's great."

The second half of the game repeated the first half. Initially, the margin hovered at ten or twelve points. With twelve minutes to play, the two freshmen came off the bench. They were rested while their opponents were not, and it showed. Billchek made a steal resulting in a breakaway layup, and right after that Billings blocked a shot. On the following trip down the floor, Nate Smith made a three. Lackey led now by seventeen points, and the Wilson players appeared to sag. Wilson's first five were competitive. After them, they had no answer for the two quick freshman who came off the Lackey bench. The final margin, twenty points, satisfied the Lackey fans as they left the gym.

Sherry and Phil were in a good mood as they walked home after the game. As Phil put his key in the front door, he noticed a black SUV parked close to the alley beside the house. *Odd*, he thought, *I know all the cars in the neighborhood, but I don't recognize that one.* It was probably nothing, so he decided not to say anything to Sherry.

He stepped aside to let Sherry enter and followed her toward the coat closet. Just as he got to the closet, someone grabbed him from behind, and he saw another person grab Sherry. Things happened fast. The guy holding Sherry had pantyhose over his face. Panic flooded his body, and he tried unsuccessfully to wriggle free. A few seconds later, he felt a prick in his upper arm. He was being injected with something. He looked at Sherry, who was screaming, and saw the same thing happen to her. *No…* Shortly thereafter, Phil lost consciousness.

Sherry's screams spooked the kidnappers, Samantha in particular. After their two victims were sedated, Sam, Chris, and Thad looked out through the windows to check for anyone who'd been roused by the noise. They didn't see any signs of activity on the street, so they continued as planned. They put cloth gags on Phil's and Sherry's mouths. Then they lay the two victims out straight with their hands to their sides. Using strapping tape, they did three turns around each victim's legs and mid torso, pinning their arms.

"That should hold them," Samantha whispered.

"Yeah, and we can bend them at the waist if we need to," Chris added, keeping his voice low. "We might need to bend them to get them into the plane."

"Don't forget to take their shoes off," Thad instructed. "And take that purse somewhere."

"Right," Chris replied, removing Phil's shoes.

After Samantha removed Sherry's shoes and put her purse in one of the bedrooms, they turned to the two thin carpets they'd brought. They rolled Phil in the larger of the two carpets and Sherry in the other one. With the strapping tape, they wrapped the ends of the carpets. Chris hefted the carpet holding Phil. "This guy's surprisingly heavy. You and I will have to carry him out together, Sam."

"Yeah, I expect it will be easier," Sam replied. "And maybe we'll both lug her out, too. It will be simpler. Right now, I'm taking off this stupid pantyhose. I don't like having my face all scrunched up."

Thad removed the pantyhose from his face. "We ought to wait a few minutes. She really screamed loud."

Chris walked around the house looking out all the windows. Then he returned to the other two hovering over the carpet rolls. "There's not a sign of movement, and only two houses have lights on, the house across the street and their next-door neighbor. The next-door neighbor is no problem. We're going out the other side of the house. We just have to wait for the house across the street. I hope they go to bed soon. The faster we get out of here, the better I'll like it."

"You sure you checked every window?" Thad asked.

"Yep. I looked out every one of them. I only saw lights in two of the houses. Most people in this Podunk town don't stay awake very long, and it's almost ten o'clock. I'm ready to load up and go."

Sam looked out the front window. "A porch light just came on across the street." The other two came and peeked out the window.

"The guy's going to walk his dog," Chris said. "I bet it's the last thing he does before he goes to bed."

"The dog doesn't look like he's up for a big walk," Sam commented. "He's peeing already."

The man and the dog went right back into the house. The porch light went out, followed by the other lights in the house.

"All right," Thad said. "We should wait ten minutes to be sure those people are asleep. After that, I'll slip out the back door and check everything. When I knock on the door, bring the first one."

Chris paced in the living room as his watch counted down ten minutes. "That's ten minutes. You can go," he said.

On the way out the backdoor, Thad pushed some glass out of the way with one of the shoes he carried. They'd broken the window earlier to get in. A few minutes after he left, Chris and Sam heard a knock. They lifted the carpet roll containing Philemon and quickly made it to the back of the vehicle. The carpet slid into the space they'd made by putting the seat down. They'd chosen this rental because the back seat had a sixty-forty split.

"One down and one to go," Chris whispered as he and Sam headed back to the house.

After they'd put the second carpet roll in place, Sam got in the back seat and Chris got in the front seat. Thad started the car, and they headed out of Lackey. He didn't put the headlights on until just before he made the turn onto Main Street.

When they got to the outskirts of Lackey, Chris asked, "Can I take off these rubber gloves now?"

"No, you ninny!" Sam exclaimed. "We didn't want any fingerprints in that house, and we don't want any in this rental car. Your dad emphasized that. Right Thad? You're all going to keep your gloves on until we leave the car at the drop-off location."

"Right. We don't want to leave any clues in this car. There was no way to avoid leaving some fragments from the carpets in the house. We can avoid doing so in the car. We're going to use the charter company's vacuum on the back of the car when we get to the hangar. We've talked about all that. With a kidnapping, the authorities are very likely to know about the crime. They'll scour that house for clues. If we keep our gloves on and clean out the car really well, there'll be no way they can trace anything they find in the house back to us."

They encountered very little traffic until they merged onto the interstate. They made good time and turned into the private-plane airport where Chris worked on schedule. They came to a stop in front of the hangar, and Chris hopped out and rolled the door open. Thad drove into the hangar and parked beside the plane. Chris rolled the door shut before he walked over to turn on the lights. He'd gassed up the plane in the afternoon and prepared it for the trip. The two seats he'd removed were in one corner of the hangar.

The plane was a Cessna 340A, a twin-engine plane with seating for six. With the two back seats removed, all three of them fit in as well as their two carpet rolls. While the whole process turned out to be a little awkward, Chris and Sam were able to get the two captives in the place where the third row of seats normally were. They were glad they allowed for the possibility of bending their victim's waists. It made it much easier to get them on the plane.

"They're just dead weight," Sam said. "I guess that stuff you injected them with put them out for quite a while."

"According to what I read, they'll be out for six to eight hours," commented Thad. "Since she's lighter, I guess she'll be out longer. With their shoes off, I can get at their feet if we need to inject them again."

"I like the idea of keeping them sedated," added Chris. "We don't want to have to listen to them on the flight. At least I don't."

"Those gags we have over their mouths should make it difficult for them to make much noise. I don't want to use the sedative again if we can avoid it. We don't want to kill her. She's a valuable commodity."

"I sure hope the gags work," Sam said. "We're stopping in Kansas City and Albuquerque, right?"

"Roger that," Chris replied. "It's going to be a long flight, no matter how you cut it. I expect we'll need to get them both back to sleep before Kansas City. If the gags don't work, they might start hollering when we stop to refuel."

"What about Albuquerque?" Thad asked.

"The airport I plan on using in Albuquerque is a small one. We've been there before on our way to Show Low. It's self-service at their pumps. Those two can yell all they want."

"And remember, when we get to Show Low, we'll be able to taxi right into the hangar," Chris added. "Manuel is bringing the Jeep from the cabin. We should be able to transfer our cargo to the back of the Jeep and drive away."

Sam broke in at this point. "We've gone over this all before, you guys. It's time to get moving. Chris, you're supposed to be sleeping on the cot in the office. We need you rested for tomorrow. And Thad, after we clean up this car, I'm going to follow you to the place to drop it off. Right?"

"She's right, Chris," Thad said. "Get some sleep. We'll be here in the morning."

"Six o'clock."

"That's it. Sam is going to pick me up at five thirty, so we'll be sure to be here by six."

CHAPTER THIRTY-SIX

AS PHIL STARTED to rouse, he felt trapped. He couldn't move his arms or legs, and some cloth covered his mouth. He had a flashback of being grabbed from behind, and then he remembered someone grabbing Sherry. Why had they been captured? As his senses began to come more fully awake, he smelled dust and some kind of fiber. He recognized the smell of a carpet that hadn't been cleaned in a while. He wiggled his hands, feeling the thing trapping him. It felt rough, like the back of a carpet. Phil wasn't sure what good it did to know he'd been wrapped in carpet. Nevertheless, he decided it was a breakthrough.

He tried to calm himself with little success. His throbbing head made it difficult. Then he remembered being jabbed in the upper arm. Now that he thought about it, he could feel the place where whoever they were had injected something into him. He and Sherry had been doped. He wondered how long they'd been out.

A noise entered Phil's consciousness next. He didn't notice it at first, because it sounded fairly steady, like an airplane, not a jet, a prop plane. Just as he recognized the noise, the plane hit some turbulence and shook a little. This confirmed his suspicion. He figured he'd been rolled in a carpet and put in a plane flying some place. He'd started to piece things together, and he didn't like the emerging picture.

The more he thought about it, the few things he'd discovered were dwarfed by what he didn't know. Where had Sherry gone? Who were the people who'd grabbed them? Where were they going? What was going on? He had lots of unanswered questions, and he was trapped in the roll of carpet. He tried to wriggle and found he could bend at the waist a little, not that it did him any good.

Phil heard a woman. "Look, the guy's starting to wake up."

"Okay, he wiggled or stretched or something," a male voice said. "Remember, we use numbers from now on. No names."

"Sure, Number One," the woman commented. "I still don't know why I'm Number Three. Whatever happened to ladies first?"

"Hush Three, we've already heard you on the subject. For now, keep an eye on them. Let us know if the other one starts moving."

Phil figured Sherry must be on the plane with him. The people, numbers or whatever, referred to him as "the guy," and he thought that implied "the other one" would be a woman. It made sense. They'd grabbed Sherry at the same time they grabbed him. He'd seen her being injected with the sedative before he lost consciousness. Phil pushed his backside and ran into something, either the side of the plane or Sherry. There was no way of telling. Phil found the whole thing frustrating and incredibly scary. Whoever had grabbed them had to be evil. All he could do was lie still and hope his headache would dissipate.

A little while later, Phil felt the plane losing altitude. The engines weren't straining as hard, and he slid a little toward what must be the front of the plane. Finally, he felt a bump and heard the plane's wheels squeal as the plane landed. The plane didn't taxi for long before coming to a stop.

"Welcome to Ka—"

"No names, Number Two, at least one of them is awake."

Phil heard the door to the plane open. Just after that, he felt movement on his side and heard a little groan. *Sherry must be coming to*, he thought.

"The woman's starting to wake up," the woman announced.

"That's fine, we'll just stay in our seats, unless you have to hit the head. Number Two's talking to the guy in the fueling truck. We won't be on the ground too much longer."

"Is there any radio in this thing, Number One? The way I figure it, we are only about half-way there. Is it possible to get some music on for the next leg?"

"So, you're tired of playing with your phone?"

"No, it's almost out of charge. I don't want to run it all the way down. It's not good for them."

"I'll check with Number Two."

As the people were talking, Phil smelled gasoline. He figured they were on a long trip, a bigger trip than the plane could make on one tank of gas. Phil didn't have any idea about the range of prop planes. Then again, it probably depended on the weather and a lot of other factors. And besides, he didn't know if they were going north or south or west. It wouldn't be east because of how long they'd been flying and from where he figured they took off.

Phil heard Sherry moan again, so he tried to answer. Unfortunately, he wasn't able to make much noise. He tried to scoot a little closer to where she made the sounds.

The woman, Number Three, spoke up as he tried to move closer to Sherry. "Should we inject them again?"

"No, here comes Number Two, it looks like we're fueled up. I don't think it hurts anything to have them awake while we're just flying. I'll inject them again right before we land. It will be easier to load them into the Jeep if they're asleep. The transfer will go better then."

Phil heard the plane's engines starting. After the plane started to move, he sensed when they were taxiing, when they were racing down the runway, and when they were airborne. He hoped Sherry could tell these things too. Despite having little success, he continued to try to loosen whatever held him in place. As the plane settled into its cruising altitude, he figured he'd have to wait. These people were clearly taking them somewhere where they'd be loaded into a Jeep. Based on what he'd heard, they'd be drugged at that point. Phil decided to try to go to sleep. He remembered reading in some mystery that being rested would be important, so he tried to relax.

Phil didn't have much luck with his efforts to rest. He found it very uncomfortable, and he had an overpowering urge to scratch. He remembered his leg being in a cast after he'd been wounded in Viet Nam. He'd experienced many itches he hadn't been able to scratch. Now that he thought about it, the carpet felt much rougher than his plaster cast. The time dragged by. The plane's engines droned, and the people, whoever they were, didn't talk.

As before, he sensed the changes when the plane approached its next destination. This landing was rougher than the last. The ride smoothed out after a rather large jolt. A few minutes after the plane stopped, he smelled gasoline again. *Another refueling stop*, he thought. The plane took off again, and the monotony continued.

After what seemed like a shorter time than the last flight, the plane landed again. As the plane taxied, one of the men said, "Look, the hangar door's open. We can taxi right in. We'll close the door before I inject them again."

After the plane came to a stop, Phil heard the cabin doors open. Cool air filled the cabin. After a few minutes, hands grabbed him and started to drag him out of the plane. They stopped dragging when his feet were sticking out. He felt a sharp stick in his foot. *Oh no, they've injected me with the sedative again.*

CHAPTER THIRTY-SEVEN

WITH THEIR TWO hostages and their other gear under blankets in the back of the Jeep Cherokee, the three kidnappers drove to the cabin. The cabin sat in an isolated part of a forest. Getting there required about ten miles on Route 60, southeast of Show Low, and then five miles of dirt road. The cabin sat in the middle of a twenty-acre tract. Moss got the cabin in the divorce. It had been in her wife's family, and she didn't want it. Thad felt it would be the perfect place to keep the hostages. It couldn't even be traced back to him. He'd never changed the name on the deed. Also, the cabin sat more than a mile from its nearest neighbor, a cabin with few occupants even in the summer. In the fall there would be no one.

Sam was impressed. "Wow, this is nice. I like the high ceiling in this, what do you call it, great room?" Sam spun around, taking in the view of the nearby mountains out the big picture windows. "How many bedrooms are there?"

"There are actually four. We only need to use the two downstairs ones," Chris answered.

Chris led Sam to a bedroom off the main room on the right. "I figured we'd put the hostages in the queen-sized bed in here, and you'll use the single next-door. That way there'd be no reason to mess with the upstairs at all."

Thad came in with an armload of stuff. "Let's get the stuff out of the car. We can bring in the hostages after we get set up."

When they had all their gear in, Chris explained, "We're going to have to feed them, and we're not going to give them their meals in bed, so I'm going to put this big eye bolt in the floor by the table in the back. When you bring them out for meals, take their handcuffs off the bars in the bedroom and attach them to this bolt."

"I get it," Sam replied. "That'll give them at least one hand to eat with, and they'll still be contained. Getting the long chains on the handcuffs makes sense to me now. Maybe they can use both hands. What do you mean about bars in the bedroom?"

Chris held up three elongated, u-shaped metal bars. "These are used in bathrooms for the elderly. They are attached in bathtubs and showers to help people get up. They keep them from falling. We're going to put one on the floor on either side of the bed. One end of the handcuffs should be on the hostage, and the other end goes on the bar. That will give them some room to move. At the same time, it will keep them secure."

"So, what's the other bar for?"

"The bathroom. You don't want to have to be in the bathroom when they're doing their business. It'll be the same arrangement. You hook them up to the bathroom bar and then leave."

"You guys have thought this all out. I like it."

Thad, waving the large drill, said, some annoyance growing in his voice, "Let's get going. The sooner we can get this stuff mounted, the sooner we can get back to the airport."

"Okay, Dad. I've been explaining things to Samantha."

Chris watched Thad drill a hole near the table in the kitchen-end of the great room. After completing the hole, Thad dropped the big eye bolt through the washer and into the hole. Chris ran out of the house with a nut and a crescent wrench. The two in the house heard him yelling from under the house to hold the bolt while he tightened the nut. Thad put a big screwdriver in the eye bolt to keep it steady.

After putting the nut on the eye bolt, Chris came back into the cabin. "That's not going anywhere," he said. "Let's put the bars in the bedroom."

They drilled the holes and again Chris ran under the cabin to attach the nuts. It turned out to be easy work, and the two bars were secured in short order. The bar in the bathroom caused no problem, since it attached to the bathroom wall and didn't require going under the house.

After the bathroom bar was secure, Chris and Sam unloaded one of the hostages, the woman. They unwrapped her from the carpet and put her on the bed. Thad put a handcuff on her wrist, making sure to tighten it. He put the other end of the handcuff over the bar on the floor and secured it. Obviously pleased with his work, he said, "She's not going anywhere."

Thad bent over Sherry with a smile, and declared, "This will teach you to try to steal from Thaddeus Moss, Ms. Ahearn. I bet you won't feel so pleased with yourself when you wake up."

Samantha asked, "Shouldn't we take the gag off? That thing's probably real uncomfortable. Look, it's making a red mark on her cheek."

"Sure, take it off," Thad said. "They can scream all they want. There'll be nobody to hear them."

Samantha removed the gag, and then she and Chris headed out to get the man. When they had him in place, Thad announced, "It's time to haul ass. We'll point the way to the grocery store when you're taking us back to the airport. I've already given you the phones, and you have the numbers on you, right?"

"Yes, and I have the blindfolds for them. I'm set to go here. I'm kind of looking forward to it, roughing it out here in this cabin. You're right, we should get going if you guys are going to make it to Albuquerque tonight. Let me check for cell service here."

"I wondered about that too," Thad commented. "It's no big deal. You can go into town in the evening to check for messages or to tell us anything."

"I'm going to have to do that. No bars here."

Grabbing their tools, Chris and Thad followed Sam out of the cabin and made sure she locked the front door. The trip back to Show Low went quickly. Sam gave Chris a kiss and hugged Thad as they all got out of the car at the hangar. She waved as they taxied out for their flight home. Next, she had to shop for supplies. If things went according to plan, she wouldn't need to keep the hostages for more than a week; however, she decided to get food for about three days. After babysitting the two captives all day, she'd probably be going bonkers. On one of her nightly trips to check on the phone, she'd make another trip to the grocery store.

That same evening at the Pittsburgh airport, Beth and Ralph walked to the baggage claim area to pick up their luggage. The honeymoon on the Virgin Islands had been wonderful. They'd spent quite a bit of time on the beach. This time Beth used plenty of sunscreen.

"I wonder where Phil is," Ralph said when they reached the carousel for the luggage from the Miami flight.

"The flight got here a little early. I'm sure he'll show up soon," Beth replied.

After they'd retrieved their luggage, Ralph said, "It looks like I'll have to give Phil a call. He might be stuck in traffic or something."

"Good idea."

Ralph didn't get an answer on Phil's cell phone, so he left a message. Five minutes later, Ralph decided to call Phil and Sherry's home number. He got no answer there either.

"Call Sherry," Beth suggested.

"She's not answering either."

"That's odd," Beth said. "I'm not surprised Phil didn't answer. He's not good about having his phone on all the time. Sherry's much better. I thought you'd get her."

After they'd waited another twenty minutes and made several more attempts to phone, Ralph decided they'd have to find another way to get home. They decided on a cab. While a cab would be expensive, they had plenty of cash.

Thad and Chris made it to Albuquerque in good time. They gassed up the plane, tied it down in a space they had rented, and took a cab to a motel close to the airport. After they checked in, Thad took charge. "You want to come to my room to listen to the call?"

"Sure, I'll drop my bag in my room and come quick—107, right?"

"That's it."

When they were together in Thad's room, Chris sitting on the bed and Thad in the chair by the little desk, Thad took out one of the burner phones and dialed the number for Gladys Ahearn, Sherry's mother. The phone rang four times before she answered.

"Mrs. Ahearn?" Thad asked.

"Yes, who's this?"

"I have a short message for you. We've kidnapped your daughter, Sherry. She should have known better than to mess with me. If you follow our directions, nothing will happen to her. You need to arrange to pay the ransom. We'll need one million five hundred thousand dollars, and we'll need it in cash, unmarked bills. Payment will be due on Friday. Don't involve the police. I'll call again with more instructions."

With that, Thad hung up.

"Wow, you kept it short."

"You don't ever want to have long conversations with these people. I'm sure the FBI will be called in. Ahearn's son is a police chief in South Carolina. Despite my instructions, I bet she's calling him right now. Eventually, they'll be trying to trace the calls, so those calls will have to be even shorter if we can manage it."

CHAPTER THIRTY-EIGHT

THAT EVENING, PHIL came to first. As he tried to get oriented, he recognized he wasn't on the airplane any longer. He had a pounding headache. It hurt to move. At least the carpet wrap had disappeared. He looked around in the dim light. He was lying on a bed, and Sherry slept beside him, probably still drugged. He moved his arms and heard a jangling sound like chains moving. He felt, and at the same time saw, a handcuff on his right wrist. He tried to pull that hand towards his body, but it didn't come far. *The other end must be attached to something on the floor.* He slowly scooted on the bed to see what held the other end of the handcuff. Looking over the side of the bed he saw the handcuff on the other end of the chain and the bar that held it. The bar appeared to be bolted to the floor. When he yanked on the chain, the bar didn't budge. Whoever had taken him wanted to keep him in this bed.

Twenty minutes later, Sherry started to stir. Phil had been waiting patiently for this to happen. When she opened her eyes, he said, "Sherry darling, I'm right beside you. We've been captured by someone."

"Phil?" Sherry asked in a shaky voice.

"Yes, I'm here."

Sherry responded to the voice and turned toward Phil. As she turned, she found she couldn't move her left hand very far. A handcuff held it.

Recognizing what she had to be going through, Phil told her, "The chain from your handcuff is probably attached to a bar bolted to the floor. At least that's my set up."

"We were on a plane, right?"

"Yes, and we took a long flight. We made two stops."

"And when we were awake, the people didn't talk too much. They used numbers instead of names. It's starting to come back to me now, and I have to say this headache isn't making it easy. They grabbed us when we were coming back from the basketball game. I saw them inject you with something. And I guess I got the same treatment. I don't remember much after that."

"The sedative, or whatever they injected us with, wore off part way through the flight. When we got here, wherever here is, they injected us again, in the heel."

"Yes, I remember that. The bottom of my foot still hurts."

"Otherwise you're okay?"

"So far as I can tell. I'm stiff and sore more than anything else. I hope this headache goes away. How about you?"

"I'm the same, stiff and sore with a headache to boot. What I need more than anything else is a kiss."

By stretching their outside arms, they scooted close and shared a long kiss. Phil spoke after they broke away. "That's nice. I needed it. I don't know what's going on, or if we'll ever get out of this. Still, there's no one else I'd rather share the experience with."

"Thank you, Phil. You're incredibly sweet. Nevertheless, I have an awful bad feeling about this. We've been kidnapped. While I've only been rich for a little while, isn't this the kind of thing that happens to rich people? They get kidnapped."

"Oh my God," Phil said. "I guess you're right. It has all the hallmarks of a kidnapping. We've been abducted, and now we're in a secure place. It's getting dark out there now. From what I saw before you woke up, we're in some western forest. I only saw the outlines of the trees. I think they were pines."

Just then car lights flashed across the window, and they heard a car parking. A door opened somewhere in the building. Five minutes later, the door to their room, a bedroom they guessed, opened and a large person appeared. Whoever it was wore a mask on his or her face, and his or her clothes were baggy, a track suit or something. The person turned on an overhead light and Phil and Sherry both instinctively moved their free hand to cover their eyes.

"So, you're awake," said the person. The voice sounded high pitched. Phil thought they were dealing with a woman. She continued, "You haven't eaten anything for most of a day. I'm going to go fix you some dinner."

"Wait," Phil asked as the woman started to close their door. "Who are you? What are we doing here? Why are we handcuffed? What's going on?"

"You sure have a lot of questions, Mr. Philemon. You'll get your answers soon enough."

"You're Number Three, aren't you," Sherry added.

"Good for you Ms. Ahearn. Sure, you can call me Number Three, or if we want to be less formal just plain Three."

"What are we doing here?" Sherry asked.

"Look, I'm sure we'll get around to that eventually. Now, since it looks like you'd rather talk than have me fix dinner, let's go over the ground rules."

"Okay. I guess," Sherry responded.

"As you have already discovered, one of your hands is cuffed, and the handcuff is securely attached to the floor. You will always be constrained that way. There will be two exceptions. First, we will have meals. When I come for you, I will release the handcuff from the bar on the floor, and I will escort you to the table and secure your handcuff in the floor there. When one of you is in place, I'll come for the other. Second, you will need to use the bathroom on occasion. We will use a similar procedure. I release you and take you to the bathroom. In the bathroom you will be attached to another bar. When you have finished, I will take you back here. It's simple, and there is no reason for any of us to have any difficulties. Now I am going to fix dinner, and then we can practice our dining procedures." With that, Three turned off the light and closed the door.

In the dim light, Phil and Sherry looked at each other quizzically. Finally, Phil spoke up. "It looks like Number Three has this all figured out. I wonder where Number One and Number Two are. Maybe we can ask her."

"I have to agree, everything appears to be well planned. I wonder if these people are experienced crooks. You know, people who've done lots of kidnappings. Some rich people just pay off kidnappers, and the careful kidnappers get away with it. You certainly hear about that sort of thing in Central and South America."

"Yes," Phil said. "And this group is on top of their game. It pleased me to see a plastic bag on that chair. My wallet and keys are in it. I'm taking it as a good sign. They're keeping my things so they can give them back to me."

"I hope you're right, Phil. Unfortunately, I haven't spotted my purse anywhere."

Twenty minutes later, Three came back. She had a metal rod of some kind her hand. "This is a cattle prod," she said holding up the rod. "If you give me any trouble, I won't hesitate to use it."

Using one foot to stabilize the handcuff on the bar on Sherry's side of the bed, Three inserted a key, unlocked the handcuff, and removed it. The entire time she worked with the key, she didn't take her eyes off Sherry. With the handcuff in one hand, she waved the cattle prod she held in her other hand. "As I just told you, I won't hesitate to use this if you try to get smart. Now get up."

Sherry felt shaky on her feet as she got up. She walked stiffly. Three guided her. After she sat down at the table, Three attached her free handcuff to a big ring in the floor. Fairly soon thereafter, Phil sat beside Sherry. Dinner consisted of a frozen entrée Three had heated up. All things considered, Phil found the food tasted better than he'd expected. They were offered and accepted water, served in plastic cups.

While they ate, Phil and Sherry looked around at their accommodations. The table almost filled one end of a large room. A kitchen ran along the wall in that end of the room with the table. The kitchen end of the cabin had a normal eight-foot ceiling. A spiral staircase let to a second floor over the kitchen end. The other end of the first floor had a high, arched ceiling and big windows. Since darkness had settled, they couldn't see anything out the windows. The furniture in the end away from the kitchen looked to be hand-me-downs—well-worn and not very well coordinated. Some of the stuff might have been nice at one time. Now it looked old and thoroughly used. Phil noticed a couple of carpets draped over one of the sofas. He figured they were the carpets they'd been wrapped in. The walls were made of wood—pine, Phil figured.

Though they'd spent quite a bit of the day drugged, Phil and Sherry found they were very tired after Three had let them linger over dinner and introduced them to the bathroom routine. They were pleased to be offered blankets and fell asleep quickly.

CHAPTER THIRTY-NINE

TRICK AHEARN HAD taken the panicked call from his mother the evening before. He tried to calm her down without much success. "There isn't anything we can do at this point," he said. "Write down all you can remember, then go to bed. I'll be over first thing in the morning."

After he got off the phone with his mother, he'd tried to call Sherry. He got no answer on the home phone or Sherry's cell or Phil's cell. He didn't worry. His watch said ten thirty. They might have turned off their cells. They could be at a movie or out somewhere. He finished getting ready for bed. A half an hour after his first attempt, he called again. Still no answer. He started to worry.

In the morning, Trick made quick work of breakfast and hurried out of the house, telling his wife he had to go check on his mother. On his way, he tried phoning Sherry again and got no response. It didn't look like anyone was stirring at the retirement community. Not his mother; he found her up and dressed.

His mother had coffee fixed for him. They sat by the table in her little kitchen area. "Did you manage to write anything down to jog your memory about the call, Mom?" Trick asked.

"I tried," Gladys answered, looking at a notepad she'd brought to the table. "First, I talked to a man, not a woman. He said they'd kidnapped Sherry. Second, he warned me to start getting money for the ransom—one million, five hundred thousand dollars in unmarked bills. Finally, he said they'd call back today with more details. That's all I can remember."

"You did very well, Mom. The call came in after ten, didn't it? Were you asleep?"

"No, I read right before I go to sleep. I guess I'm pretty tired at that point. I don't get many calls, particularly at night. Every time I get a late call, I'm afraid something has happened to Sherry, or you, or one of the kids. All my friends around here wouldn't call that late. I guess, this time I had reason to be worried."

"It looks like you might have. I haven't been able to get ahold of Sherry or Phil. While we can't be sure this isn't a sick prank, I'll make a couple of calls. I'll use my cell phone. We need to keep your line open. They didn't say when they'd call, did they?"

"No, they just told me they'd call today."

Trick's first call went to the Lackey police. He got right through to the chief of police. The chief assured him he'd send someone to check on Phil and Sherry's house. Trick felt glad Lackey was such a small town; the chief knew Phil and Sherry, or at least knew who they were.

After the Lackey police, Trick called the FBI. They handled kidnappings. After he explained his concern and his identity, the person who'd answered the phone told him to hold. The next person he talked to identified himself as Agent Albert Harrison. Trick repeated his story to the agent.

"Okay, we're going to advise you to do a few things. We don't know yet if it's really a kidnapping. Our advice is to proceed as if it is. You've got to figure out a way to record any call you get. Can you do that?"

"Yes, I can have my people get me a recording device. If they don't call in the next half hour, I'll be able to record it."

"Good, the recording might be really helpful."

"Second, if they call, demand to speak to your sister. That's important because we need to know they really have her and if she's okay."

"Makes sense, and I guess you want me to keep them on the line as long as I can?"

"We won't be able to trace the call, so it doesn't matter so much. Still, the longer the recording is, the better. Finally, call us the minute you hear from the police in Pennsylvania. If it looks like they're missing, we might be able to get help to you sooner."

When he got off the phone with the FBI, Trick called his station. He gave them a quick briefing and told them to get something to record a phone call at the retirement community as fast as possible. Finally, he told them to clear his calendar for the day. He had a terrible feeling this wouldn't be a normal Monday.

Back in Lackey, Ralph and Beth woke up a bit late. They'd gotten in at a reasonable hour after their cab ride from the airport, nevertheless traveling tired them out. When they'd made it home, they tried calling Phil and Sherry and again didn't get a response.

After he'd had breakfast and dressed, Ralph told Beth he'd drop by Phil and Sherry's to figure out what had happened to them.

"Tell them hi for me," Beth commented. "And tell them to turn on their phones."

"I sure will. I bet Phil forgot all about picking us up."

When he approached Phil and Sherry's house, Ralph saw a police car pulling up in front. Ralph recognized Miguel Torres getting out of the car.

Ralph shouted as he approached. "What's up, Miguel?"

"Oh hi," Miguel answered. "We got a call to check out Professor Philemon's house. Sherry Ahearn's brother is a cop somewhere, and he called. I don't know what it's about, he talked to the chief. Anyway, I got a call to check out the house pronto."

Ralph followed Miguel up to the porch, and they checked the front door. It was locked. They peeked in the windows. "It looks fine to me," Ralph said.

"Let's go around back. They have a back door, don't they?"

"Yeah, off the kitchen."

When they got to the back of the house, they saw the back door had been breached. "Look, this door's been opened," Miguel said. "Ralph, don't touch anything. This might be a crime scene. I'm putting on my latex gloves."

Ralph didn't know what to think. *What could have happened to Phil and Sherry?* He nodded to Miguel. "I won't touch anything."

Miguel pulled open the door and pointed to the shards of glass on the floor. The two of them then walked carefully into the quiet house.

"There are two bedrooms on this floor," Ralph said. "And there's a finished attic. They mostly use it for storage."

"Okay, let's check out the bedrooms."

"This one's the master," Ralph said, leading the way. "Nothing is out of place. Wait, it's weird. The bed hasn't been slept in, but that's Sherry's purse on the chair."

In the spare bedroom, Miquel spoke up. "This one looks funny. They must have taken out some of the furniture to paint. It still smells a little like paint."

"I haven't been in this room before. You're right. It's been recently painted. We'd better check the garage. Phil had planned to pick me and Beth up at the Pittsburgh airport yesterday afternoon. It was weird. He didn't show. I'd wondered whether he'd had an accident."

"That wouldn't account for the broken glass and the open back door."

"I guess you're right."

Ralph opened the garage door and saw both cars.

"Their cars are here—both of them. I wonder where they are," Ralph said.

"I don't know, let's check the attic."

In the attic, Ralph noticed their suitcases. He recognized them from the Cayman Islands' trip.

"These are their suitcases, Miguel. It doesn't look like they've taken a trip of any kind."

After they came back from the attic, Miguel concluded, "They're not here, and, except for the back door, there's no sign of anything amiss."

Ralph started to get very concerned. "What's happened to them?"

"I have no idea. I'd better get back to the station and report what we found. Do you want to come along?"

"No, I can't. I've got to open my store, and I'm late already. Come and tell me what this is all about? I can't figure out what happened to them. This has me a little shook up."

"I can see that. I'll be sure to let you know. Come on, at least let me drive you. I'll drop you at your store on my way."

CHAPTER FORTY

TRICK STRUGGLED TO control his nervousness. He'd paced every inch of his mother's small apartment and answered as many of her questions as he could. At nine o'clock, Trick almost jumped out of his shoes when his cell phone rang. It turned out to be the Lackey police. They'd sent a patrolman to Phil and Sherry's place. They told him it looked like the place had been broken into. They found no signs of Phil or Sherry, and their two cars were in the garage.

Trick called back the FBI and told Agent Harrison what he'd learned. Harrison told Trick they'd be sending a team to help him. If this really had been a kidnapping, they'd be taking over the case. They had the ability to track phone calls, and they would be able to give advice about how to handle things.

"When will you be here?" Trick asked.

"It might be a couple of hours," Harrison answered.

"What if I get a call before that?"

"Record it. You've got that capability, haven't you?"

"I do. I can't trace the call, and my mom's phone doesn't even have caller ID."

"Let's just hope they don't call before we get there. If they do, remember to tell them you won't do anything until you hear from your sister."

After the call to the FBI, Trick resumed pacing nervously, hoping the next car entering the complex would be full of agents who knew what to do in kidnapping cases. While he had been a chief of police for three years, he'd never had to deal with anything like this.

At ten thirty, the phone rang again. Trick put on the recording device and answered, "Ahearn."

"This isn't Gladys Ahearn, is it," a male voice said.

"No, it's her son, Richard."

"Okay Richard, here's what you and your mother are going to have to do. If you ever want to see Sherry again, collect one million, five hundred thousand dollars in cash—"

Trick broke in. "Look, whoever you are, I'm not doing anything until I hear from Sherry. I've got to know she's okay."

The person on the other end of the line didn't pause at all. He simply announced, "Seven o'clock tomorrow night," and hung up.

Trick found his pits were sweating up a storm. He turned off the recording device. After he'd calmed down, he played the short recording. The guy mentioned the same amount of money his mom remembered, otherwise the guy on the other end of the line hadn't said much. While Trick knew he was supposed to try to keep him on the line longer, the guy'd hung up abruptly. He kicked himself for interrupting the guy when he started talking about the ransom. All things considered, he couldn't give himself good marks.

The FBI got there an hour later. Agent Harrison, a tall blond who looked to be in his late forties, exuded authority. There were two other agents, both of whom carried electronic gear. They didn't introduce themselves.

He said, "Let's listen to your recording."

"Sure," answered Trick. "It's real short. I doubt it'll be useful. I'm not sure I did a good job."

"Don't worry, and you'd be surprised. We'll take it and analyze it.

Sometimes we can pick up clues based on the background noise."

Trick played the recording for the group, and they all listened.

"You're right, it's short. The bad news is it looks like we're dealing with sharp people. They were ready for you to ask to speak to your sister, and they kept the call short."

One of the other guys picked up the recorder and asked, "Can I take this back to the lab? We might find something."

"Sure," Harrison responded, looking at Trick who nodded.

He continued, "Now we've got to do something about hooking up the rest of our equipment. I take it this is your mother's apartment."

"Yes, I forced her to go to her regular bridge game at ten. I didn't want to offend her. Still, she got on my nerves."

"It's going to be a mess in here with all the gear and people. We ought to try to either find a place for us to move or find a place for your mom to move. We'll essentially be living here for a while."

"We might be able to find an empty apartment we'd be able to move to. I know the management. I'll ask them to transfer her phone to an empty unit. Why don't you come along with me, Agent Harrison? The presence of the FBI might make the management more cooperative."

Two hours later, the FBI completed their set up in one of the empty apartments. They checked and double checked the phone set up. Gladys' number rang on the phone in the new apartment. Trick explained the new arrangement to Gladys, and she said she'd be happy to not have to share her apartment with a bunch of FBI agents. Still, she came to the new apartment and hovered for a while.

Nothing happened the rest of that day, and Agent Harrison guessed nothing would happen until seven o'clock the next day.

Thad hadn't been surprised when the Ahearn guy wanted to speak to his sister. He thought it came right out of kidnapping 101. The kidnappers had to prove they actually had the victim. He turned to Chris. "The mother, and her son I guess, won't do anything until they know for sure we have their daughter. So, we've got to get Sam to do a call. I told them we couldn't arrange the call until tomorrow. Tonight, tell her to make the call tomorrow at five o'clock. I have the number she's supposed to call."

"Five o'clock. I thought you told them seven o'clock."

"Remember time zones, Bozo. Arizona is on mountain time, and we're on eastern time, so five o'clock in Arizona is seven o'clock here."

Chris slapped his forehead. "Sure, time zones. I don't know how I forgot them. Do you figure the FBI's involved? Aren't they called in on any kidnapping?"

"Yes, I bet they are. Asking to speak to Ms. Ahearn sounds like them. We have to assume they're going to be poised to try to trace any calls. That's why I got all those phones and kept my call short. Sam has to do the same thing, keep the call really short. When Sam puts Ahearn on the phone, all she can let her say is that she's okay. Only one sentence. The FBI, or whoever, will try to extend the call. Don't let them. Tell Sam she should just hang up after Ahearn says her bit."

"Okay, I've got it. And Sam should destroy the phone she used on that call."

"You're right. In fact, have her destroy all the phones she's used already. We left enough phones for her. She shouldn't use any of them more than once."

"Tomorrow night you're going to call them after they've heard from the woman."

"Right, that's when I'm going to tell them about the shoe box full of money we want on the dock at the lake. What we should do now is write out the explicit instructions for that part. Again, they'll be trying to trace the call, so we have to be quick."

"Yes, and then we destroy the phone ASAP."

"You got it. So, what do we have to tell them? I need your help, because I want to get it right. While I know you've been practicing with the drone, you can't pick up just any shoebox, or can you?"

"I guess it would be better if we specified a particular size of shoe box. I've got all the stuff in my car. I have the Nike shoe box I've been practicing with. I'll go get it."

"Good."

A couple of minutes later, Thad heard Chris coming back in the front door. He glanced and saw Chris carrying an orange shoe box.

"This is it," Chris announced. "It's a little scarred up because the drone's picked it up a bunch of times. This size works perfectly. I'd probably manage to pick up something a little bigger. I'd rather not try, though. Better safe than sorry."

Why did he have to go on about the stupid shoe box, Thad thought, about to lose his patience. He told himself to calm down.

"Go to the junk drawer in the kitchen and get a measuring tape," Thad said. "We ought to give them the dimensions."

Chris came back with the tape and measured the box. "It's thirteen by five by eight. It's probably a standard size."

"I'm sure it is, and it will fit all the cash we're demanding with no problem."

"We should tell them to put tape around the box," Chris suggested. "I almost always grab the box and keep it steady. I just want to be sure nothing goes wrong."

"Okay, let's go into my office so I can draft the message."

After they got to the office, Chris paced as Thad wrote. Finally, Thad stopped and picked up the paper.

"Try this out," Thad said.

Chris read,

> *If you ever want to see your daughter alive, place one million, five-hundred thousand dollars in unmarked one-hundred-dollar bills in a*

regular-sized shoe box, thirteen inches by five inches by eight inches. Securely tape the box shut. Put the box on the end of the pier at the west end of Lake Whipple in Pennsylvania. The shoebox should be in place no later than Friday night at six o'clock.

After Chris looked up, Thad said, "I tried to keep it short. Did I leave anything out?"

"No… oh wait. There's one problem. I don't want to have to pick up the box if it's right at the end of the dock. I need it back from the end. The arms that grab the package might get fouled up if the surface around the shoebox isn't flat. Tell them to place it three feet from the end in the middle of the dock."

"Okay, I understand. Good catch. I've never seen how the drone picks up the package."

"Is that it for now?" Chris asked.

"Yeah, just be sure to talk it through with Sam about the call where Sherry Ahearn has to verify she's alive and safe. Five o'clock her time tomorrow night."

"You were going to give me the number to call."

"Yeah, sure. Here it is." Thad pulled out a folder from a pile on the top of his desk and wrote down a phone number he found in the file.

Chris took the piece of paper and headed toward the door. "I'll send you a text message after I've talked to Sam," he called over his shoulder when he got to the front door.

Later that evening, Sam called Chris. When he answered, she said, "It's good to hear you, Honey. I'm bored out here in the not-so-wild west."

"Boring is good, Sam. That means nothing's gone wrong."

"Yeah, it's routine. I'm real tired of wearing that mask and messing with those two. I only had to use the cattle prod once. The woman, Sherry I guess, tried to take a swing at me this morning during our walk to breakfast. It didn't work out for her. I shocked her good. They've been gentle as lambs ever since."

"Sounds good."

"How much longer is this going to last?"

"Things are moving," replied Chris. "And we've got something for you to do tomorrow evening."

"Great."

"The people we're talking to, Ahearn's mother and brother I guess, want proof she's alive and unharmed. We've arranged for them to expect a call tomorrow night. You should call a number I'll give you at five o'clock your time. Put Ahearn on the line and have her say she's alive and unharmed. Don't let her say anything else, and don't you say much of anything. When they answer the phone, just say, 'Sherry Ahearn has a message for you.' After Ahearn says her bit hang up, and immediately destroy the phone. Zap it with the cattle prod and then smash it to bits."

"I'm going to have to figure out how to keep Ahearn contained while the call is taking place. I can't use the handcuff arrangement we rigged up in the house."

"I'd use duct tape. Tape her ankles together and pin her arms to her side. That'll keep her still while she's with you in the car. You get enough cell service on the outskirts of town. You don't have to go all the way in."

"Sounds like a plan. Okay, five o'clock my time tomorrow, I can make it work. You'd better give me that number."

Chris took the piece of paper out of his pocket and repeated the number to Sam.

CHAPTER FORTY-ONE

MONDAY EVENING BETH and Ralph reviewed all the details they knew. Ralph had called Beth at the hospital to tell her Miguel reported it looked like Phil and Sherry had been kidnapped. Miguel came by the store at about eleven to tell Ralph the news. The chief had received a call from Sherry's brother, Richard. Apparently, someone called Sherry's mom the night before demanding ransom. Ralph called Beth right after Miguel left his store. Unfortunately, she had to break off the call quickly. This evening gave them their first chance to talk in detail.

"I'm sorry your call caught me at a bad time this morning. I was about to go into surgery. It turned out to be a long one, so I wasn't able to get back to you. Do we know anything more than what you learned from Miguel?"

"I went to the house after I closed, and some techs from Pittsburgh were there. They had yellow crime tape around the house. Miguel had gone off duty, but I saw Frank. He told me the techs were collecting fibers they found. The fibers they were interested in didn't match anything else in the house. They also dusted for fingerprints, I guess. I have no idea what they found. Like I said, they had the house blocked off. Frank told me he and Miguel had interviewed all the neighbors. None of them had seen Phil or Sherry for a couple of days. Other than that, none of them noticed anything suspicious. I didn't learn anything, really."

"Kidnapped. I've been wondering about it since you called. Who would want to kidnap Phil and Sherry?"

"I've been giving that some thought too," Ralph added. "The obvious thing is money. Sherry, her mom, and her brother just came into a ton of money from the sale of their property."

"Yeah, that just happened. Not many people know about it. I don't think it's the only thing."

"The local paper publishes the information about property transfers on a regular basis, and there's no telling how many people know about the big pot of money the Ahearns just got."

"Do you think a local kidnapped them?"

"It's certainly a possibility. Look, someone broke into their home and took them. The person would have known which home to break into, and they must have known about Sherry and Phil's comings and goings."

"You said someone broke into their home using the back door."

"Yes, the door has a pane of glass. You remember. Half of that pane of glass had been shattered. It's easy to break in with no glass in the door."

"And there were no signs of a struggle, no furniture out of place or anything."

"That's right. Where are you going with this?"

"My guess is that the people broke into the house when Phil and Sherry were away. If they were there, they would have heard the glass break. And this probably all happened at night. Otherwise, one of the neighbors might have seen or heard something."

"Okay. I follow you."

"My bet is that it happened Saturday night. Phil and Sherry would have gone to the basketball game. Everyone in town knows they're big basketball fans. The crooks probably broke in at night and waited for Phil and Sherry to get back from the game. It would be dark, a little after nine."

"It all makes sense. The neighbors reported they haven't seen either of them for the last two days."

"Unfortunately," Beth concluded. "Figuring out when it happened doesn't help us figure out who did it."

"Frank told me the FBI has been called in. They get involved in kidnappings. There will be a lot more high-powered people working on the case than us."

"Yeah, I guess they'll be trying to trace any phone calls they get from the kidnappers and stuff like that."

"Actually, with cell phones involved, they can get quite a bit of information. I bet you're right. They'll be tracing the calls and lots of other stuff too. I sure hope Phil and Sherry are okay. It gets real dicey if the FBI advises them not to pay the ransom. I wouldn't want to be in Sherry's mom's position."

Beth nodded and then filled the silence. "I bet it's her brother who'll be making the decisions. He's some kind of cop, right?"

Ralph answered, "He's a county police chief."

"There's nothing we can do, Honey. We should say a prayer for Phil and Sherry."

Phil and Sherry were thoroughly bored as they lay on their backs on the beds, handcuffed to their anchors on the floor. Sherry's side still hurt where Three had used the cattle prod on her the previous morning. After that experience, which Phil heard as he waited on the bed, they figured it best to obey Three.

They whispered to each other most of the time, because they didn't want to be overheard. All things considered, there hadn't been much to say. They were in some cabin in the western United States. That much they knew for sure, but they didn't have a clue about anything else. While Three didn't say much, the way she brandished the cattle prod said a great deal. Sherry told Phil she thought Three had liked using the cattle prod on her.

They decided Phil should try to catch the license plate on Three's car. Phil's position allowed him to look out the side window, and he might be able to see the plate if Three went out in the afternoon. If they saw her license plate, they might know which state they were in.

Phil recognized that finding out the state might not help much. Still, they wanted something. Otherwise their situation appeared to be hopeless. At least they were being fed. Phil figured they wouldn't bother if they were planning to kill them. It didn't feel like much to hang on to.

Back in South Carolina, Trick and the FBI agents didn't expect anything until seven o'clock, so not much happened during the day. Agent Harrison called Trick in the early afternoon to tell him the lab hadn't been able to find anything useful in their analysis of the recording. "It was a longshot," he said. "Let's hope we can keep them on the phone longer the next time. And we'll have the trace equipment, too."

"I'm not surprised. The short call didn't give you much to work with," Trick replied.

"We should get the whole team together tonight at six thirty. The call is supposed to be at seven. We want everyone in place well before then."

"I'll probably be at my mother's apartment. She's pretty upset. My wife will be with her this evening. I'm sure we won't be able to keep her there at seven. She'll want to hear the call from Sherry."

"I'm sorry she has to put up with this. There's no way around it," Agent Harrison concluded.

CHAPTER FORTY-TWO

IN PITTSBURGH, KRISTEN hoped she had all her ducks in a row for the Tuesday afternoon meeting of the paper's legal committee. She'd never been to one of these meetings. Mike told her it had to happen before this story broke. Just yesterday evening she'd finally managed to meet Judy Hughes. Kristen had gone out on a limb and written up the story as if Judy had backed up what her ex-husband had reported. Luckily, it turned out to be a good strategy. She'd stayed up late Monday night inserting quotations from Judy, who'd been happy to have her name used. This morning she'd turned in her story to Mike, and he'd told her to leave while he read it.

Fifteen minutes after she left his office, Mike called to tell her about the legal committee meeting. When she heard about the meeting, she recognized she didn't know much about the legal committee. She went to her friend Ramon, who'd been at the paper for about ten years. He filled her in. Apparently, it consisted of the paper's lawyer and two outside lawyers Mike picked from a list of local attorneys. Ramon said he thought the committee didn't convene very often.

"You must have something really hot," he commented. "Care to tell me what it's all about?"

"No, I'm sorry I can't. I promised Mike. If there are no hang-ups with this committee, you'll hear about it soon."

"Front-page stuff, huh?"

"If I'm lucky."

At three o'clock, Kristen entered the paper's conference room. She saw the paper's lawyer, Jack Betts, sitting at the conference table with Mike and a woman she didn't know. Mike introduced the woman as Marcia Kennedy. Kristen didn't catch which law firm the somewhat stout, gray-haired lady worked for. After a few minutes, a short, bald, elderly man entered.

"Horace, what are you doing here?" Marcia asked as she got up and hugged the new entrant.

"Oh, hi," the man said, extracting himself from the hug. "Mike called me. I served on this committee several years ago."

Everyone shook hands, and then Mike introduced Kristen to Horace Kemp.

"Bill Sims turned out to be busy?" Marcia asked. "I expect him at these meetings, not that we meet very often."

"The reason Bill's not here will become clear in a minute. Let's start. I know you two are billing me by the hour. I'm going to let Kristen start. It's her story. You'll all find it very interesting."

Kristen stood up and switched on the projector. The first slide showed the instructions sent to her with the thumb drive. She explained she'd received a thumb drive, which she held up for them. After everyone finished reading the slide, she told them she has no idea who XYZ was. Then she showed the slide show, providing a commentary where needed. She identified Jim Simmons as the attorney for Wilson Enterprises, Judge Moss's house, and Quinn Calcott, and she pointed out Calcott had been represented by Frank Martin.

The two guest attorneys gasped a couple of times when it became clear the videos were about a judge being bribed. They didn't ask questions until the slide show finished.

Mike picked up the story at that point. "When Kristen first showed me this, I didn't know what to do. I know you lawyers are going to tell me this kind of evidence, evidence obtained illegally, wouldn't be admissible in court. We're in a little different territory here. Unlike a courtroom, we can use anonymous sources. This XYZ is just that. As you know, sometimes we go to great lengths to protect anonymous sources. Since we don't know XYZ's identity, we won't have to worry. Still, we wouldn't publish a sensational story like this based only on one source."

"What you have here is really damning," Horace Kemp said. "I know Thad Moss, not that I think too highly of him. This will cause a sensation at the courthouse."

"Now I understand why Bill Sims isn't here," Marcia said. "Those lawyers, Jim Simmons and Frank Martin, are from Johnson, Sims, and Fox, aren't they?"

"Yes," Mike replied. "Why don't you continue, Kristen?"

"Okay. After Mike and I talked about it, I started investigating. First, I tried to gauge the magnitude of the problem. While we knew about two lawyers, there might be more. To get a handle on this, I looked at the records in Judge Moss's court to determine how well those two lawyers did when they had cases there. I found Jim Simmons won every case he brought before Moss in the last three years. Frank Martin lost his first case in Moss's court but followed the loss with a string of five straight wins. My boyfriend, who teaches at Pitt, told me what I had wouldn't be very convincing. Instead, I may have just proved these two are really good lawyers, or they only take easy cases."

"He's right. I don't find it convincing," Marcia said. "Granted, it's consistent with your other evidence. Still, it's not convincing on its own."

"As a result of his sensible criticism, I looked at similar data from all the other courts. I found both Simmons and Martin were quite average, maybe a little worse, when they tried cases before other judges. They were great in Moss's court and very middle of the road in other courts. There were a couple of other lawyers who were very good in Moss's court. In their situations, they were just as good when they tried cases before other judges. Simmons and Martin stood out."

"That's starting to be more convincing. In my experience, statistical work like this isn't going to do the trick," Marcia commented.

"That's what I told her," Mike reported. "Go on, Kristen."

"My work with the data did uncover another suspicious Johnson, Sims, and Fox lawyer, Phillip Gestner. Just like the other two, he did spectacularly in Moss's court and turned out to be ordinary when facing other judges. I agree this isn't enough for a story. Still, it gave me my targets. I started to interview the clients of these lawyers. All the clients who won their cases were happy as clams. They didn't have any misgivings about what had happened. My break came when I interviewed Mildred Posey, one of Phillip Gestner's clients. Her husband, who died last year, turned down Gestner's suggestion to bribe Judge Moss. She is still so proud of her husband. In any event, she witnessed the entire discussion and is willing to have her name used in the story and to testify if legal proceedings follow."

Mike jumped in. "I told Kristen she didn't have enough yet. She didn't have two sources on any one lawyer. She only had the statistical stuff on Gestner, which I agree is only suggestive, and Mrs. Posey. The XYZ people didn't have anything on Gestner. I told her she had to continue digging, and she persevered."

"Though I have a very demanding boss, like he suggested, I persevered," said Kristen, who got some laughter from the group. "Anyway, I tracked down one of Frank Martin's clients, Vernon Hughes. At first, he didn't want to have anything to do with me. The second time I saw him, he finally broke down. Martin offered Hughes the chance to bribe Judge Moss. He didn't take it. His wife Judy wouldn't have anything to do with it. She told him she'd divorce him if he went along with Martin's scheme. While Mr. Hughes told me all this, he didn't give me permission to quote him. Finally, I tracked down Judy Hughes, his ex-wife. After their dealings with Martin, she divorced him anyway. I interviewed her last night, and she's willing to be quoted and to testify if things wind up in court. I stayed up half the night drafting the story."

"So, there you have it," Mike concluded as Kristen sat down. "We're going to run a front-page story tomorrow unless you three talk us out of it."

"Congratulations, young lady," Marcia Kennedy said. "You did quite a good job of developing the story, and your presentation was excellent. I don't know, Horace, what should we tell them?"

Horace Kemp rocked back in his chair and looked at the ceiling. After a long pause, he finally spoke. "There's no reason to advise them to stop publication. They didn't do anything illegal. While these XYZ people broke all kinds of laws, the paper didn't do anything wrong. I don't see a reason to stop the story. I presume you've given Mike the same advice, Jack?"

Jack Betts, who'd also been silent throughout the presentation, answered, "You're right, Horace. In my view, Mike and Kristen have handled this completely appropriately. I'm not surprised you agree. And you, Marcia?"

"Yes, the paper is on firm legal ground."

Jack continued. "We called this meeting mostly to seek your advice about how we should handle this with Johnson, Simms, and Fox. As you all know, they are my former employer, and we all have friends and respected colleagues who work there. I told Mike we should give Bill Simms a heads up before we publish. After all, he's normally a member of this committee. We shouldn't blindside him."

"That's very considerate of you, Jack," Horace said. "When were you planning to drop the bomb on them?"

"You think I should?"

"Yes," Horace replied, and Marcia nodded when Jack looked at her.

"Horace is right," Marcia added. "It's very considerate of you to give them a warning. This is going to be awful for the firm. They'll have TV cameras in their faces right after the story breaks. It will be much easier for them to have talking points ready. This is going to be big, really big. It might even make the national news. If I were Bill Simms, I'd pray that some other newsworthy stuff crowds them out."

"You're right, Marcia," Mike said. "Jack and I will set up a meeting with Bill for four-thirty or five. If he can't clear his calendar, we'll meet with one of the members of the management committee who can. I want to do this after the story has been edited. Kristen has a little polishing to do. In any event, Jack, why don't you make the call and set up the meeting. Try to find a neutral place to meet."

"Okay," Jack said as they got up, shook hands all around, and hurried out the door.

"I'd better be going too," Kristen added. "As you said, I have some polishing to do. Nice to meet you all."

CHAPTER FORTY-THREE

IN ARIZONA, THREE came into Phil and Sherry's room at four thirty. Phil glanced down at his watch. *Unusual*, he thought. *Dinner is usually closer to six.*

Three commanded, "Lie still, Ms. Ahearn. I want your legs together and your hands at your side. You and I are going for a little ride."

She waved the cattle prod, and Sherry obeyed. Using duct tape, Three taped Sherry's free hand to her side. After she assured herself Sherry couldn't use that arm, Three picked up Sherry's lower legs and wrapped them with duct tape. Next, she had Sherry sit up and wrapped duct tape around her upper torso, trapping Sherry's arms at her side. After she finished, Three unlocked Sherry's handcuff from the bar on the floor. "Now you're ready for your trip, okay?"

"Do I have a choice?" Sherry asked, worried about what was going on.

Three chuckled. "No, I guess you don't."

At that point, Three lifted Sherry off the bed and stood her up. Then she bent Sherry over, put her over her shoulder, and carried her out of the room. The way Three carried her made Sherry feel like a sack of grain.

Outside, Three put Sherry on her feet beside the car, opened the car door, and shoved her in. Since Sherry's arms and legs were wrapped in tape, she wasn't able to move much. She scooted so she was more or less comfortable.

When Three got in the driver's side, Sherry asked, "You going to fasten my seat belt?"

Three chuckled. "Sure, I believe in always using seat belts."

After fastening Sherry's seat belt, Three started the car, backed up, turned around, and headed down the driveway. Sherry tried to pay attention to everything. She and Phil had been correct, they were at a cabin in the mountain west. The trees were almost all some kind of pine, mostly little ones. The driveway, just two tracks with some gravel, didn't deserve the title driveway. At the end, they turned right on a good gravel road. The soil beside the road looked to be reddish brown. As they drove, Sherry saw Three check her cell phone frequently. *She's checking for reception*, Sherry thought.

"Trying to get cell service?" she finally asked.

"Very clever. Yes, I am. And when I have service, and the time is right, I'm going to put you on the phone. You are going to tell whoever is on the other end who you are, and you're going to tell them you're okay. That's it, that's all you're going to say. Got it?"

"Who I am, and I'm okay. Do I mention Phil?"

"No, leave him out of it. Just who you are and you're okay."

"I understand."

Three drove for what seemed to Sherry like another couple of miles, and then she parked the car, some kind of Jeep station wagon, on the side of the road. For the ten minutes or so they'd been on the road, there'd been no other traffic. Three checked the clock on her phone and announced, "Five more minutes. I'll put the phone so you can speak when I want you to, and I'll use the cattle prod on you if you say anything you're not supposed to. Got it?"

"Okay."

"Just who you are and you're okay."

They sat in silence for a few minutes. In the distance, Sherry saw another vehicle coming toward them. Three saw it too, so she put her head down so it wouldn't be so obvious she wore a mask. Sherry couldn't move her arms or legs, so all she was able to do was put a stricken look on her face. It didn't have any effect. The driver of the other vehicle, a pickup, had a cell phone in one hand, and he didn't pay any attention to them. Sherry thought the truck had an Arizona license plate, but dust covered most of it, so she couldn't tell for sure.

Three looked at her clock again. "Show time; who you are and you're okay." She took a piece of paper out of her pocket and dialed the number she found on it. Stretching her neck slightly, Sherry saw it was her mother's number at the retirement community.

Sherry recognized her brother Trick's voice saying, "Hello."

Three answered, "Sherry Ahearn wants to talk to you."

Trick asked, "Who are you? Where are you?"

"Quiet," yelled Three, and she put the phone up to Sherry's mouth, and nudged her in the ribs.

Sherry spoke into the phone in a shaky voice, "This is Sherry Ahearn, and I am okay."

Three pulled the phone back and disconnected the call. "Well done, Sherry," she said. Three started the car again and soon found a wide place where she was able to execute a U-turn. Though Sherry tried to pay attention while they were driving back, she didn't learn anything she hadn't learned before.

Three carried Sherry back into the house and plunked her down on the bed beside Phil. After attaching Sherry's handcuff and removing the duct tape, she said, "That went very well. Dinner will be in an hour or so. Ta Ta."

Sherry told Phil what had happened.

"I'm relieved," Phil said, his voice shaking. "When she took you like that, I didn't know if I'd ever see you again. It's been an awful forty minutes."

"I'm sorry, Phil. I couldn't do anything."

"Yeah, I know, and I guess Trick and your mother would want to know you're okay. It probably happens in lots of kidnappings. The kidnappers have to prove somehow they do in fact have the people they say they've captured."

"I just said what she told me to. She had the cattle prod. There wasn't any percentage in disobeying."

"No, and probably your mother and Trick liked hearing your voice."

In South Carolina, Trick hung up the phone. The line had been disconnected right after Sherry spoke. The call had been incredibly short. He looked at Agent Harrison. "I wasn't able to keep them on the line."

"Yes, I heard. Was it your sister?"

"Yep, it sounded like Sherry all right. And it sounded like a woman for the other person. Yesterday's call came from a man. Did you have any luck tracing the call?"

"Get anything, Jim?" Agent Harrison asked one of the techs, staring at his screen.

"Really short," the tech answered. "All I can tell you is that it came from the western half of the U.S. If I'd had a few more seconds, I could have been more specific. The call was so short, that's all I got."

"So, they really have Sherry. Is that what we're supposed to conclude?" Gladys asked.

"Yes, Mrs. Ahearn," Agent Harrison said. "That, and Sherry said she was okay. Hang on to the second part. We're going to do everything to make sure she stays okay."

"I'm sure you'll try. Still, to my way of thinking, you've got mixed motives. You people at the FBI want to catch crooks. I'd like to do that too, but it's not my first priority. My first priority is to have my daughter back. Catching crooks is second."

"Mrs. Ahearn, there's no conflict, we want to get your daughter back too,"

"What have you done to help me get the ransom money together? It looks to me like these guys know what they're doing. If it's true, I'm willing to pay them what they're asking. I want my daughter back safe and sound. I've got the money, and there's no better way of spending it. Tell me how to get that much cash. It can't be easy."

"I don't know if I'd advise paying the ransom, Mrs. Ahearn. It's early. These people might slip up and make a mistake. We might be able to find your daughter without having to spend a dime."

"Yeah, you might. Then again, you might not. I just want some action about the ransom. I'm willing to pay it, if we need to. Right now, I need help getting the cash. I can always deposit it again if I don't need it."

"Okay, Mrs. Ahearn. I'll call someone to help you get the cash. I hope you don't have to use it."

Trick spoke up at this point. "Mom, I understand what you're saying. In my view, we should listen to the FBI. They're the experts. Neither of us has ever had to deal with anything like this before. Still, I guess it's better to be ready to pay the ransom, if we decide that's the best thing to do."

"That's all I'm saying," Gladys concluded.

"Now we wait for the next call. Is that it, Agent Harrison?" Trick asked.

"Yes, it's the only thing we can do."

CHAPTER FORTY-FOUR

BACK IN PENNSYLVANIA, Chris and Thad sat in Thad's office nursing their drinks when Sam called Chris.

Sam started with a report. "Ms. Ahearn did a great job. The call lasted only a few seconds. She told them her name and that she was alive and well. Now I've got her back in the cabin safe and sound."

"Great, and you destroyed that phone?"

"Zapped it with the cattle prod and smashed it big time like you told me. No problems there."

"Good, you'll have to sit tight until Saturday. I'll call you on Friday night when I get the ransom money, and then we'll meet in Albuquerque on Saturday. You'll have about a six-hour drive. When you get there, we can take the plane back."

"And if something goes wrong, if I don't hear from you on Friday night, we activate the abort procedures we talked about?"

"Yes, you drive them into New Mexico and leave them where we talked about," Chris said. "You won't know what happened here, so drive as far as you think you need to and drop the Jeep. Remember to take the license plates off before you park it and use the money we gave you to get back here."

"Yeah, just to be prepared, I've been looking at maps. If it comes to that,

I'll leave the car in Amarillo, Texas. That should be far enough away."

"If it comes to that, be sure Philemon and Ahearn don't have a chance to see anything. I'd suggest blindfolding them."

"I already thought of that. I haven't used the blindfolds here. When I move them, I'm wrapping them back up in their carpets again."

"Good idea. I'll meet you in Albuquerque in a few days."

"Here's hoping."

"I've got to go. Dad and I are about to make our call with the instructions."

Ten minutes later, Thad called the Ahearn number in South Carolina. Thad impressed Chris with how calmly he handled it. He used a broad southern accent as he gave the instructions. Chris thought it didn't sound like him at all.

He simply said, "Listen, I know you are recording this, so I'm only going to say this once."

Then he read the instructions he and Chris had written out the day before and hung up.

In South Carolina, Trick put down the phone and looked up at the FBI agents gathered around their computers. "Any luck tracing that one? Luckily it turned out to be a little longer than the one from Sherry."

"Yes," replied the tech, Jim. "It came from a cell phone located in Pittsburgh, and I've got the number."

"We'll try to figure out who owns that cell phone. Unfortunately, most likely we'll come up empty," Agent Harrison said. "If these people are good, and it looks like they are, I'll bet we'll find it's a cell phone purchased at some drug store or something, and my guess is they'll never use it again. The real information is that the call came from Pittsburgh."

"Yeah, too bad that's not so helpful. Pittsburgh's a big place," Trick commented.

"Isn't it odd," Gladys added. "You said the call from Sherry came from the western half of the country. Pittsburgh doesn't fit. Also, this southern guy didn't sound at all like the first guy who called me."

"You're right," Agent Harrison replied. "It looks like these people are spread out. It's unusual, but not unprecedented. Usually the hostages are kept close to the place where the ransom is supposed to be dropped. I've never heard of Lake Whipple. Is it close to Pittsburgh?"

"Yeah, I think so," Trick answered. "Anyway, it's not in the western US."

"Yeah, so somehow they moved your sister all the way across the country. They must have the use of a private plane, or they did a lot of driving after they picked her up on Saturday night. All this suggests a large group. It looks like we're dealing with pros."

"All the more reason to start to collect what we need for the ransom," Gladys said emphatically.

"Yes, we've heard you on that, Mom. We're going to start that first thing tomorrow morning," Trick reported.

"And I've got a lot of work to do," Agent Harrison added. "We have to get this recording to the lab, get someone checking on that phone number, and we have to send a group of agents to Lake Whipple to scope out the dock. We don't have much time, only three days."

WEDNESDAY MORNING, RIGHT after she finished reading the front-page story in the *Post-Gazette*, Sybil Watson called Beth. They'd had a long talk on Sunday night when Beth called to give a report on their honeymoon. This time Beth heard the excitement in Sybil's voice.

"The paper has a big story. It's all about Judge Moss and bribery. The reporter you fed the information to found lots of cases. The story's long. It starts on the front page and takes up three columns on page four. The judge is going to be in big trouble."

"Wait a minute, Mom. I'm going to pull it up on my computer. We don't actually get a paper. We have a digital subscription."

Sybil heard Beth shouting, "Ralph, get in here. I have something to show you."

After a couple of minutes, Beth said, "I've got it now, Mom, and Ralph's here too. Let us read the story. I'll put you on speaker phone when we finish."

Sybil became impatient waiting for the two in Lackey to finish reading. Finally, she couldn't contain herself. "Isn't this something? I mean, one of the cases they're talking about has to be our case. They've got him dead to rights. Two people are willing to testify about their lawyers, suggesting they bribe Judge Moss. It looks like this newspaper reporter did a fantastic job."

"I'm not quite finished, Mom. I have to agree. So far, the story's good. It's just what we wanted. I told you Ralph sent the reporter a bunch of information from the surveillance we did on Moss's house. Apparently, the information we sent the reporter didn't turn out to be enough. That must have been what took so long."

"Wait, Beth," Ralph interrupted. "She's got a lot more here. Like your Mom told us, the reporter found two people we knew nothing about, and those two people are critical to her story."

"What you guys sent didn't use any names—anonymous, right?" Sybil asked.

"Right," Beth answered. "Ralph signed the note XYZ."

"Yeah, I wanted to give them a name, not our names."

"And Phil mailed the package with the note and the thumb drive from Cleveland," Beth added. "There's no way they can trace it back to us."

"Sybil—er, Mom," Ralph said a little nervously. "You should get ready for some phone calls. It's not going to take people long to put two and two together. Think about what you're going to say."

"Ralph's right, Mom. I guess I'm a little surprised the newspaper reporter didn't contact you already."

After a pause Sybil spoke up. "My best strategy is to act outraged. There's no way I knew the Calcotts bribed the judge. In fact, it outraged me when you told me about it. It won't be difficult to dredge up those feelings again. I guess I should demand a retrial. Maybe I should contact my lawyer, Thornton Reed."

"That's good," Beth said. "Take the initiative. Based on the story, you should demand a retrial. I guess a lot of other people will be doing the same thing. You won't stand out at all. You want to put in your two cents, Ralph?"

"It's perfect," Ralph answered. "It would look funny if you didn't have a reaction. Find out Thornton's opinion. Don't let on you know anything more than what's in the paper. There are enough details there for you to call Thornton."

"I'm glad you guys approve. I liked Thornton, and he did a good job. I'll call him right after I get off the phone with you two. I guess you'll be calling your friends Sherry and Phil, won't you?"

"No, we won't," Beth said. "I guess I haven't told you. It looks like Phil and Sherry have been kidnapped. Someone broke into their house Saturday night. Remember I told you on Sunday Phil hadn't been at the airport to drive us home? On Monday morning, Ralph went to their house and found the police investigating. We learned later that it looks like they've been kidnapped. While that kind of thing doesn't make the news, it's caused a big stir here. We're worried sick about it all."

"Kidnapped, oh my God how awful! What do you know about it?"

"Nothing. It's really frustrating. It's all happening in South Carolina where Sherry's mom and brother live. We don't know anything. Ralph and I have been really upset. There's nothing we can do. The FBI's involved. I'll let you know when we find out anything."

"Okay, you do that. Kidnapping. I can't believe it. I guess I'm going to call Thornton. I'll get back to you when I know something."

Wednesday night, Sam made her nightly call to Chris. After a quick greeting, she gave her report. "Everything here's going smoothly. My captives are starting to look a bit ragged, and they're starting to smell. All things considered, I'd say things are fine. How's it going in Pittsburgh?"

"Things here are a mess! My father is incredibly upset. There's a front-page story in the *Post-Gazette* implicating him in a bribery scandal. It's got him all tense and nervous. I've never seen him so out of control."

"Is he really in trouble? Will he be arrested? The timing couldn't be worse."

"Come to think of it, even if the police come and arrest him, we don't need him. He's not at all necessary to the rest of the plan."

"Wow. I guess you're right."

"It's a big deal here in Pittsburgh. Clearly some lawyers are in trouble. People the paper interviewed said the lawyers suggested bribing Dad. The two people quoted in the paper reported that they didn't take the lawyers up on the suggestion. The article implied there's evidence other people bribed him. At this point, it looks like the lawyers are the ones in trouble. I'm not sure it's going to stay that way."

"Sounds dangerous. It's got nothing to do with us, right?"

"Right now, we're in the clear, and maybe we can walk away from this with his share too."

"Okay, I'll sit tight here. My part of this operation is going fine."

"Same here. The next thing is the pick up on Friday night. I'll be sure to call you when I have the package."

"You've got the cell number for the phone to call that night."

"Yes, I do. No problem."

At ten on Thursday morning, Chris went to Thad's house. Based on a phone call the previous evening, Chris knew his father was starting to panic. The *Post-Gazette* story clearly had thrown him for a loop. Chris remembers wondering how his father was able to live as well as he did. While they'd not been poor before his dad became a judge, they hadn't been rich, either. After the divorce, he'd figured his dad would be in bad shape. Chris assumed he paid alimony, and he knew his mom got the house. The big house and all the trips to the Caribbean didn't make sense. Now the story about bribes made pretty clear how his father's financial turnaround happened.

Chris's own financial turnaround depended on the kidnapping, so he wanted to be sure everything stayed on track. He didn't think he needed his dad. He'd made this visit to be sure.

Chris used his key to enter, and after a quick search, he found his father sitting in his office chair staring off into space.

Chris interrupted his thoughts. "What are you going to do about the newspaper article?"

"I've been sitting here avoiding phone calls. I'm due in court this afternoon, so I saw no reason to go to the office any earlier. I can't understand how the *Post-Gazette* got its information. Those bozo lawyers must have messed up. The two people the story talked about refused when the lawyers suggested the bribe idea. If that's all they have, I can just tough it out. I can deny everything. I'd say the lawyers were just trying to line their own pockets. If that's all they have, it will be a mess, but I'll survive. The lawyers are in more trouble than I am. I'm just afraid one of the lawyers will crack."

"Look Dad, you should bail," Chris said, shocked at the pained look on his father's face. "The article implied they had other information. It's more than just the two people they interviewed. I think you should get out of here. Sam and I can handle the kidnapping from here on out. If you can get to the Caymans, you have enough money to disappear, don't you?

"Yes, I guess I do."

"You should just leave. We'll hold your share of the kidnapping loot until you can tell us where to send it."

"I don't know, Chris. I've been mulling over the idea of bailing like you suggested. What about Catherine?"

"She'll dump you the minute there's any hint of scandal. Has she called you since the story broke?"

"No."

"There you go. I wouldn't worry about her. You need to get the hell out of here before everything blows up. Don't worry about the kidnapping. Sam and I can handle the rest of it."

"I don't know."

"Think about it. There's not really anything holding you, and if, like you said, one of the lawyers cracks, you'll be in deep shit."

"You're right, Chris. I'll be gone in an hour or two. Keep this cell phone." Thad opened his desk drawer and gave Chris an unused phone. "I know that phone's number. Don't expect to hear from me for quite a while."

Chris took the phone and rose from his chair. "I've got to get to work, so I guess this is goodbye Dad." He and his father shared a brief hug. "Give me a call when you get settled. I'll get the kidnapping money to you."

"You can count on it. Good luck."

"Good luck to you too."

CHAPTER FORTY-SIX

EARLY THURSDAY AFTERNOON, the FBI took Gladys to a bank. They had arranged for her broker to sell some of the stock she bought with the proceeds from the sale of her land. Following her instructions, the broker had sold the stock and deposited the funds in her bank account. The last step, taking possession of the cash, turned out to be easy. Large withdrawals of cash raise all kinds of red flags in the banking world. The FBI smoothed the way for Gladys, so she had no trouble withdrawing the cash.

Gladys couldn't help smiling as she walked into the apartment Trick and the FBI people were using. "Here's the loot," she reported.

"Thank you, Mrs. Ahearn," Agent Harrison said. "We're going to put it in a shoebox and fly it up to Pittsburgh. It has to be in place before six o'clock tomorrow evening."

"I guess there's nothing else to do, is there?" Gladys asked.

"No, there's not. We don't have any way of contacting the kidnappers, so we're stymied here, Mom," Trick answered.

"You should go back to your apartment and take a nap," Agent Harrison suggested. "It doesn't look like you've been sleeping well since this started. Nothing is going to happen here."

"Why thank you, young man. I guess I will. Now you be sure to contact me if there's anything I can do."

Watching his mother walk away, Trick thought, *it's been incredibly tough on her.* Turning to Agent Harrison, he announced, "I'm going to go home too, at least for a few hours. I haven't been sleeping well either. I'd have never thought about it. When you said that to my mom, it really hit me. I just live fifteen minutes away. Call me if you need me."

"Sure, get some rest. We might all be up for quite a while tomorrow night."

At three that afternoon, Gladys Ahearn heard a knock on her apartment door. She had recently awakened from her nap and was just about to go to the FBI place to see if anything had changed. When she opened the door, she recognized the young woman standing there. "Melissa, what a surprise. What are you doing here?"

"Can I come in?"

"Of course," Gladys replied, backing up and hugging Melissa before offering her a seat.

"I work in DC now, and when I saw Sherry's name on one of the readouts of FBI activities, I just had to come down to help. You must be really worried."

"I am. I'm worried silly. It's nice to have my favorite FBI agent here. Agent Harrison is okay, I guess. He's certainly not Mr. Personality."

"This is way more serious than our last encounter. I had easy duty staying with you and Sherry when you were in witness protection. This is much more serious. I know you've gone over this with the other agents. Still, can you tell me what's happened?"

"Sure, if it will help."

"It might."

"Well, my role got cut off real fast. I called my son Richard, you remember Trick. Anyway, I called him right after I got that first phone call. I've been just a spectator since then."

"Tell me about the first phone call."

"Sunday night, late. I'd just about stopped reading in bed. I always read for a half an hour or so before I go to sleep. A man called. While I think he also made two of the other calls, I'm not able to swear to it. Anyway, he told me he'd kidnapped Sherry, and the ransom would be one million and five hundred thousand dollars."

"Anything else?"

Gladys paused, shutting her eyes. When her eyes opened, she started, "Yes, one more thing. He said something like… like this will show Sherry she shouldn't have messed with me. Something like that."

Melissa looked startled. "The reports I've read didn't mention anything about that. What did you suppose he meant?"

"I don't have the faintest idea. I'm sorry I didn't remember that part of the conversation until just now. Is it important?"

"It might be. Would you mind coming with me to the apartment the FBI's using? We need to see how they react to this."

At the same time in Pittsburgh, the police finished searching Judge Thaddeus Moss's house. They'd called his son Christopher to get the keys. They found nothing. An empty spot in the attic looked as if a suitcase might have been parked there. Chris had told them he thought Thad kept his suitcases in the attic.

They hadn't been able to open the judge's wall safe. They didn't have the authorization or the equipment for that. They just did a search to determine whether anything obvious explained Judge Moss's absence.

The search had been triggered because Judge Moss didn't show at the courthouse on Wednesday afternoon and Thursday morning. The newspaper story about bribes in Moss's courtroom had been big news, and it looked like the judge skipped town to avoid getting questioned.

It had been easy to convince another judge to grant the warrant for the search. Now the police had to deal with the swarm of reporters outside the Moss house. They'd been aware of them collecting while they searched the house. Someone at the police station must have tipped them off.

"Did you find anything?" shouted a reporter as the first policeman left the house.

"No comment," said the patrolman. "The lieutenant will be out in a minute or two."

When the lieutenant came out, he strode up to the reporters. "There's no story here. Judge Moss didn't show up for his cases yesterday or today. We're treating it as a missing persons case."

"Did you find anything?" asked a reporter.

"Not really. The judge's car is gone. Otherwise, the house looks like you'd expect it to look. There's no evidence of any wrongdoing."

"Does this have anything to do with the bribery scandal?"

"We have no way of knowing. Sorry guys, that's all. There's nothing here."

CHAPTER FORTY-SEVEN

ON FRIDAY, THE FBI sent a team to Lackey to figure out who had it in for Sherry. Gladys' recollection had given them something to do. Given her familiarity with Lackey, Melissa Jacobson had been assigned to lead the team.

Beth got one of the first calls from the FBI. At ten thirty, a short, trim blonde woman in a blue suit walked up to the nurses' station. Beth overheard the woman say she was with the FBI and needed to speak to Beth Williams. Beth approached the woman with her hand extended. "I'm Beth Williams, what can I do for you?"

The woman responded with an outstretched hand. "I'm Melissa Jacobson with the FBI."

Beth shook her hand and looked at the badge the woman held out for her.

Beth looked around and pointed. "There's a conference room down this hall."

The two women walked to the conference room in silence. After they were seated, Melissa started, "I'm here in conjunction with the FBI's investigation of the kidnapping of Sherry Ahearn and Phil Philemon. I understand you're a good friend of theirs."

"Yes, I know both of them very well. We're all real concerned about the kidnapping. I don't think I can help. It's been horrible being so out of the loop." Beth paused. When the FBI agent didn't say anything, she continued, "Actually, our relationship with Sherry and Phil starts with my husband, Ralph. He'd been a student of Phil's during Ralph's undergrad years at Lackey College. They stayed friends. And when Phil and Sherry started going out, I eventually met Sherry. Since we first met, we've become good friends. Phil and Sherry were in my wedding last month. Oh, I'm jabbering on. I guess I'm nervous. I've never talked to the FBI. Sometimes I talk too much when I'm nervous."

"No, it's refreshing," commented Melissa. "Lots of people clam up when we come to talk to them."

"I mean, Sherry's great. She's as nice as she can be. Sometimes really pretty girls are stuck up. Sherry's gorgeous, but she's real down to earth. There's not a nicer person. I can't think of anyone who'd want to harm her."

"Actually, I've met Sherry, and I have to agree. She's really nice."

"How do you know Sherry?"

"You remember when Sherry had to play dead and go into witness protection?"

"Oh, and she went to South Carolina, and her mother's still there."

"I handled her in witness protection. After she came back, I came here for the hearing, and I met Phil Philemon then. He's nice, too."

"Yeah, Phil's great. He actually works at Ralph's computer store. He quit at the college after his wife died. I knew her too, Mary Jane. Anyway, she was killed in a car accident, and Phil got a big payout from a life insurance policy. Like I told you, he quit at the college. Eventually he got bored, so he's helping Ralph now. Ralph and I just got back from our honeymoon on Sunday. Phil had been scheduled to pick us up at the airport. We were surprised when he didn't show. While I guess we should have suspected some problem, we just thought he forgot. Ralph went to their house Monday morning and found the police searching it. There I go, jabbering away."

"No, that's fine, Mrs. Williams."

"Beth, call me Beth."

"Okay, Beth. Do you have any idea why anyone would want to kidnap Sherry and/or Phil?"

"Ralph and I talked about that, and we're stumped. Like I said, they're both incredibly nice people. My guess is it's about money. Sherry and her family sold their farm to one of those oil companies. They got like a ton of money for it. Lots of people around here have heard about it. The property transfers are in the local paper. The Ahearns aren't the only farmers around here who've sold out to the oil companies."

"I'm sure the money's important. It doesn't make sense to kidnap poor people. It appears to be about more than just the money. Sherry's mother remembers during the kidnappers' first phone call something being said about getting back at Sherry. Do you have any idea about anyone who'd want to take revenge on her?"

Beth's eyes got big, and she went silent.

After a minute or two, Melissa asked, "Mrs. Williams… Beth?"

Finally, Beth spoke up. "Look, Melissa. Can we go to Ralph's store? This is complicated, and I'd like Ralph to be in on the discussions."

"So, you know something?"

"Yes, it's complicated. I can get a half an hour off. Please be patient."

Five minutes later, Ralph, Beth, and Melissa were seated in the back room of Ralph's computer store.

Beth spoke up. "So, Ralph, Melissa wants to know if anyone would want to take revenge on Sherry. I can only think of one person. Judge Thaddeus Moss."

Ralph felt on edge. It wasn't every morning his new wife and an FBI agent barged into his store demanding a private meeting. Now he knew why, and he started to perspire. Beth looked stressed, too.

After a pause, Melissa asked, "Okay… Why Judge Moss?"

Both Beth and Ralph started to talk. Beth held up her hand. "Let me talk. I've had more time to make up my mind about what to say." She took a deep breath. "It all started when my mother got sued. Anyway, sparing you the details, even though the charges were bogus, she lost the case. The judge in the case turned out to be Thaddeus Moss."

Ralph jumped in. "And it just looked rigged. The trial, I mean. It looked to me like every ruling went against Beth's mom for no good reason. I got really suspicious."

"So, what did you do?" Melissa asked.

"Okay," Ralph spoke up after an uncomfortable pause. "I set up some surveillance equipment outside Judge Moss's house, cameras and phone intercept stuff. And what I found confirmed my suspicions. Judge Moss had been bribed. It's a big scandal now. The *Pittsburgh Post-Gazette* ran a story earlier this week. He's been taking bribes from a bunch of lawyers."

"And another story this morning claimed Judge Moss has gone missing," Beth added.

"So how does this involve Sherry? Let's get to the point."

Beth continued. "Initially, we weren't able to figure out how to get back at the judge. What we did listening in to his phone calls and so on might not have been legal. We couldn't take it to the police. Among other things, we learned that Judge Moss had planned a trip to the Cayman Islands. To make a long story short, Sherry played a big role when we stole the stash of cash the judge planned to deposit in his Cayman bank."

"Wow, I understand why you might be reticent to tell this story to the FBI," concluded Melissa.

"Yes," Ralph said. "If it helps get Sherry and Phil back, it'll be worth it."

Beth added, "We didn't think stealing the money Judge Moss had received from bribes would be illegal. I mean, what is he going to say? These people took the money I got illegally."

"I'm not so sure about that, Beth. Crime is territorial, so you didn't break any U. S. laws, but theft is illegal in the Cayman Islands. You'd better steer clear of there."

"We sure will," Beth said.

"You just told me you successfully stole the money. How did Judge Moss identify Sherry?"

Ralph looked up at the picture on his shelf. "Oh my God! I bet that picture did it." He took the picture off the shelf and showed it to Melissa. "It's a picture from our wedding. It ran in the *Post-Gazette*. Moss must have seen it."

"It's a nice picture," Melissa commented. "The wedding happened recently, didn't it?"

"Yes."

"Anyway," Ralph continued. "I bet dollars to donuts Moss is behind the kidnapping. Sherry just doesn't have any other enemies. There's a first husband she divorced. Heck, that has to be almost thirty years ago."

"And Moss is a crook," Beth added. "He took bribes. We're sure about that much."

"Thanks for telling me this. It's going to be incredibly helpful."

"Can you tell us what you know so far? Maybe we have more helpful information."

"I have to get your information to the rest of the group, so I'll be brief. We don't have much, so this won't take long. Sherry's mother got a call from a man on Sunday night. Then Richard, Trick, took a call on Monday. He told the kidnappers he needed to talk to Sherry. They were able to record the second call, but they weren't able to trace it. The third call came from a woman who put Sherry on the line. By the time of that call, while we had tracing capability, the call didn't last long at all. We learned the call came from the western US, that's all. The final call with instructions about where they wanted the ransom lasted longer. As a result, we traced it to Pittsburgh and a particular cell number. It turned out to be one of those phones you can buy in a drug store, and the store didn't have any record of who'd bought it. That's about it."

"Where is the ransom going to be dropped off?" Beth asked.

"At a dock on Lake Whipple. It's on the other side of Pittsburgh from here."

Ralph stood up. "Judge Moss has a vacation cabin in Arizona somewhere. I bet that's why the trace came up with the western US. I bet that's where Phil and Sherry are."

"Wow, it makes sense," Melissa exclaimed. "Thank you so much. You've been incredibly helpful. I've got some urgent calls to make."

"Are we going to be in trouble?" Beth asked.

"No, probably not. I'd avoid the Cayman Islands if I were you. And Ralph, you didn't do any breaking and entering with your surveillance equipment, did you?" Melissa asked with a gleam in her eye.

"No ma'am," Ralph answered.

"Good. I bet you're clean."

Beth and Ralph hugged after Melissa exited, reaching for her cell phone.

CHAPTER FORTY-EIGHT

THE FBI WENT to work quickly after Melissa called with the information Beth and Ralph provided. Albert Harrison in South Carolina coordinated the effort. Agents from Pittsburgh started an investigation of Thaddeus Moss. Agent Harrison emailed them tapes of the two phone calls from the kidnappers, and Moss's secretary in the courthouse told the agents the voice on the first recording sounded a little like Judge Moss, but the one with the southern accent didn't at all. Progress on the case stopped at that point. The local police were already investigating Moss's disappearance, and they told the FBI Moss must have skipped town because of the bribery scandal.

Agents in Arizona were assigned to find Moss's mountain cabin. This turned out to be no easy task, because they had very little to go on. There are thousands of mountain cabins in Arizona. Agent Bill Turner in Phoenix had been put in charge. He called all the counties likely to contain Moss's cabin and asked about property. The agents were stymied, and Turner reported as much to Agent Harrison.

The agents in South Carolina decided they would have to follow the kidnapper's directions and leave the shoebox with the ransom on the dock in Lake Whipple. Melissa Jacobson, who'd joined the Pittsburgh team, accompanied them to the lake. At five thirty, an agent put the shoebox on the dock, following the instructions of the kidnappers precisely.

After placing the box on the dock, the agent drove away. Melissa and two other agents were positioned in a lake cottage with a good view of the dock. Other agents were scattered around in position to follow whoever picked up the package. They had every possibility covered. They guessed the kidnappers would use a boat to pick up the package. Anticipating that agents were in place by the roads leading from the cabins on all three sides of the lake on which there were cabins with docks, they positioned an agent posing as a fisherman in a boat out on the lake. They didn't want to capture whoever picked up the ransom. They wanted to follow him.

As time passed, Melissa and the other two agents in the cottage took turns looking through the night-vision telescope they had trained on the dock and the package. Tension ran high. As dusk settled, other fishing boats joined the one with the FBI fisherman. It looked calm on the water. Nothing happened until seven fifteen. One of the other agents heard it first. "Is that a drone?" he asked.

Melissa perked up. "Yes, sounds like it."

Just then, the agent looking through the telescope yelped and backed away, holding his eyes. The drone had turned on a bright light as it hovered over the package. The agent had been momentarily blinded and didn't see anything through the telescope. The others saw the drone lower on the package, pick it up, turn off its light, and fly away. The whole thing happened in just a few seconds.

Melissa got on the radio and checked in with her agents. "Did anyone get an idea where that drone went? It's got the package."

"It flew off to the east," came the response of the agent on the boat.

"How far?" Melissa asked.

"I can't tell. It didn't slow down, and I lost it pretty fast because of the trees," the agent reported.

None of the other agents were of any help. They didn't see the drone.

Melissa reported their complete failure to headquarters. The package had been picked up by a drone, and they had no idea where it was now. They'd been completely outfoxed by the kidnappers.

The FBI's first break on the case came in St. Johns, Arizona, the county seat of Apache County. As she left work, Isabel Ramos, the woman who'd taken the call from the FBI in Phoenix, discussed this unusual event with her friend Carol Pierce, who worked in the county treasurer's office.

"Wait a minute," Carol said. "Did you say Moss?"

"Yes, Moss—like on the north side of trees," Isabel responded.

"Well, I might have something. Most of our property tax checks come in from the property owners. For example, Samuel Jones owns the property, and Mr. Jones writes the checks for the property tax. Some don't match, and I notice them. One of them involves someone named Moss. He's not the property owner. He pays the taxes."

"That might be important. Let's go back in and find this Moss's address. The FBI will want this information."

Isabel called Bill Turner in Phoenix with the information on the cabin on which Moss paid the property taxes. She gave them Moss's full name and address. The agent was thrilled. It turned out to be Thaddeus Moss at a Pittsburgh address, and they had a bulletin about him just yesterday. Turner relayed the information to Agent Harrison. Harrison told them to get the cabin under surveillance as soon as possible and standby for further orders.

"That's not going to be easy," grumbled Agent Turner in Phoenix. "We've looked the cabin up on the topo maps we have here. It's in a really remote part of Arizona. I'd say it's a six-hour drive from here. We can get there faster with our helicopter. Still, it will take a while. And it's real remote out there near Show Low where this cabin is."

"Can you get any help from the locals?"

"I'll try. You don't want them going in with lights and sirens, right?"

"Right. It would be better if they went by the cabin in an unmarked car or something. I just want surveillance. No action. The hostages might be in jeopardy."

Agent Turner made a quick list. First, he had to call his guys back. Most of the people he wanted to take north had left that afternoon. Second, he had to call the Apache County Sherriff and the Show Low police. One of the two of them might be able to come up with what he wanted. Third, he had to alert the helicopter pilot and get him out to the airport. Five minutes later, he'd finished his list. While he'd had to put up with some griping from the agents he called back, eventually they came around.

The Show Low police had been his most successful call. Luckily, he caught the chief of police. Chief George Hunter turned out to be very cooperative, and he knew the road the cabin sat on. "It's just past the Apache County line," he told Agent Turner. It wouldn't be hard to find the cabin.

"I don't mean for you to have to go," Agent Turner said.

"No, that's all right, I'd like to do it. It shouldn't take you guys long to get here to relieve me, right?"

"We'll be getting into the Show Low airport in a couple of hours."

"And you'll need local transportation. Won't you?"

"You're a step ahead of me, Chief."

"So, I'll have a squad car waiting at the airport, and he can show you the vehicles you can use. Will two pickups be enough?"

"That should do it."

"After I get that arranged, I'm going to head out to that cabin. I'll drive by it and park beside the road a half a mile up. Then I'll walk back to where I can get a good look at it. Don't worry, I'll hear you coming. Park near my truck. It's a big Ram pickup. You can't miss it. Then wait for me. I'll show you where you can get a good look at the cabin."

"Have you done this before, Chief? You sound awful prepared."

"No, Agent Turner, this is a first," Chief Hunter answered. "It's not rocket science. You need vehicles and you want the cabin watched. I can help you with both."

"Okay. Thanks. I'll be there in a couple of hours."

CHAPTER FORTY-NINE

PHIL CHECKED HIS watch when Three came in and turned on the light in the room he shared with Sherry. Five fifteen in the morning. He'd heard her stirring around for the last half an hour. She'd come in and out the front door a couple of times. Phil figured something was about to happen. His stomach twisted with nerves.

"Okay, professor, put your legs together and hands at your side," Three ordered.

Phil complied. Three put a little duct tape on his arms and then wrapped his legs two times with the tape. Her actions repeated what she had done when Sherry had been taken out for the phone call. Three wrapped his arms and unlocked his handcuff. Next, she lifted him up and carried him out to the living room. The pieces of carpet had been laid upside down on the floor. Three put him down on one of the carpets and rolled him up tightly in it.

Phil's eyes were covered, but he heard Three going back into the room. Then he heard her say, "Same deal for you, Sherry."

After several minutes and lots of scuffling noises, Three picked Phil up and took him outside. It felt cold. Three put him down, and he heard what must have been the back of the Jeep opening. Next, he felt himself being lifted and plunked down in the back of the car. A few minutes later, he felt a weight being loaded beside him. "Sherry?" he asked.

"Yes, it's me," Sherry answered.

"Quiet, I don't want you talking," Three yelled. "Look, this time I've put the back seat down to load you guys. That means all I need to do is lean over the front seat to zap you with the cattle prod. While you may not be aware, I have a view of the top of both of your heads. I don't expect you want to be zapped in the head, so keep quiet."

Phil then heard Three throw some metal things, probably their handcuffs and chains, in the back beside them. A minute later, the car started, and they bounced their way down the driveway.

The FBI team noted the lights come on in the cabin at five o'clock. From their perch behind a tree, they saw a large woman moving around inside the house. They kept silent and watched. The woman made a couple of trips to the car. Then she took the two hostages out of the room they'd originally been in. When she opened the door and put the roll of carpet in the back of the Jeep Cherokee, Agent Turner thought he knew what might be happening. He figured a hostage had been rolled in the carpet. A second carpet roll came out, confirming his suspicion. The woman moving the hostages. He ordered two of his agents to get back to their pickup, so they were in position to follow the Jeep. He instructed them to stay way back. They had the license number of the Jeep, so they didn't have to be close.

The Jeep started and drove away. Turner radioed the agents he'd sent back. They answered, reporting they'd heard the car start, so they were on it. A couple of minutes later, their pickup went by slowly with its lights out.

Turner and the other agent approached the cabin cautiously. Hearing no noises as they waited, they finally decided to enter. The front door turned out to be unlocked, so they put on their latex gloves, opened the door, and went in. The cabin had clearly been used, dirty dishes in the sink, stuff in the trashcan, and a spill on the stove. One of the bedrooms had an obviously used single bed. The other ground floor bedroom had a double bed. The agents scratched their heads when they saw the bars on the floor on either side of the bed.

"Those must have been used to tie the hostages up or something," Agent Turner suggested.

The other agent had gone into the bathroom. "Yeah, and there's a similar arrangement in here. Another bar they used to tie them up."

Turner took out his phone and found he had no cell service. "I was going to call the local police to get a team out here to dust for prints, but my cell won't work. There's nothing more we can do here, let's go. I bet there'll be cell service when we get out to the main road."

On the walk back to their borrowed pickup, Turner used his radio to check in with the two agents following the Jeep.

"They turned right when they got to sixty, so they're headed toward Springerville," the agent reported.

"There's two options then," Turner said. "Either they're going to turn east just outside of Springerville and head to New Mexico, or they're going keep straight toward Alpine and the Coronado Trail. I'll try to get people in place to cover whichever option they take. Get closer to them when they approach Springerville. The turn off on sixty toward New Mexico is north of town."

When Agent Turner got to route sixty, he found he had cell service. He called the Show Low police and to his surprise Chief Hunter answered. "Don't you ever sleep?" he asked.

"You guys got my adrenalin going, so I just stayed up. What do you need?"

"The woman who has the two hostages loaded them up and took off east on sixty. I have the other pickup trailing them. I figure they'll either head east on sixty into New Mexico or keep going toward Alpine. When we find out which way they're going, I'm getting in the copter to be part of the group trailing them. What I need from you is to have someone secure the crime scene out at the cabin. And we need to dust for prints. There's no problem with you guys being there, we saw the two hostages."

"Okay, I'll put a team on it," said Chief Hunter said. "It's really out of our jurisdiction, so I'll call the Apache County Sherriff. He won't mind."

That morning in Pittsburgh, Melissa Jacobson and the FBI team were licking their wounds. They'd completely blown the pickup of the ransom. Frequently kidnappings unraveled for the kidnappers at that point. They had to come to the pickup spot to get the ransom, and the authorities can then trace them back to their hide out. The mood had turned somber. Melissa's pride still hurt from the dressing down she'd received from Agent Harrison.

One of the agents, Molly Gilbert, who hadn't been part of the team the previous evening, came in and listened to the story. When she heard about the drone, she said, "Wait a minute," and rushed to her computer.

Everyone came to see what she had in mind.

"So, I remembered something. Moss has a son, Christopher. Yes. Here it is." She pointed to her screen. "Moss's son is a pilot. He works for a charter outfit that runs out of a private airport in Pittsburgh. A pilot would be good with a drone, wouldn't he?"

"You don't have to have a pilot's license to use a drone," commented one of the agents.

Melissa spoke up. "No, you don't. Still, I think Molly, it's Molly isn't it, is on to something. From all we know, Moss is running away from this bribery scandal. Maybe he gave the kidnapping over to his son. Or maybe his son took part in it from the start."

Molly responded, "And the business about the hostages being in Arizona makes sense with the pilot being involved. He could have flown them from here to Arizona right after they were taken."

"Yes," Melissa said. "Oh Molly, this is big. Someone call the charter company and find out if Christopher Moss is there."

One of the agents hurried to the phone and everyone moved beside his phone. The agent put the call on speaker phone. The secretary at the charter company reported that Christopher wasn't there. He'd taken a flight out early that morning.

"Ask if he took a charter," Melissa ordered.

"No. Sometimes our pilots use our planes for their own personal travel. We charge them a much-reduced fee," the secretary responded.

"Did Christopher take a similar flight last weekend?" Melissa asked.

"Let me get the records," the secretary answered. "Yes, on Sunday. Oh, and on Monday. He didn't get back until about three on Monday."

"Do you have any idea where he's going?"

"No, but he'd have to log a flight plan with the tower here. They would have his destination."

"Do you have the number for the tower?" Melissa asked.

"Sure," the secretary replied, and she gave the number.

Another agent hurried to his phone and called the tower. Though it took a while for him to get someone to pick up the phone, finally he did. After a brief chat, he turned to the group and reported, "Kansas City, Kansas City both times."

"Let me get this information to the group in South Carolina," Melissa said.

When she got Agent Harrison on the phone, he thanked her and said, "That just might fit. The Phoenix guys found the cabin the hostages were in, and they watched them being loaded into the back of a car. Right now, they're trailing the car. It looks like it's headed to Albuquerque."

"The plane might just be gassing up in Kansas City," said Melissa. "It could be headed to Albuquerque from Kansas City. I'll have one of my guys here call the Kansas City airports to check on other flight plans."

Melissa put her hand over her phone and instructed the agent who'd found about the flight plan to call Kansas City. "You'd better find any private plane airports as well as the main one." Turning back to Harrison, she asked, "Did it look like the hostages were okay?"

"Yes, but the Phoenix team didn't get a great look at them. Early morning out there, still dark. Nevertheless, it looked to them as if the hostages were in good shape. Their captor wrapped them up in carpets before she loaded them into the back of her car. The car's under surveillance now."

Melissa looked at the agent calling Kansas City. He took down a number and then dialed again.

"Just a minute. We're making progress on our call to Kansas City," she said.

Two minutes later, the agent on the phone yelled, "Albuquerque, both times. Last weekend and today. The plane just took off for Albuquerque."

"I heard that through your phone," Agent Harrison reported. "Great work, I'll contact the people trailing the car. Do you have the call numbers for the plane?"

"Yes," Melissa answered, and she repeated the letter and numbers for the plane.

CHAPTER FIFTY

THE PICKUP TRUCK that had been following the Jeep from Arizona peeled off at Pie Town in New Mexico. The helicopter had made one pass and saw no other traffic close to the Jeep. The road traveled through one of the most desolate parts of the whole United States, so they knew where it had to be going for quite a while. There was no need for close surveillance. Only one question remained; what would the Jeep do when it got to Interstate twenty-five just south of Socorro? The FBI from Albuquerque were going to handle that. While they strongly suspected the Jeep would turn north, they had two cars at the relevant intersection to pick up the surveillance whichever way it turned.

Agent Turner in the helicopter headed the operation, and he felt good with the cooperation he'd received from the Albuquerque people. The pilot told him he'd need to fuel up, and so they headed to the airport in Albuquerque. On their way there, they got a message from Albert Harrison in South Carolina.

"I'm just headed to the Albuquerque airport myself," Agent Turner answered. "I'm in a copter, and I need fuel. Do you want me to hold the pilot?"

"Yes, take him under custody when he lands. He's going to a private plane airport, not the big one. I believe that's where the car you're following is headed. Be ready to arrest the woman driving the car if she gets there."

"Okay, it sounds like it's all going to happen in the next hour or so."

"Yeah, I just checked with the Kansas City airport. The plane refueled there. They thought the plane ought to make it to Albuquerque in the next hour. We missed it by about an hour or so in Kansas City."

"I'll be in touch," Turner responded.

"You do that. I've got some nervous relatives here."

Turner then contacted the Albuquerque FBI and got the promise of backup at the private plane airport.

After the helicopter landed, Turner went to the area where a private plane would tie down and waited for the plane coming in from Kansas City. He and the other agents spotted the plane as it taxied in. Without any difficulty, they placed Christopher Moss under arrest as he walked away from his plane.

Meanwhile, the FBI agents at the intersection of route sixty and the interstate were surprised when the car they were set to follow went into Socorro. Both cars moved into position to trail the car through the streets. The Jeep turned into an underused industrial park and went behind one of the buildings. The agent in one of the chase cars got out and peeked around the building. The Jeep had stopped, and the driver opened its back end. The woman took out a roll of carpet and put it down beside the building. She repeated the operation with another roll of carpet. Then she hopped back in the Jeep and took off.

One of the cars followed the Jeep, and the other went to investigate the carpet rolls. The agents from the car that stayed behind cautiously approached the two carpet rolls. When they got there, they saw the tops of people's heads in the rolls of carpet. They wondered if they were going to be discovering dead bodies. They both put on latex gloves.

After one of them went back to the car to get something to cut the tape, they unrolled the first carpet. A woman stared back at them, very much alive and crying loudly.

"It's okay, Miss," the agent said, smiling. "We're the good guys. The FBI. You're safe now."

"Hallelujah," came a male voice from the other carpet roll.

The agents unrolled that carpet and discovered the man. They cut the tape trapping his arms and legs and then went back to do the same for the woman.

"You okay, Sherry?" Phil said, straining to get a look at her.

"No, you idiot, can't you see I'm bawling?" Sherry answered through her tears.

"We're safe, Honey."

"I know, but I… it's just been so awful. I don't have an idea what to feel."

One of the agents looked at Phil. "Can you get up, sir?"

"Probably, if you'll help," Phil replied as he slowly got to his feet. He felt a little unsteady, not bad. He wished he had shoes.

After Sherry had been freed from tape, Phil helped her to her feet. They shared a long hug. Then they turned to the FBI agents, and Phil asked, "Is there somewhere we can get a shower and some new clothes? I think we're really disgusting. By the way, where are we?"

"You're in Socorro, New Mexico," answered the agent. "It's a little town in the middle of the state. We can arrange a shower eventually. First, you'll want to come with us to Albuquerque. Come on, let's get you to our car."

The agents told Phil and Sherry as much as they knew about what was going on. They were astounded. Their car caught up with the car following the Jeep just as it reached the outskirts of Albuquerque. Following the Jeep posed no problem in Albuquerque because they knew just where it was headed. The woman driving the Jeep didn't put up a fight when the FBI agents surrounded her Jeep right after she parked. She looked incredibly surprised to see Phil and Sherry, who were standing off to one side.

As soon as they got to the FBI Albuquerque headquarters, Sherry had a long phone call with her mother.

While Sherry talked, the FBI debriefed Phil. The head of the FBI in Albuquerque and Agent Turner from Phoenix were there in person, and Albert Harrison from South Carolina and Melissa Jacobson currently in Pittsburgh were included on a Skype call. Phil couldn't answer very many questions. He hadn't even gotten a good look at any of the kidnappers. He'd been drugged for the early flight, and the woman called Three kept her mask on the entire time they were in the cabin together.

Mostly Phil learned about what had happened. Melissa Jacobson told about Beth's help in breaking the case. They really didn't have any clues until Beth suggested Thaddeus Moss. Moss himself hadn't been located.

"Try the Cayman Islands," Phil suggested.

"We have," Melissa said. "He's already come and gone."

CHAPTER FIFTY-ONE

TWO MONTHS LATER, Phil and Sherry threw a big party. The invitation didn't say much. It read, "Come Welcome Katie Ahearn Philemon—presents welcome! We need onesies, diapers, baby toys, and advice."

It had been a whirlwind two weeks since they got the call from the adoption agency. They had just recovered from the ordeal of the kidnapping and had faced endless questions from the FBI and then the press. They claimed complete ignorance about why Judge Moss or anyone in his family would kidnap them. The pressure eased when, three weeks after they returned to Lackey, the judge had been arrested in a small village in Italy. They were pleased when he claimed the kidnapping had been entirely his son, Chris's, idea.

They still were worried their actions in the Caymans would come to light. So far, they seemed to have dodged that bullet. They already were indebted to Melissa Jacobson, and now the debt had increased. All that disappeared from their minds when they got a call from the adoption agency. Katie entered their life a week after the call. Her mother died in childbirth, and no one had any idea about the identity of the father. The mother wouldn't tell anyone. Her parents, both disabled, were in no position to care for a child, so she'd been put up for adoption. Phil and Sherry were thrilled to get the call from the agency. They met Katie's grandparents and agreed to keep them in the child's life. After hurrying to buy a car seat, crib, and a changing table, they took Katie home from the hospital. Phil and Sherry were amazed and overjoyed.

At times, the idea of a baby seemed far superior to the reality of a baby. Katie didn't turn out to be one of those magic babies who slept through the night quickly. By the time of the party, she still only slept three hours at a stretch.

"I don't understand how nursing mothers do it," Sherry said one morning as she held Katie, swaying back and forth. "You were up giving her a bottle two times last night."

"It must be really tough," Phil added, standing at the range cooking breakfast. "I've heard my friends say God had a good plan when he decided to give babies to the young."

"I guess that's right. I probably would have handled this much more easily twenty or thirty years ago. Now we have this party to prepare for, too."

"At least Andy agreed to cater for us. We won't have to worry about preparing food or drinks."

"Yeah, we just have to get the house ready. I like the idea of the tent for the back yard."

"Yes, the weather is supposed to be reasonable, and given the number of people you wanted to invite, the house will be overflowing. If it does turn cold, we can still send the people out there to get drinks. They won't have to stay outside."

"Moving the queue for drinks outside is always a good idea," Sherry said with a grin.

At that point, they were interrupted by a knock on the door. Phil went to open the door and found Beth there.

"I didn't want to phone. Katie might have been asleep. I have some news."

"Come in. I just scrambled eggs, and I have bacon." Phil said. "You want some?"

"What's your news?" Sherry yelled from the kitchen.

Walking back to where Sherry and the baby were, Beth answered, "No eggs please. A piece of bacon would be nice. I've had my breakfast already."

"What's your news, Beth?" Sherry repeated.

"My parents were going to try to have their first encounter with the Calcotts declared a mistrial because of the bribe. Yesterday, the Calcott's lawyer contacted Thorton Reed, my folks' lawyer. He said the Calcotts want to repay my parents the entire one million fifty thousand. They want nothing to do with another trial. They just want to put the whole thing behind them."

"So did your parents take them up on the deal?" Phil asked.

"Yes, they did. Thornton told them the idea of having a judge declare a mistrial wouldn't be a sure thing, and the Calcotts offered a generous settlement. The lawyer for the insurance company agreed. According to my mom, he was thrilled to be getting the insurance company's money back."

"This means the Calcotts bribed the judge and got away with it," Sherry concluded. "I don't think they should get away with it."

"I'm not so sure," Beth said. "According to Thornton, the Calcotts might still be in trouble. All this does is ensure any trouble is not the result of my parent's actions. Apparently, the mess involving Judge Moss is going to take a long time to settle."

"You sure you don't want a second breakfast?" Phil asked as he dished the eggs and bacon onto plates.

"No, just a piece of bacon."

Phil put a piece of bacon on a small plate and gave it to Beth, who sat down at the kitchen table. "It looks like you're getting the hang of eating with one hand while you hold the baby."

"Yes, it turns out there are quite a few things you can do with one hand.

Still, it would be better if Katie would let me put her down every once in a while. Sometimes she's okay in the bouncy chair we got. Other times she's not too happy, particularly if I go out of the room she's in."

"So, what does the latest information tell us about our crime doesn't pay discussions?" Phil asked. "I remember us agreeing it looked like crime paid off for the Calcotts. In the long run, it didn't. They were losers in the whole deal. There's no way they'll get the fifty thousand bribe back from Judge Moss, and they might still be in trouble."

"Crime paid for us," Beth responded. "We'll eventually get the money we took from Judge Moss in the Caymans, and now we don't have to use it to make my parents whole. They'll be getting all they need from the Calcotts."

"Our share's going into a college fund for Katie," Sherry reported.

"She's going to be brilliant. I'm sure she'll be getting loads of academic scholarships," Phil said with a laugh.

"That may well be. Still, I wouldn't count on it. A big fat college fund is a good backup."

"I don't know what Ralph and I will do with our share," Beth commented. "In any event, we'll have some savings for the first time in our life. Crime paid for us."

"Maybe the lesson is—steal from crooks," Sherry said. "Judge Moss didn't report our thievery to the authorities in the Caymans. We were successful crooks. I agree crime paid for us."

A week later, the party for Katie turned out to be a big success. Katie looked great with the bow on her headband. Andy did a wonderful job catering, and the weather stayed relatively warm, so some people lingered in the tent. Everyone had a good time.

Beth and Ralph stayed to help Phil and Sherry clean up. They'd been able to transfer Katie to her crib, so they had some time to make progress on the clean-up, but they had to keep quiet.

Sherry had her hands full of the rented stemware as she walked back to the kitchen to get them washed when she saw Beth and Ralph sharing a grin. She asked, "What are you two so happy about?"

Phil took the glasses from Sherry, and asked, "Yeah, I didn't see either of you without a smile the whole night."

Ralph and Beth looked at each other, still grinning. "You go, Beth," Ralph said.

"Okay, we didn't want to upstage Katie and your party. We've got some news."

"Yes?" Phil and Sherry asked in unison.

"I'm pregnant!"

"What? When? Oh my gosh!" Sherry exclaimed, as she and Phil hugged Beth.

ABOUT THE AUTHOR

Robert Archibald was born in New Jersey and grew up in Oklahoma and Arizona. After receiving a BA from the University of Arizona, he was drafted and served in Viet Nam. He then earned a M.S. and Ph.D in economics from Purdue University. Bob had a 41-year career at the College of William & Mary. While he had several stints as an administrator, department chair, director of the public policy program, and interim dean of the faculty, Bob was always proud to be promoted back to the faculty. He lives with his wife of 49 years, Nancy, in Williamsburg, Virginia.

www.ingramcontent.com/pod-product-compliance
Lightning Source LLC
Chambersburg PA
CBHW021308190726
48288CB00003B/747